BALLIN OUTTA CONTROL

Sullivan Phillips

Fulton Books, Inc.
Meadville, PA

First originally published by Fulton Books 2018

ISBN 978-1-63338-256-5 (Paperback)
ISBN 978-1-63338-709-6 (Hardcover)
ISBN 978-1-63338-257-2 (Digital)

Printed in the United States of America

FOREWORD

by Cosby Lorenzo Burch

Who is Sullivan Phillips? My boy...

A friendship that has existed for greater than 25 years began when he arrived in/on the island of Bermuda. He joined my elementary class, at Bermuda Institute, in the sixth grade. When he first arrived, he was the odd man out - an American who liked baseball, NFL (the other football) and basketball. In Bermuda, we mainly played football (soccer) or cricket and, at an early stage, it was a rough game, with little rules. With his American accent and his tall stature, he stood out like a sore thumb. Nonetheless, he was quick to learn the games and soon became a top athlete. This is just one example of how he made the best out of a situation, which would drive him to excellence.

Not letting other peoples' actions control yours was an important lesson Sulli learned quickly. He could have retreated and allowed the teasing and stress of a new environment overwhelm him, but rather, he rose to the challenge and used his circumstances to rise to a level beyond anyone's expectations.

At first, we didn't get along, but this soon changed and our bond became inseparable. We challenged every parental rule while growing up. We knew our boundaries and how far to go without getting into too much trouble. We both had a strong spiritual background, which you will see in reading his book, and how critical this is to a young person's character. I believe this made all the difference in who we are today. "Train up a child in the way he should go: and when he is old, he will not depart from it." (Proverbs 22:6). Truer words have never been spoken

Sulli's journey is one that many young people can relate to and hopefully grow from. Why reinvent the wheel when we know it has to be round in order to produce a smooth ride?

This book is a true prodigal son's story, with a modern-day back-drop. Sullivan has traveled extensively and thus is sharing many "Do's and Don'ts" learned - some the hard way, as he navigated through his life. He has had many opportunities and many life experiences that have shaped him to the man he is today - one who fears the Lord and strives to be and do better.

For parents, this book will hopefully give a different perspective on the challenges their youth face today.

I can see God moving in Sulli's life and it has inspired me in many ways. God is real in protecting and guiding us through life. He is intentional in all that happens to us and this book is a fine example of how God shapes us to be who He knows we can be. Ultimately, fulfilling a vital plan to not only make us better, but also allowing us to help others either fulfill their purpose or become one step closer to Him.

CHAPTER 1

WHERE THE MARK OF GREATNESS BEGAN

He not busy being born is truly busy dying.

—Bob Dylan

February 9, 1979. Man, the world would never be the same, thanks to a gift from Leroy and Sharon Phillips in the form of a bouncing baby boy of nine pounds and thirteen ounces: Sullivan Bervin Phillips. My parents had to be thinking, *This kid's going to break our bank based on just his size.* Being raised between Texas and Louisiana in my formative years, there was little excitement in my life, but I was always learning lessons along the way that would later mold and shape me.

My father was a Seventh-day Adventist minister (you may later see me refer to this as SDA), and my mother was a schoolteacher. You can gather from these two facts three important things about life for my older sister, Lori, and myself: (1) Church was nonnegotiable. The only way you didn't go was if you were ill to the point where death was around the corner from you. So rain, sunshine, or snow—church was a mainstay. The funny thing is going to church was all I knew, so it didn't really bother me. The only time I can remember ever missing church was probably for a Pathfinder retreat. (Pathfinders are like boy and girl scouts, but Adventists combine both.) (2) Manners and respect were also nonnegotiable. Step out of line, and your butt would be beaten thoroughly until you understood and practiced both regularly. (3) Education, articulation, and excelling academically in school were mandatory; this particular rule, I'd have issues with.

In Texas, we had a close-knit congregation, and we were all like one big happy family. However, as a minister's kid, you're taught never to get too comfortable in one spot because the call can come, and you can be moved to another congregation at any time. When I learned we were moving to Shreveport, it was the first time I can truly say I was mad with my parents for making us pack up and go to another place. I never knew why I was born into such an environment, and believe me, I let my parents (especially my mom) know with my whining how much I didn't like Louisiana. However, these moves would serve as the foundation for my career and other important events in my life.

Shreveport, Louisiana, was a drug-infested city, and our neighborhood wasn't exempt from this fact, which was why I wasn't allowed to go to the park even though it was only three blocks from our home. As a kid, I was told not to do a lot of things, but what my parents and many older generation parents failed to do was explain why I shouldn't go or be in that environment.

No matter what, I always seemed to learn the hard way, and the curious boy in me always ventured to this little pavilion in the park. I was a kid who was never inside and was always out in the streets. Of course, there were rules that had to be followed; but for the most part, my mom and dad let me go out and explore. Usually I'd tread carefully, but I'd end up at the courts under the pavilion, knowing full well that if I were caught, I would get the beating of a lifetime. However, that was me as I am now, always living on the edge. At eight, nine, and ten years old, I was out there with grown men, listening to absolute foolishness. My mom will read this and be shocked because I don't think she or my dad had a clue I was going out there. As a parent, what I've had to learn and now admonish other parents is this: sometimes you need to talk to your kids so that they can understand the reason why you do certain things. Having said that, there are also times where they shouldn't have a vote or say in the situation, no matter what. It's a very fine line, one that, over the years, even I still haven't mastered.

But on one particular day, I saw our blue Isuzu pull up by the pavilion (that was my parents car and if my dad caught me I knew I was dead). Boy, in the middle of the game, I dispersed like a cockroach when the light came on. I was ghost—you have no idea how fast I was outta there. I literally ran nonstop until I was about three hundred yards from my house. It was only then that I stopped and paused to catch my breath.

I slowly edged up to the door and walked inside the house. My dad was in his usual position, book in hand, reading something, but he paused with an inquisitive look, and he asked, "What's up, son? What brings you in so early?" My reply was swift and unconvincing as I said, "I am tired." And he bought it! Man, that was the first time, and one of the few times, I lied to my dad and lived to tell the story without too many bruises from a beating. Looking back, I can honestly say I never got caught, and I grew more brazen with the lies, and the seeds of deceit began to grow.

Truthfully, our three years in Louisiana were cool, but the violence and the school we were attending weren't good at all. My parents grew weary of this, especially since my sister, Lori, was due to graduate from eighth grade soon. While in Louisiana, I had my first crush. Hello, Ms. Jackson, brown skinned and about five feet seven inches tall. Man, she was so amazing to me; but of course, I was so much younger than her, and in the fourth grade, there was no way she would give me the time of day, no chance at all. However, I had learned at a young age how to massage a woman's brain and ear, and soon she was my girl. Yes, I'm going to say it, I was Mr. Sweet Talker, or so I thought. Little did I know that short relationship would end, and we would move to the place I have always called home—Bermuda.

Mom and Dad went to Bermuda to explore a possible move and left us with an elderly couple from church. I can honestly say I was so not impressed about being there and couldn't wait for my parents to walk in and rescue us. They lived on a farm, so you know how life on the farm is. I was totally bummed about being there, but my parents soon came back, and I was made aware that we would be moving to pastor in Bermuda. I longed to stay in Louisiana now that I had my queen, or so I thought at the tender age of ten. However, the year soon ended; and after many promises to keep in touch, we were off to Bermuda, which at the time was like heaven.

In Louisiana, you had to have three locks on each door, and maybe a rail too; that's just how violent it was. In contrast, in Bermuda, you could leave the door open and come back to find everything in the exact condition as you left it. This was definitely foreign to me. I'd always loved the culture and dialect in Bermuda. We usually visited every summer to see cousins and my mother's family, so I was slightly familiar with the country. However, I had no idea of the impact moving there would have on my life.

At ten years old, kids get jobs packing groceries, and I was no different. It was a great way to learn a craft and earn cash to spend as well. Sentinel Hill (in the Southampton Parish of Bermuda) was my stomping ground, and it was amazing to look out and see palm trees and the ocean; it was like heaven. Soon I found a partner in crime, Mr. Rhaji, who is still a dear friend of mine to this day. We ran the streets all the time, from morning until night, nonstop. His big brother was like an OG (an older-brother figure to school us on life) who gave us the lowdown on girls, and he had an earring (if you're old enough, you know this was a serious unspoken no-no in the SDA community). The way I looked up to him was crazy; anything he said was like the Bible.

My mother, my sister, and I went to Bermuda first, and then my dad finally came over to join us from the States in Bermuda later. The school year started with me going to Bermuda Institute, and I can honestly say that the fifth and sixth grade years there were brutal. It was crazy! I was unanimously hated, no girls looked at me, and I was constantly teased. I got beat up by Mich, who later became and still is my close friend to this day. First off, I really had a crush on her but said the wrong thing to her one day, and we ended up meeting at the train tracks to brawl (what in the world was I doing fighting a girl?).

Needless to say, I got slapped, and I ran like it was no tomorrow. Luckily, I was superfast, and no one could catch me.

Sixth grade was more of the same. I disliked my teacher so much it was unbelievable, and I would act on my disgust for her. The demons of anger toward her was unleashed on her, and I stole money from her purse on two separate occasions. When my parents discovered the thefts, they were so shocked. I think they thought I was selling drugs. After the beating of a lifetime, I was forced to give her every penny back and apologize. It was so humbling the second time when I had to apologize in front of the class— talk about being shamed to no end. My dad was no joke! He was a military man, so if you did wrong, he knew how to get you right for sure, with that good old black belt.

Athletically, I was a laughingstock (in soccer as well as cricket). Academically, I struggled, and I attended summer school in both the sixth and seventh grades. Yeah, it was ugly. Around this time, the new, aggressive me appeared. We were at a small church, Somerset SDA Church, and I remember telling my dad, "This place is a funeral home. Can't you move?" Having to go from school to this place, I was miserable; but fortunately, we would end up in a much better social situation for me at our new church home, which would become my church home, Hamilton SDA Church.

Truthfully, during these middle school years, I became quite the avid footballer (soccer player). In those first years of being teased, I told my classmates, "Laugh now, but later you'll all pay to watch me play." Of course, they laughed and mocked me, but they never understood how that would fuel me to excel. Other than having to attend summer school in the seventh grade, things were shaping up well for me. I caught on to the pace of life in Bermuda, thing became cool. During this time, the trinity crew was formed. It consisted of Morissa Francis-Rodgers (a.k.a. Ris), Lorenzo Burch (a.k.a. Renzo), Tanaeya Ingham/Burch (a.k.a. Ingy or Nae), and me. When I say we were inseparable, it's not just words. We literally did every-thing together. Whether it was Camporee in Colorado, music clinics (mind you, Nae went to another school, but we worked it out so she could attend our trips), or leadership conferences—you name it, we all went together.

Let me stop here to give the first lesson I've learned in my years, and I'll share more insight I've gained through my life as I go along.

> *Lesson 1: When choosing friends, don't just look at how they treat you or act with you. Take stock of where they come from and observe if they have qualities that will elevate you to be your best.*

You see, all of my friends came from two-parent Christian homes. They all went to church and school with me, the whole nine. (Please don't take this the wrong way. I'm not saying someone is better because they go to church or that their parents are together because I know some great kids who have come out of single-parent homes with non-Christian parents.) Seeing this family dynamic around me helped me see what I wanted for my future and help me seek to create that type of family for myself. It also helped me identify the characteristics I wanted to emulate in my life. Very soon, I'd see this important lesson of organic truth revealed in my life.

The years rolled by, and the eleventh grade came around, and soccer-wise, my skills had evolved from playing under the tutelage of the mighty Devonshire Colts Soccer Club. As a young boy of sixteen they helped me develop my skills and before the drama wagon came to my door, I was truly coming into my own. However, on one cool winter morning in October, I made one silly mistake that totally changed my life.

We used to have these bump-up sessions (basically we would beat up someone without really harming them too seriously just to have a little fun). One day, my man Flurbal called a guy up to the lockers just to mess him up a bit. The original plan was to bump him up, sadly it turned out to be far more brutal. The bump up turned into a beatdown, and it was superugly. The ended up with a swollen head from being hit with a locker padlock. Afterward, we shot out of there like a cannon, but it wasn't going to be a quiet, pushed-under-the-rug type of situation. It was so ugly, and he had no clue what really happened.

It was a perfectly executed crime, but like any crime, all it takes is one witness to ruin everything. Word traveled like the flu in a kindergarten class, and soon names were listed, and people were being brought in to find out what happened. Forty-eight hours later, I was being *expelled*! You don't understand the magnitude of this sentence—I was a prefect. (For my non–Bermudians, a prefect is a teacher's aide who helps bring the students into the classrooms in the morning every day; it's a leadership position.) I was about to join the under-twenty-three national team, as well as the under-twenty national team for soccer. Why was this happening to me, I didn't know. It was just a joke. This stupid situation was starting to look like it was going to ruin my future.

The school called my dad right then and there and informed him. Man, this was the fastest ride from school home on my moped. After locking my bike and taking off my helmet, it was time to meet with my dad. I knew this was a death sentence for me as soon as I entered the doors of the house. At 6'2" tall and 245 pounds, you can imagine my fear, but where could I run? I had to face the music. As I opened the door gently, he just sat there with no book, or belt, just a serious face as he beckoned me to the couch. It was a weird feeling. To this day, I really can't explain it, but it was surreal. He simply said, "I'm going to ask you a few questions, and I need you to answer me honestly." I acknowledged him and said I'd comply, as if I had a choice.

First question: "Did you beat up the boy in the locker room?" No, sir." This was true. Second question: "Do you know who did this?" Since I was present, I answered, "Yes, sir." With a pleading look, he asked the last question: "Are you going to tell who did it to get reinstated in the school?" I hung my head and told him, "I'm not going to be snitch, Dad." He looked at me with a look of utmost sadness, as if he thought my schooling career was over. I knew the thought of how naive I was being was in his head and that telling me I was ruining my future was on the tip of his tongue. He simply told me to head to my room and grabbed his book, but I could see the disappointment in his eyes. When my mom came home, she wasn't holding back her tongue for anything, and she let me have it: "You're really going to throw your life away just like that?" Seeing the tears fall from her face as she pleaded. But never for a second was I about to be a snitch! This brings me to the next important lesson I've learned along the way.

> *Lesson 2: Sometimes doing the right thing in situations where it may seem wrong can yield a result that's not fair or just. Whatever choice you make, always look to God for guidance and trust your instincts, especially when they are divinely guided.*

For me, loyalty is a must; it has been and always will be. It's a sign and a form of commitment that's needed in any relationship, especially among friends. We stood together, all five of us involved, and wouldn't tell, waver, or throw anyone under the bus. My loyalty brought so much grief to my parents. I remember my mom and dad arguing about the situation and my mom telling my dad, "Just make him say what he knows." My dad just said, "No, that's his choice. He has to understand the consequences of choices." The rumors and things I heard people say about me and my family were very harsh and rude. "Look at this boy fighting and acting a fool. What are his parents doing with him?" I remember hearing a lady say, "Apples don't fall far from the tree." I was so mad when I heard her say that I responded, "Is that why your daughter has gotten pregnant by two different men in the last couple years and isn't married?" Yeah! I know that you're thinking wow that's so rude, but it was true. That's what started to spew from my mouth, truth—a lot of it without thinking first or regard for whom it could hurt.

Emotionally I could see the effects of my choices and how real and detrimental they could be. Fortunately, after two weeks, things were sorted out, and we were reinstated back into Bermuda Institute, but it was never the same for me. I never fit in again and felt like a prisoner on guard at all times. One day it all came to a head. I came home from school, and my father saw it in my eyes, and he asked what was wrong. Well, he definitely got a full-throttle answer, and I visibly seeing my father's heart shatter into pieces at the words that followed. I told him, ***"This really sucks being a pastor's son. Having to live like you no matter what I like to do or the places I like to go. I'm judged by your title. I can't go to the movies (at that time, I had to sneak to watch movies because I was forbidden to go with no explanation), but I'm allowed to watch the same thing when it comes on cable? I can't play sports (Bermuda Institute didn't have an athletic program at the time, and I could only showcase my God-given abilities when summer came, and I played in summer leagues), and it's because I'm your child that I can't go to a public school." I hear the words like it was yesterday: "I hate my life, especially in this little fishbowl of Bermuda. I didn't ask for this life. You chose it for me. I'm a prisoner of my dreams and aspirations because of your occupation and your beliefs."***

For the first time in my life, I saw tears well up in my father's eyes. I never physically saw them fall, but I knew he cried in his room after our talk. My grandpa was a bit of a playboy who took the household's money and spent it on booze and tricked it off on women. He wasn't emotionally available or forthcoming with his kids, and my father was the same for the most part. But this day I had struck a nerve, and I know he cried some serious tears all because of my words.

Looking back now, I understand that all he wanted to do was be a father to Lori and me, give us a better life, and be a Christian example of what a good man is supposed to be. My comments had to have pierced his heart and made him feel he was failing me. In truth, I really was just going through a rough patch as most teens do, but the biggest problem for me was not seeing how I could use my talents. Like the good parents they were, he and my mother began to tirelessly look for an outlet for me where I could develop my skills and use my talents. That conversation showed two things:

1. I needed the chance to be me and not be in the shadow of their choices for my life even if they had pure intentions.

2.   If I didn't leave that school soon, I probably wouldn't finish school and would turn to major mischief, and this story definitely would be different from the one you're reading about me now.

On the flip side, when I left everything I knew and was accustomed to, would my closest friends forget me? Would our bond change? Would I even like wherever I ended up? My parents and I would have to make some tough and possibly life-changing decisions very soon.

> *Lesson 3: At the end of the day, sometimes you have to take a leap of faith in order to get to a desired place of personal, spiritual, and emotional balance in your life, even if it doesn't necessarily guarantee happiness.*

It's crazy. I sit here some almost twenty years later, and my eyes still water because of all the negative things I said to my dad that day. Now I can see the bigger picture, how my parents sacrificed to keep me in line so I could be the best me I could be. It took a huge risk on their part to take their child out of the SDA school where my dad ministered and send me elsewhere, but that's what great parents do. They don't allow situations or circumstances to dictate their kid's lives, and I'm eternally grateful for their sacrifices. Finally, after the first semester finals were taken, a new chapter in life was opened for me, and I was enrolled in Garden State Academy (GSA), where my life would change quickly, but I had no idea how and why God would allow it to happen that way.

CHAPTER 2

JUST WHEN THINGS COULDN'T GET ANY WORSE

Character is like a tree, and rep-
utation like a shadow.
The shadow is what we think of
it; the tree is the real thing.

—Abraham Lincoln

The end of January came, and I said good-bye to the trinity crew. Know question this was the hardest part for me saying good-bye to my friends, but it was a part of the sacrifice I had to make. My homie and friend to this day Bass and I were off on the journey of a lifetime (we thought so) to New Jersey. The people were beyond friendly, and most importantly, the Adventist community was so small that I knew plenty of people there, the Bermudians anyway. I can honestly say the adjustment was quick and fairly easy. However, we were coming into a different school format, and they had already begun their second semester, so Bass and I were playing catch-up from the jump. It was cool, though. The work wasn't as hard as back home, so we figured it out. Truth be told, as I think back, in spite of all the familiarities, I was missing the trinity crew. The bond with others just couldn't compare.

Soon as we got there and got caught up the dorm and overall campus life, were off to Oakwood College now Oakwood University in Huntsville Alabama. I can't even lie. For the first time ever, I was excited to see my parents and my sister and to just enjoy life away from Tranquility, New Jersey. You see, GSA is literally in the woods in the middle of nowhere! Not that Huntsville, Alabama, was a huge city, but Alumni Weekend is a huge SDA event; and since it was also the centennial weekend, it was going to be huge. For readers who aren't familiar with Alumni Weekend, it is the same as homecoming for other universities. The one difference is that this particular Alumni Weekend was at Oakwood University, a prominent SDA university that was founded by the SDA world church. Needless to say, everyone besides me attended there, so I was going to be there for the weekend.

The first night there, my brother-in-law and I went to get a bite to eat, and that's when it happened: a specimen standing five feet ten inches tall, caramel skin, baby blue eyes. Flat out! She had me from the moment I laid eyes on her, it was lust at first sight again. My brother-in-law sat back and watched me go to work. Her dad was a real West Indian–style man (very proper and didn't think anyone was good enough for his daughter) and quickly came over to shut me down. But I engaged her in conversation ever so carefully, complimented her mom, and smoothed it over with him.

Martina was of French Canadian descent. Mercy, this lady had my head spinning. Her cousins had an apartment close to campus, so you already know what time it was. My parents had finally flown in, and my mom was like babying me big-time. Shoot, I even had Ms. Martina in the mix with my family. My parents were cool like that. They never really stressed too much at this stage in my life. But if you slipped up you would most definitely be held accountable.

Hanging out with my folks was cool, but a major concern was my dad, who was walking with a cane everywhere because he had been experiencing excruciating pain in his legs. But nothing was going to keep them from this Alumni Weekend, and this time would ultimately change our family dynamic for the rest of our lives. He was due to have some medical exams the following Monday, so the weekend was straight fun and relaxation. However, even amid the fun, you could see the pain in my dad's eyes, and seeing him with a cane was hard to watch. He seemed so weak and frail.

While meeting all of my parents' friends, the question kept ringing out, "[Are] you coming to Oakwood?" I was quick to answer, "Nope. I'm good." Mom told me not to close the door on that opportunity, but she didn't know I already had. They didn't have a sports program at the time, and I didn't want to have the same experience as before. Plus, Oakwood was becoming a huge fad with Bermudians at that time. At GSA, my talents were finally being used for sports, and I wanted to play college basketball and soccer, so I knew going to Oakwood wasn't going to happen. The weekend was going so fast, and after an evening at a gospel concert, I had dinner with my folks and got the lecture to be on time for my flight in the morning. I'm usually good with time and assured them I wouldn't be late, and I stayed with Ms. Martina for the rest of the evening.

Unfortunately, it was daylight savings time, and I missed my flight. Man, if looks could've killed, I would have died twice; my dad was so vexed. Anyone who had the pleasure of knowing my dad knew there were few men cheaper than him, and to pay that $50 for the flight-change fee was like paying $350 to him. He flipped the script and said the fee was coming out of the money he was going to give me to take back to school. I was unbelievably vexed, and I don't think I spoke to my dad again until I boarded the plane. At the time, I felt hurt, and it killed my mood. And of course, my folks wouldn't let me roam the streets, so I was stuck with them until the flight—double whammy. Like a brat, I just followed them sulking until I got to the airport and wished them good-bye. This was the last time I'd ever see my father alive, leaving him with a childish attitude over money, in spite of all they had done for me. ***That's something I live with to this day.*** My selfish wants and desires overrode the opportunity to spend the final moments of my father's life together.

Back at GSA, Bass and I had so many stories, and as typical guys, we shared many of them about what went on during the weekend.

Finally, after hours of chatting, I drifted to sleep, dreaming of Ms. Martina and the great weekend we had shared together and, hopefully, we would be reunited soon. Monday morning, still all smiles, but little did I know my world was about change forever. While in the shower, Mama G (Mrs. Deria Gadsden, the unofficial principal) called me to the office via the campus intercom. Now, when Mama G calls you to the office, it usually means you're in hot water. But I had just come back, and my grades were okay, so I figured she was just checking up on me to make sure I had a good trip. Rushing to dry off, get clothes on, and hurry to the office, life was great. Heck, I was on cloud nine. Life was really starting to make sense, especially after the previous crazy months I had encountered.

I walked in the office, there stood Mama G with tears in her eyes, the school pastor, and a whole lot of people, which led me to believe either I had done something extremely bad, or something far more terrible had happened. I was beckoned to sit and take the phone. Hesitantly, I obliged and took the phone. On the other end of the line was my mother. I could hear when my mother said hello that something was terribly wrong and that she had been crying quite hard and that in her attempt to speak, she was fighting the tears. She broke the news, "Daddy's dead." No way! I had her repeat the words to make sure I was hearing correctly, but the nightmare was one I wouldn't be able to wake from and just go on as if it wasn't true. The words were true.

Immediately I began to cry and scream. They wanted me to stay in the office and just talk with them, but I couldn't. I ran through the hallway, tears running down my face like a stream. These tears wouldn't stop, and I must have cried for an hour before I even uttered a word. Thoughts of our encounter the day before ran vividly through my mind, and how I left my parents, mainly my dad, with a major attitude. And now I'd never have the opportunity to say I'm sorry or I love you again—it was an opportunity that would never be. I couldn't believe it. I didn't want to believe it. The reality for me now was that, for the rest of my life, I'd be without my father. This definitely leads into the next lesson along my path of life.

Lesson 4: No matter the magnitude of disappointment or hurt you experience in a relationship, never ever leave it unresolved with anger. There's no guarantee that you will have time to make things right!

I never dreamed that when I left Alabama that sunny Sunday, I'd never see my father alive again. To this day, I have to live with the consequences of my attitude and my behavior on that day—and **I can never apologize for what I did** ! Over the years, I've learned how to deal with the pain of my actions, but in truth, it never goes away. The pain serves as a reminder that tomorrow is never promised, so you should live and love while you breathe today. I was seventeen years old, with one parent—what in the world was God doing? He took the man who taught me to love and trust in him. What was God doing in my life and to my family? My dad definitely wasn't perfect by any means, but he was a good man. This totally wasn't right or fair. Thankfully, the GSA family was so supportive to me, and everyone in my 1997 graduating class was phenomenal. But I had to go home and bury my dad; that was something I had to do alone.

Time flies when you're having fun, or when something bad has happened and you have to face the music. Unfortunately, the latter was the case for me. I must say the trinity crew (Renzo, Nae, and Ris) was there with me every step of the way, hanging tough with me. To this day, I don't think they have any idea how much they helped me during the toughest time of my life. In the truest sense of the word, their love for me never wavered. (George and Pam Burch, Larry and Patricia Ingham [rest in peace], Morris and Rosalynn Francis—as tears flow from my face, this story will be read because of you and your kids. **You saved me!** You raised amazing people. Without all of you, only God knows where I'd be.)

Lesson 5: Good friends are like pearls. When you get one you should hold it close to you and never let go of it or forget its priceless value!

After the funeral service, we ate with friends and family, but I was feeling extremely loss, angry, extremely angry with God because my dad was a good man. I felt there were plenty of people who should've died for their negative ways, but a good man was dead and leaving so many to mourn. I can honestly say the angry black boy in me planted his roots deep in my heart to resent life, religion, and most importantly, God. Just like that, Monday morning I was on the plane back to New Jersey. My Discman (for my younger readers, this was a small portable CD player) was playing, but the entire flight was a haze to me for obvious reasons, but soon I'd be back in school and had to get back to life. It was very hard to walk back on campus and answer the questions over and over, "Are you okay?" "Do you need anything?" I couldn't be mad, and I was glad that they cared, but every mention of the situation took me back through all the pain over and over again.

I honestly have no idea how I finished the eleventh grade in good standing; the remaining semester after April 16, 1996, was a giant blur. One day my English teacher saw me in her class totally out of it; I had tears running down my face and didn't even recognize it. I was in the back of the class, and no one noticed, but she spoke with me after the class and began to issue extra work for me to do to keep up with the pace. It was beyond evident that the burden on my heart was showing on my face and was awfully heavy to carry. But I can honestly say I made it to the end of the school year in good standing. However, once again, I would be presented with some tough decisions to make in the summer regarding school, and life with my mom would become extremely rough and tedious. :"Every path to success has many detours and speed bumps that can cause failure; your success depends on you and what path you choose to take."

One thing was for certain, I was heading to Canada to see Ms. Martina and try to put the last few negative months behind me. Her dad reluctantly allowed me to come and visit. I stayed in the basement to ensure I didn't have access to her, but that didn't stop us from spending every waking moment of the week together. I could sense her dad hated me, so I had a conversation with him one day and was just straight up with him. I asked, "Why do you hate me?" He proceeded to tell me how worthless I was and how I only wanted to have sex with his daughter and take her off her path of success. I wanted to cuss him dry, but to keep the peace, I only told her about it later when we went out to a movie. Sensing from that moment we would never work out was a little sad, and on that brisk Sunday morning it was the weirdest feeling ever kissing her good bye. She cried so hard, but I knew I'd never see her again; and to this day, I haven't. This is life for me in a nutshell: God allows people to be in our lives but never specifies how long they will be part of our progression to becoming better people.

The summer before senior year would prove to be most interesting. At GSA, I had become a part of the family, but I was offered the opportunity to attend Takoma Academy (TA) in Maryland for my senior year. It was tough because TA was a good school and had an excellent basketball program as well; for sure, I'd get a lot more looks from bigger colleges by attending there. All summer I was getting calls and letters asking for a decision. Again, my loyalty was tested, but my decision was made for me the day my dad died. The entire school just surrounded me and comforted me, even though they really didn't know me. It was a no-brainer; I would return to GSA for my senior year. People quickly tried to advise me that it was a foolish decision, but if you knew me, then you know that when my mind's made up, unless God himself shows me otherwise, I'm not going to change it!

Personally, at that time in my life, I can honestly say that I did not appreciate the way the church handled my father's death, especially the housing of my mom and how she had to really scramble to keep house and home operating. To make matters worse, I had a glimpse at my father's files and saw what was going on in the church, and that infuriated me even more, especially thinking how people were acting to my mom when clearly there was a lot of dirt going on at the church. Some people acted extremely funny to my mom when she moved her membership because it was tough to attend Hamilton SDA church after my dad died. A lot of things that were said infuriated me to no end, to the point I'd just meet up with the trinity crew for lunch to avoid the services. If I went to camp meetings (when SDA churches regions meet up once a year usually for a week to worship together), you'd best believe I was in the parking lot and not in service. I stopped singing in the choir and participating in other activities. I know there's someone who can relate to my experience. You might not be as young as I was, but maybe you've left the church for something trivial, or you feel like walking away as I did. But here's another tough lesson I had to learn:

> *Lesson 6: Even the most decorated church member (pastor/reverend, elder, deacon or deaconess) is a human; they will fall and sin. That's why you should always look to Jesus's example, and then you're never disappointed. Even the most decorated human needs a shower or bath daily because we all get dirty.*

At the end of the day, God came to save us all because we are sinners. But I had looked up to a lot of people, and after seeing the files from board meetings and personal one-on-one counseling files, I was like, "I'd rather go to hell my way than pretend I'm a Christian," and that was that.

At this point in my life, work was the name of the game. I knew I was broke, and my mom couldn't afford to send money, so I saved money like I was never going to work again. The summer went by so fast, and soon it was time for me to head back to Jersey to finish my senior year of high school. On the personal front, I met a very attractive, sexy lady right before I left for school at a basketball game. I will call her *Ms. Black*. It was a very interesting and whirlwind rela-tionship. It was a crazy connection but a great one, even though she was six years older than me. It was very exciting to me, and we stayed in contact for my whole senior year. It seemed like every week, there was another letter from her; and to be honest, she kept me really focused and in contact with homelife in Bermuda. Academically, this was the first time it clicked for me. I can be honest, being in the woods and not having much to do but schoolwork and playing ball made it a lot easier. My grades reached an all-time high with a 3.6

GPA, and when I gave my mom the award letter at Christmas, her expression was priceless; she absolutely gleamed with joy. That was actually the highlight of our time together during the break because she was furious that I was hanging out with a much older lady and wanted me to stay focused on my schoolwork.

During the Christmas holidays of my senior year my sister got married in Atlanta, Georgia. It was a cool ceremony officiated by one of my dad's friends. Though small, it was very nice. Even though I wasn't that close to my sister, I told my brother-in-law, "If you do wrong by her, I'll kill you!" He laughed until he saw that I was as serious as triple bypass surgery! One of my biggest regrets in life is not being as close to Lori as I could have been, especially seeing as now we are older and the time has gone so fast; there could have been much stronger bond.

The last part of the break was spent in Bermuda with the trinity crew and Ms. Black. I even went to church, I believe, for the Christmas service. It was good to feel like I finally was taking control of my life again. The break went by so fast as it always seems to do when you're having fun. Back at GSA, basketball was quite easy; the team included a great group of guys. We weren't the best, but our play was exciting and quite fun to watch. Looking back, my stats were cool, but the one thing I gained from playing there was a sense of brotherhood at all times. Our coach, Mr. G, was the most patient and kind man on this earth. He loved to win, but he was a teacher of life. And his words, as well as actions, exemplified the love of God and genuine concern for us.

Basketball was done by the end of the semester, and it was all about finals and graduation—and boy did they come fast. I also had more joyous news: shortly after getting married, my sister became pregnant and was due to have my oldest nephew, Jereme, in September. Graduation weekend was truly a good weekend, and now looking back, I see how the prayers of my mother pushed and covered me. Her face had a glow like none other. Hell, when my dad died, I would have bet that I wouldn't finish school, but never underestimate the power of a praying woman! Summer was going to be hell on earth, trying to decide what school to attend. I had quite a few schools looking at me to attend their institutions, and I was hoping that finally my dream of being in the NBA was drawing ever nearer. However, little did I know that God had special plans for my life and would soon reveal them in the most interesting of ways. High school was done, and soon I would be in college. But until then, it was summer and time to chill. Or so I thought.

CHAPTER 3

WELCOME TO THE
REAL WORLD!

*It's possible to fail many ways…while
to succeed is possible in one way.*

—Aristotle

The summer after graduation from high school can be one of the most critical periods in your life and can basically define who you are or what, if any, value and purpose you can contribute to society. For me, I had but one intention when choosing a school, and that was to play basketball and soccer at the highest level afforded to me, nothing more, nothing less. My mother and I heard many offers about things that could be given to me, like time on court and just an array of things to cloud my judgment. However, my mom was adamant that I attend an SDA university for my first year; and after that, if I didn't like it or felt it didn't meet my needs, I could leave. But the SDA universities didn't have any athletic programs. The best of the bunch at the time was Columbia Union College (CUC), but I didn't like the vibe there and wasn't going to go there. So where else was there to go, or would I again feel as if my talents and God-given ability would be wasted?

Summer continued, and it got ugly between my mom and me. I really made her suffer for making me attend an SDA school. Now looking back, with her being a single parent, the discount to attend an SDA university because my dad had been a minister, plus the academic and leadership scholarships I had received, it would've been a financial breeze to go to an SDA school. Plus, I only had to check out a school for a year. Unfortunately, I saw things from a totally different perspective. When I say we bumped heads, trust me, we bumped heads. She even had a minister sit down with me to try and see where my head was. This made matters worse because, at that time, anyone who didn't support the vision I had for my life was an enemy, and I treated them as such, point-blank. So much anger mixed with confusion was a bad and sad combination to have in one young man who was still searching for an identity in the world.

During this time, I turned to alcohol instead of doing what I did years later and seeking professional help to clear out the inner demons in the deep closets of my soul so that I could move forward and stop playing the role of a victim. I was a live time bomb just waiting to explode! No one could tell me anything except the trinity crew or Ms. Black, and even then, sometimes I wouldn't listen to them. I was rude, cursing out people, and just out of control. The sad thing was it wasn't about to get any better for me because soon I would be forced to choose a school, but not of my own free will. It was one month before school began, and I had to enroll somewhere. Oakwood University and Andrews University were logical options for me because my friends had chosen these schools, but neither school had sports programs, so then what would I do? Columbia Union College wasn't a viable option because neither my mom nor I trusted the coach there, so it was a rap for that school.

One thing I've always been able to do is step out in faith and do things differently from others even when it's not the norm or popular, and the choice of a college to attend wouldn't be any different. I totally flipped the script and chose Atlantic Union College (AUC). My boys Butters, Bass, Scotty, Flur, Big Al, Douglas, and Gene (a.k.a. Macky) were already committed there for the college ride, so I figured I might as well too since I really had no choice in the matter.

Freshman year was a drag from day one. Attending an SDA school meant dormitory, curfew, mandatory worship, and vespers (evening or morning religious meetings), all of which I wasn't interested in. But this was part of the education there, and I had to attend. Most people at AUC already had a chosen major or knew what classes they wanted to take, but not me. I just wanted to hoop and kick a soccer ball, so I really was lost and basically had to learn on the fly, which lead me to this lesson on life's journey:

Lesson 7: No Plan + No Vision + No Guidance = Instant Failure! When you don't have a game plan or a visionary path for your life or guidance to help you navigate through life, you're headed down the quickest path to failure that could ever be imagined.

During the summer, I never paid attention to these things; I only focused on what I wanted short-term and not the long-term possibilities for my life. If you're about to go to college or even making a big decision in your life, take heed to this lesson. My freshman year was a waste education-wise! I really had no clue, so I jumped on Nae's and Ris's decision to study physical therapy. I had no clue what I was getting into at all and soon would realize it wasn't for me. School was no joke; the teachers weren't as patient with me like they were in high school. The classes went by quickly, and if I missed anything, tough cookies. It was a harsh reality for me, but one I needed to be reminded of; and at the end of the semester, I was truly humbled.

AUC did have a soccer team, and we played quite well, considering the program was a restart and no one really wanted to play us. I was very excited about playing. We had a very decent squad; we just struggled to gel at the start. During the games, I was at peace, and I didn't care about my bad grades or anything; I felt like a boss out there. In one game against the powerhouse team in our conference, I was playing defense, and I literally blanked the supposed best player of the conference and played quite well, even though we lost the game. The referee came up to me and asked me to meet him by the showers after the game. He handed me a flyer about MLS (Major League Soccer) tryouts. He told me that I played at a high level and should try out. I smiled, thanked him, and went back to the locker room and forgot about the encounter. Truthfully, I thought this dude was just blowing smoke up my butt, so I ignored it and kept it moving and blew off an opportunity that a lot of kids would have died to have.

As soon as soccer finished, tryouts for basketball shortly followed. I just went as a formality, honestly I could do anything with the basketball. I could honestly do anything I wanted to with a basketball. Playing basketball is my God-given talent. People are born to do many things, and for me, I learned early on that I was born to shoot hoops. My downfall in my early years was I never wanted to shine; I just wanted to fit in. Now, if we were playing one-on-one or if you pissed me off, then you'd see the animal come out of me. After soccer was over, I usually worked out alone and got some shots up alone. I did play openly for recreation like many others did, but a lot of times, I wouldn't do anything because I was too lazy and cocky.

The tryout consisted of drills to show your skill set and then scrimmages so the coaches can see you play. Truthfully, I just breezed through. At this stage in my life, there was nothing I couldn't do as far as basketball was concerned. When I flipped the switch to do what I wanted to do, you were at my mercy. I knew I'd make it, but others kissed up to the coach and thanked him for the opportunity to try out. I just left the gym and showered, but little did I know that I'd be humbled and made to realize that things in life did not revolve around me. Due to NCAA (the National Collegiate Athletic Association), restrictions and requirements that had to be met in order to play sanctioned basketball, I found out I wasn't eligible to play. This year was just going from bad to worse. I started thinking that maybe college wasn't for me and that I should try my hand in something else. But what could I do with no degree and no means to support myself?

Outside the sports scene, in the first week of school, I met my homie, and still good friend to date, Mrs. MC, who is one of the coolest people I've ever met in my life. We straight vibed together from our first conversation. I did a little homework and found out she came from a good crop (good parents/family). She was just a down-to-earth sister in every sense of the word. The problem was that I met my college sweetheart Ms. J around the same time. They came from different crews and people, and this wasn't going to fly. Ms. J was not one to share or tolerate shaky friendships. She was five feet nine inches tall, and from head to toe, she was a classy lady to a tee, and she had me under her spell from the first time I saw her. I couldn't even lie; I have never worked so hard to be part of and establish a presence in any one person's life as I did with hers.

Here's another lesson I learned:

> *Lesson 8: Real women require real attention! If you're dealing with a real woman (her race or ethnicity doesn't matter) and focus solely on pleasing her and making her happy, you'll never find time to play with girls!*

Ms. J truly made me grow up and understand life from a relationship perspective. She schooled me and taught me I had better grow up or step off and stay in the kiddie lane of life. I'm not proud of how I handled the situation with Mrs. MC because she was a good friend, and I totally blanked her in order to keep Ms. J. Now that I'm older, I'm thankful that time allowed me to mend that bond and remain friends with her to this day.

> *Lesson 9: No matter the relationship (friend, boyfriend, girlfriend, etc.) never lose your identity in order to make others happy. It's okay to make sacrifices, but to totally give up your identity and lose focus of the best you can be isn't a good look at all.*

It was tough, but I wanted the relationship, so I did what I had to do to maintain it, and soon I saw how others viewed and began to talk and treat me. At lunchtime, I would walk with her from class to eat with her and her friends and then walk her to her dorm afterward. She made it clear: "If you want me, you have to openly show it, privately mean it, and show it at all times." After a strong year, I finally was received as her boyfriend both publically and privately. My Bermudian friends kind of distanced themselves from me as well. They felt like I was whipped and that I gave Ms. J too much power over me, but with the guys, they were just teasing me. Macky, Butters, Douglass, and Big Al all had relationships as well, so they had some of the same issues. It's just that their girls kind of rolled with the Bermuda posse, but I didn't have that luxury with Ms. J.

The first semester was finally over, and I was placed on academic probation. My GPA was an awful 1.67, just pathetic. Ms. J straight sat me down and was like, "If you can't get a degree, you and I definitely can't be. You have to push yourself, and if you're not interested, forget you and me." During the semester break, my mom expressed the exact sentiments with a bit more ammunition, threatening to make me come home and work. That's all I needed to hear. Trust me, I knew what time it was: time to turn on my nerd switch. My nephew Jereme had been born by this time, so it was cool to see him and hang out with my sister and her family during this time. I was still trying to hold on to Ms. Black as well. You can imagine how busy I was during break, making calls to the States and hanging in Bermuda with friends and family—it was an interesting break. But like all good times, soon it was over, and it was time to head back to school.

Still salty about not playing ball, I decided not to waste the whole year pouting, and my main man Max invited me to play in a church league. I figured it would be harmless and I would get to head to Boston ever so often for games, so shoot, I was down for it. All was well until one winter evening, the most unforeseen injury occurred. While playing, I used a crossover move to separate myself from the defender, but he fouled me and stuck his elbow right under my right-armpit shoulder socket. Next thing I know, my shoulder was dislocated and my rotator cuff was torn. Trust me when I say it was the most excruciating pain I've ever been in, and I've been injured a lot. It was twenty-five degrees outside in the freezing cold, but the sweat was profusely dripping from my body. My arm was still out of socket, so it was agonizing, to put it nicely.

Right then, college offers from big schools **had gone** because this was a major reoccurring injury; no school would risk taking me no matter what potential upside there was. Frustration was running through my head. I was like, *Here we go again. Just when things start to look good, something bad always happens.* Truth be told, these dreadful, painful moments shaped me and made me stronger for the upcoming battles I would soon encounter.

> People grow through experiences if they
> meet life honestly and courageously.
> This is how character is built.
>
> (Eleanor Roosevelt)

This is so real, and I didn't understand this saying to be so true, especially with the drama I was experiencing. But what doesn't kill you can only make you stronger. A few months later, after a lot of rehab, my arm was better, and my GPA was 3.3; meaning, my academic probation was lifted. I would have to sit and really think about what I wanted to do in life because, clearly, my latest injury had proven there was no guarantee in playing sports.

During the summer, my aunt Carolyn pulled some strings in the Department of Social Services, and I got a part-time job working at a home for kids with behavioral problems. This was the job that confirmed what I wanted to do with my life. Seeing their actions, behavior, attitudes, and just bonding with them and learning the tricks of the trade made me really look into the profession, not for the money but as job where you can actually see the fruits of your labor by changing people's lives. So it was settled: my sophomore year, I'd major in social work. Ms. J and I were still going strong, so instead of just messing around all the time on the PlayStation with the fellas, I was in the library. I was definitely on top of the schoolwork. My freshman year definitely showed me that only the strong and rich survive. I sure as heck wasn't rich, so I needed to work hard to make this work.

It was during this year that my best friend from high school, Sheldon Oliver (but from now on, I'll refer to him as Shel), reconnected with me when he returned to the area—and man, it was on like Donkey Kong all over again. But Ms. J knew of Shel's tendencies and warned me that he was trouble, but this time, I had to let her know, "I don't choose your friends, and you can't choose mine. I understand your concerns, and I'll respect them, but he's my dude." So Shel and I hung out. We weren't always in the clubs, but sometimes we would work out together in the gym. However, it was always genuine brotherhood. One thing was for sure: I loved some alcohol, and in college, the weed was often passed, but never ever would it come my way. If Shel was there, he would instantly stand guard as a good friend and brother should. Unfortunately, on the court, things weren't as good as I'd like them to be.

It's crazy how sports and life mirror each other, how some interesting characteristics can make a huge difference for you.

1. **Timing**. It is so crucial. Moving too fast or too slow can alter a play in a game and affect the whole season. The same happens in life when it's not your time yet and/or you rush things that aren't supposed to happen in a particular space of time, the results can be awful. That was my sophomore year for me in a nutshell with basketball and life—just bad timing.

2. **Discipline**. This means doing what works the right way every time even when no one is watching you. It's the same with life: doing what's right when others try and steer you to do wrong, or even when no one's watching you, takes discipline. I didn't have that in this phase of my life.

3. **Vision**. It's not just the ability to see the play but the ability to visualize past the present, being able to anticipate the future, and having the mental fortitude to counteract whatever comes your way. If you can't see where you want to be on a daily basis, then you'll be stuck where you stand

forever. That was me. I had to open my eyes past where I was and allow my vision to show me the path I should take. This was a tough lesson to learn and grasp.

4. **Execution**. This comes into play when the timing is perfect. Everyone's on the same page, discipline hasn't wavered, the goal and game plan are seen and followed, and the vision is in sight and everyone sees the goal. When these criteria are met, the game plan must be executed and carried out. I was nowhere near ready to be in this phase, but I would soon learn through losing how to get to this point on and off the court.

The second semester began, and after a tough first half of the year, the games were going well. We beat the top seed for the first time in our school's history, got a few other notable and comfortable wins, and life seemed to be on the rise for our team, the good old Flames. Then out of the blue, and as has been the story of my life until now, the injury bug bit me. We were at a road game in Vermont on a windy and snowy afternoon. The game was going well, and we were actually in control. But before the halfway mark of the half, my shoulder popped out again. One of the other team's henchmen, who was sent in to hack and hurt me, pushed me as I jumped for the ball. The precaution you have to take with dislocations is to never allow the shoulder to be in the pledge position because that's when you're most vulnerable for a repeat dislocation. Unfortunately, it was my day, and man, the pain and agony was ever present again. I was looking at another four weeks of my life in a sling and rehab before there would be any remote chance of a possible comeback. I was so gutted and upset.

The playoffs came, and we went out in the first round. I'll be the first to admit that I was shaken and played like it when it mattered most, and we lost by six points. The rest of the school year was just a formality really. The soccer tryouts came around again, but my fear of being hurt lingered from basketball, so I punked out on the opportunity again and just went on with my life, hoping that the chance would come my way again. As the school year came to an end, rumors were circulating that the AUC Flames were invited to some huge tournaments in the next season, including a huge tournament in Bermuda, so things were looking up for me. The question was, could and would I be able to maintain my health and get my shoulder ready?

On a more personal front, Ms. J wanted to enter my world and see what and how I lived, and I promised to take her to Bermuda to see and experience it firsthand and meet my people. In truth, she wanted to see and hang out with a few Bermudians whom I didn't like to associate with, and I wasn't down with that. We had a small quarrel, but we quickly smoothed it over. We resumed our lovely trip as was my job as host. It truly was a great weekend. Then Monday abruptly came, and she was gone. We wouldn't see each other for a few weeks, but the time we did spend together was special. For the remainder of the break, I was still on the grind, going to physical therapy and working on my game to try and better myself for the upcoming year.

Junior year came much faster than I had expected, and to be fair, like most students, I wasn't ready to take classes. I hadn't gotten supplies or anything, but I wasn't worried. I had worked out a foolproof plan to get my textbooks and some extra cash—**I stole them**. At the time, the AUC bookstore didn't have a security camera, so basically, all I needed was someone to be a lookout and an accomplice to help me get the books that were on my list. The key to being successful was to buy some things to avoid suspicion. In my sophomore, junior, and senior years, I stole my textbooks and took orders for others to make extra cash (I regretfully admit that I stole textbooks for hire). I think now about how stupid I was. If I had gotten caught, I would have been expelled with no chance of graduating, and I would have caused so much embarrassment for my poor mother. But I didn't stop to think of the consequences. It was lightweight fun until Ms. J found out what I was doing, she was thoroughly disgusted with me on every level, and immediately threatened to break up with me. She was extremely infuriated by my actions, and it took the better part of a month to get back in her good graces. But it was never the same, and rightly so. My actions were reckless and stupid, and she wanted nothing to do with me.

Sports-wise, soccer had started, and I was eligible to play. But this year, I had a different mind-set. I was not looking for the glory but wanted to make my teammates better. This was the leader in me beginning to grow. Understanding the bigger picture is always better than the private one you may hold dear. So I changed my position on the field and tried to help maintain coverage on every part of the field, thus making us strong enough to compete with the best teams. Rattery, Butters, Macky, Scotty, and of course, Big Al, and I balanced ourselves throughout the field and let the Bermuda connection take over the field. I played defense and still remained captain, but I played defense because it was the most challenging job on the field, keeping our opponents' best attacks out. It was crazy, but I became a natural, and it was great to help my team; though occasionally, I would run forward and score just for the thrill of it. You couldn't tell us we weren't *bud* (Bermudian lingo meaning "too cool").

We didn't win as much as we should have, but it truly was a great experience. In the last game of the season, in order to clinch a playoff berth, we needed to beat the best team in the conference. Unfortunately, we lost 3-0, but oddly enough, the same referee from previous times who had spoken with me about potentially playing professionally pulled me aside. He spoke something profound to me that really made me stop and take notice. He said, "It's nice to be a big fish in a small pond, but you never can grow bigger than the size of your environment." In other words, if I wanted to cultivate my talent, I needed to step out on faith and see what the tryouts would bring. His final words still echo today, and they were: "Don't waste another year of time working for your school when you could be getting paid to play a game you're good at." I was superexcited and began to share with some people of what my plans were and how excited I was to finally be able to try and execute this next phase in my life. I learned another valuable lesson in this situation, and if you're truly looking to be successful in this life, you'll have to accept it.

Lesson 10: Sometimes you have to understand that not everyone will share the same dreams or visionary path for success as you do. You can't let their hate for

your drive, vision, and ability to make your dream
a reality deter you from greatness.

I told Ms. J about the negativity I was getting from some people, and she just smiled and softly said, "Haters are *motivators*. Use their hate to propel you, and trust me, they will be back on the bandwagon when they see that your mental strength trumps their hate." As much as I played it down, it was a tough pill to swallow when you have known people for so long and have experienced some things with them as well that, at a drop of a dime, they would flip the script. But that's life, and as this chapter's title states, this was my welcome into the real world. In going through this, I came across one saying in passing in my literature class that summed up the reality of living your dream, and others hating because their gifts aren't like yours:

Envy and hate are just taxes paid on success.

(Dania Nichols)

Well, after swallowing this tough pill, I immediately registered for the tryouts. A teammate of mine also decided to head to the combine, which was sweet because now I'd have a ride to get there. And having someone I knew there was a plus. But first, basketball season was upon me, and there wasn't a lot of rest in between seasons. However, I enjoyed the challenge and loved to push myself. This season on court would be extremely different as we would soar to new heights and exceed a lot of expectations. First and foremost, I came in with a different mind-set and was focused on what can I do to stay healthy and make everyone around me better, so I began to work out my shoulder more. I had committed to doing this all season to make sure my shoulder didn't pop out. I also started playing more pickup games with my teammates and was getting a better feel for how they played. I began to know their tendencies better and discovered new ways to get them going, which in turn made life easier for me.

Boy, did all of it pay off! Shoot, we obliterated teams left right, and center. The real test was heading down to Vermont right after

Thanksgiving and playing the big boys on their court to see what we were made of. Like a fine-tuned guitar, we didn't miss a beat; and going into the season break, we were tied for the top of the conference standings, and this was major for our school. On the personal front, I finally had the opportunity to head to Ms. J's home and spend time with her family and see her environment and where she grew up. To my surprise, it was quite cool, and I really enjoyed Brooklyn to the fullest. Her mother and family showed me so much love I was definitely excited that things were cool. But unfortunately, I could sense that there would be tough days ahead; I always had a sixth sense with relationships.

Finally I was headed home for the break to see my crew. I missed hanging with them just to chill and get away from sports, and even Ms. J. As much as I loved her, the relationship was becoming too much, and I didn't know how to juggle everything and keep everyone happy. I remember talking to Renzo about it and asking him how, even from a distance, he always made time for Nae, even neglecting what he may have wanted to do for himself and his well-being. In his deep voice, Renzo just said, "That's a sacrifice I'm willing to make for her, man. She's worth it." It was profound truth that struck me to the core. Was I really that committed, or did I want to be free to explore? Was I having second thoughts about this relationship? Pushing this to the back of my mind, I began to enjoy the family. My nephew was a toddler, so I was with him everywhere, just playing and loving on him big-time. He was, for sure, my birth control. He definitely reminded me I didn't want kids and that kind of responsibility. It was so fun to see Jereme growing and developing, but like all good things, this visit was soon to end, and it was time to head back and finish off the basketball season.

We had the annual high school tournament coming up, as well as a few games for us to showcase what we had going on with our program and the progress it had made over the past few years. We played well and were great hosts, but around the corner was a cross-country trip to Walla Walla College in Washington State. Oakwood, Walla Walla, AUC, and Southwestern University would play in an epic round-robin tournament. We started Thursday facing Southwestern.

I went bananas and made twenty-six points, eight rebounds, and eight assists, and we won against a good team. Friday saw us pitted against the home team right before evening vespers. It was a nail-biter, and we went back and forth. But they were slightly more organized; thus, they edged us out by five points. It was a pretty solid game. The last game was somewhat of a rivalry game against Oakwood College, and we pretty much smacked them from the get-go. One thing about our offense on that Saturday evening was that we ran it crisply and methodically. They gambled, and we punished them. At the end of the game, we had won by almost twenty points and had to wait and see if Southwestern would win so we could finish in first place. However, we ended the tournament in second place, and I was named to the All-Tournament Team.

The one thing I remembered most about this trip was me apologizing to Mrs. MC and asking for her forgiveness for my brash and rude dismissal of our friendship. She was dating my homeboy Mr. MC, and I just wanted life to be normal. When I mentioned this on the phone to Ms. J later that evening, boy, it got ugly so fast. But at that point, I didn't care because I could sense our bond growing thin, and she was about to graduate. Truthfully, I was at that point where I felt, *If you can't deal with it, oh well.* It was ugly for a bit; and even when my mom, sister, and brother-in-law came to visit, they could sense the distance between Ms. J and me and asked me if things were cool. At this stage of my junior year, my mother became my confidant, and I began to open up and discuss the situation with her. In turn, she began to dissect a lot of things for me to make me understand what I needed to do to be ultimately happy with myself. I had a blast with my family, and Jereme was getting so big and was so much fun, but they had to leave before our home game the following Sunday. However, their presence reassured and relaxed me for the following months to come.

On the court, we were pushing for a great seed and our first home playoff game in years, so we fought like heck, ending with a 9–3 record, which meant we would host a playoff game. The city of Lancaster, Massachusetts, was straight on pause from 7:00 p.m. to 9:30 p.m., and the evening belonged to the Flames, and we didn't disappoint anyone who showed up. From start to end, we controlled the game and managed to hold their star player down. The atmosphere in the small gym was electric; even the faculty came out and supported. It was a great feeling and a great experience to be a part of. At 9:30 p.m., the court was stormed by rowdy kids screaming out, "AUC! AUC! AUC!" Man, we had finally put things together, and this was our year to do it big, going to the final four and winning the conference championship. These are moments you dream of as a sportsman. You long for those days when it's all or nothing, put up or shut up, and you have to show up and prove you're the best.

Unfortunately, the following weekend at the final four, the dream would end against the eventual winners. We played a close game throughout, but in the second half, we hit a dry patch. They were a great shooting team who punished us, and that's the way it went—we were out. It was the hardest and most difficult lesson I had to learn, knowing you're better than someone but, on that day, they got the better of you. We'd beaten them both home and away in conference play, but we just didn't come through in the clutch, and that pissed me off big-time. But the wheels of time never turn backward.

Around this time, I started going to vespers not just for credit, but I actually enjoyed the vibe, and my attitude to many things and people began to shift. I disliked our dean of the dorm to no end, but I got the urge to be kind and open-minded to him and his culture, regardless of our run-ins and how we bumped heads. I also looked at some worthwhile severed relationships and started to mend them and be more open-minded to life. I had to face the fact that, for over three years, I was closed-minded and only sought to please my lady. The few people who accepted this choice were my close friends, but as the year came to a close, the drama began.

The soccer trials took place inside an artificial dome because it was March and the weather was still inclement. **There were about 3,000 people** trying out, and believe you me, I was slightly intimidated at first. However, like I do with any game, I watched my opponents—in this case, it was everyone—to see how I matched up in talent and technique. After some serious observation, I saw a few cats who were really good, but I wasn't afraid anymore. I actually felt released from the pressures of school, the haters, and just anything that was bothering me. For those two hours, I was free.

All I kept telling myself was that I was built for the grind, and sure enough, that's how I kept going. The combine tryout was on Friday, Saturday, and Monday. In these three days, the number **went from 3,000 people to a final twenty-two**. Shoot, after one of the first drills, the **number went down from 3,000 to seven hundred**—the cut was that concise and precise. My teammate got axed after the first day, but they pulled me aside and talked to me at length and began to pry into my life a bit. Honestly, I didn't know how to take it, nor did I understand the coach's thick Scottish accent. My teammate left me at the combine because he was so mad that he had gotten cut. Luckily, there was guy there who lived in the next town over from Lancaster, and I was able to get a ride from him. This experience taught me another bitter lesson.

Lesson 11: Hate can consume you or can propel you to be greater!

I was invited to the second day of the combine, but in truth, the first day was by far the hardest. The second day covered the technical side of the game, understanding positioning and things I was more than comfortable with. On Saturday, we played games, and people were picked to play in 5v5, 6v6, and so on until we were in 11v11 games. Basically, the staff just analyzed everyone's strengths and weaknesses. Come Monday, I had a problem. The final tryout made me miss my advisor's class, and she made a huge fuss. She was such a loving and honest lady she allowed me to go after praying with me. However, I had to write an extra paper, but I was cool with that. Papers were easy for me to write, so I was off to see if I was going to be asked to be a professional soccer player.

The last day of the combine was again just games and they rotated a few other guys and me all over the field and we never had a break. I can honestly say that the third day I had picked up on the other players' tendencies, and with my ability and size, I bullied my way around the field a bit, but the technique really carried me over.

One thing I had learned from young watching people in Bermuda was that they limited themselves to what was comfortable, meaning only using one foot. I always practiced using both, figuring that if you can use both feet, then you eliminate more weaknesses in your game and your technique. It's tough to deal with a player who is highly skilled with both feet.

Those two hours went by so fast, and finally, the final whistle was blown. We were called in for a small chat to tell us who would have no chance and whom the officials would be in touch with. Right before the names were called, my mind reverted to the days at BI (Bermuda Institute), where I was the joke of the class, and no one gave me a chance at all to play, to the grind and the years I played and tried to master my craft, my respect of the game I loved, and how I wanted to represent Bermuda to the fullest.

The names were being called fast, and finally the official stopped. He didn't call my name, so that meant I'd be getting a call later to either invite me to camp as a player or to offer me a contract, or so I thought. They told me to stay behind after, which I did, and I was told that the GM (general manager) was on his way to talk with me and offer me a contract immediately. I couldn't believe it. I thought we had to wait, but they told me they wanted to sign me from the first day but wanted to see how my body and mind would respond over the weekend with a day off in between.

They gave me the option to sign immediately or to come in for a sit-down meeting the following Monday to proceed. I took the latter option and went back to AUC, just smiling because I had accomplished another goal I had set for myself as a kid, and I had proven all the haters wrong. The Boston Bulldogs, an A-League soccer team, was going to help me obtain a lifelong dream of being paid to play soccer professionally. Wow, things were looking on the up-and-up for me. Wait, someone's knocking on my life's door. Ah yes, the neighbor. Everyone hates drama. What lies around the corner?

CHAPTER 4

DON'T LET IT GO TO YOUR HEAD

Progress is a nice word. But change is its motivation, and change has many enemies.

—Robert F. Kennedy

A week later, I was embracing a true dream and signing my first professional contract to play for money. However, once you sign, you've got to produce. I sat in the GM's office and discussed a suitable salary. I had just purchased a vehicle to get around in, and they reimbursed me for that, so life seemed great. I was given special days to work and some deference because, unlike me, my teammates were finished with school, and playing soccer was their primary job or major hobby, and their work schedule coincided with the Bulldogs' schedule. I would train three times a week when permitted, but usually only two times until school ended. At the end of the year, they had an apartment for all the players, and I would go there to live, and it was basically like a frat house. I finally began working out with them, and the practices were hard and were mentally draining. I fared well, but the problem for me at first was the speed of the game. However, after a week, I had almost gotten it down to a science.

After a few weeks of training, the preseason was done, and I was to catch a flight out to San Diego to meet the guys for the trip to the first game of the season. Usually trips went like this: train the day before in the morning and then fly out that evening as a team after having lunch together. The week went by so fast. I couldn't even sleep Thursday night, but Friday a.m., I woke up way early and made moves because morning traffic in Boston is no joke, and I couldn't blow this opportunity. Up to this point, I had told my mom not to tell a bunch of people about my place on the team, just my close friends' parents. I mainly wanted to keep it on the low because of the major hate I received from the people closest to me, and she kept her word. On the day before I flew to San Diego, my mom and I had a really good talk. She reassured me that I was more than capable for this opportunity and promised that she was praying over me. That was a great thing to know.

On the relationship front, things were bad at this time. I was speaking with old friends again and hanging out with Sheldon way more than before, and it got ugly. But this trip was a safe haven. A few days away from it all and flying first-class to San Diego to play professionally wasn't a bad way to start my weekend. Game day came with the usual routine. After brunch, Coach gave a strategy breakdown and named the starting eleven, and then we got the time we needed to be down in the lobby for the team bus. Riding to the stadium, my stomach was full of butterflies. I had started a routine while playing basketball in high school, and that was to listen to gospel music on game days, and that is something that sticks with me today—it has always put me in a serene place.

The game presented a challenge to us, and it was against a strong San Diego squad that jumped out to an early lead in the twentieth minute with a strong, towering header from one of their forwards. Our coach was never one to panic; he always breathed confidence into the team and encouraged us to play as a team. Unfortunately, on the stroke of halftime, we let in another easy goal, and things weren't looking so great. Before Coach came in to give the halftime talk, he told me to warm up and not come in for the talk, so I stayed outside with an assistant and went through a lot of drill work. It was on the outside of the field. I hated playing winger, but if that was what was going to get me paid, I was up for it.

The second half began and we looked flat, it was blatantly obvious changes were needed. I had thirty-five minutes to show that I belonged, and buddy I couldn't have asked for a better introduction on this sort of platform at this stage in my career. I was extremely fast and utilized pass and move masterfully. With my speed and a better technique, I was cooking this left-side defender and leaving him in my dust. In the seventy-eighth minute after leaving him for dead again, I sent in a low cross (delivery of a ball along the ground from either side of the field across to the front of the goal); and to my astonishment, it slipped through the maze and slid into the corner of the goal. We had a lifeline and twelve minutes to complete the comeback. At this point, the strategy was to get the ball to me and let me cook my defender, and that's exactly how it went down until finally in the eighty-fifth minute, when he received a red card (second yellow card, which meant he'd be ejected and couldn't continue to play). As the ball came rolling to me, I could sense he was coming as well, so I flicked the ball around him and proceeded to run around him into the open space to recollect the ball for twenty yards of free space and for my teammates to join me.

Regardless of my somewhat explosive first game, we lost 2–1, but I had definitely set a tone for myself. I had shown that I belonged, but to be honest, in the locker room, I could sense that people didn't believe in me. A scout from the prestigious LA Galaxy team found me after the game and gave me his information and told me that if I kept playing like I did, they might snap me up. Man, all this happened after just one game! I was superhyped, and my coach saw it and wisely pulled me aside before I went into the locker room and gave me this warning with his thick Scottish accent: "Keep your feet on the ground. Only true stars are permitted in the sky." I got the message and shut it down and was superquiet on the bus ride back to the hotel. I wasn't in a terrible mood, but I had gotten humbled. I turned on my Discman and didn't say a word at all about the game or what transpired afterwards to anyone.

I learned so much under Coach Stevo's tutelage. He really took me under his wing, but never in a group setting. He would always make me stay after practice and made it looked like he was giving me the rookie treatment. This was the greatest learning experience, being separated from the pack. Stevo was a player on the iconic Liverpool FC (one of the greatest European soccer clubs ever), and he was a defender by trade. Thus, he would give me insight on how to get around defenders and ways to expand my game. Let's face it, by my third game, people began to kick the crap out of me, hoping to kick me off the pitch instead of dealing with my pace. But that's why you always go back to the laboratory (whatever it is you wish to be great in, go back to the basics) to redefine yourself so that your opponents can't get a strategy to hold you down. You should evolve and expand your game to a point where, hopefully, they just can't deal with you.

Personally, back at school, my relationship was coming to an end. We had many rough patches, and Ms. J and I had maintained through the struggles and drama, but graduation was coming up soon. What would be next for us?   We talked about it and agreed to keep pushing through. And since I'd be playing soccer, I would come up to New York some weekends, and we'd work it out like that. It was a good plan in theory, but it didn't pan out that way. We struggled to get back to our previous bond, and we never did.

The season was going so well for me individually, but as a team, we were struggling to maintain an identity. We also had a lot of injuries in key positions, which definitely put a damper on our success as a whole. We lost so many games in the last fifteen minutes of the games when our concentration and focus should be at their highest to keep us from making mistakes. As the summer began to draw to an end, we had an opportunity; but unfortunately, on a road trip in Montreal, my shoulder popped out again. It slid back in, and I just played the ninety minutes of the game in pain. Two days later in Rochester, the season ended with same thing happening: my shoulder popped out and slid back in. As soon as we got back to Massachusetts, they took me to the doctor, and I learned that I would need surgery to fix my shoulder and rotator cuff, using pins and wires to secure my shoulder in place. I was scared out of my mind, but Ms. J and her mom came and looked after me. I can honestly say they saved me because the pain was unbelievable.

Ms. J was going to head to North Carolina to go to school, and since the flights were so expensive, I volunteered to drive from Massachusetts to North Carolina to help her out. Plus, I couldn't fly for a month because of my shoulder surgery. It was a peaceful ride, and we had a blast, but it would be the last time we would ever spend time together. After a few days there, hanging with the family, I headed back to Massachusetts to rehab and got ready for my senior year. Word on the street was that it would be AUC's last year of existence. I had my ear to the ground and was looking for other places to play with my last year of eligibility; and because of the fiasco of my freshman year, I needed the extra time to finish school as well. I can honestly say that during my last year, I mended a lot of torn and severed relationships that I had previously discarded. I also had a good bit of fun, maybe a bit too much, but I learned this:

Lesson 12: Relationships have their place, so do friendships. When you honor both, you become a much more well-rounded person.

Realistically in previous years, I didn't value friendships; and that year, I vowed to do so. Some were open-minded and understood what I had done wasn't right, and they forgave me. Not everyone did, and that's life. People don't necessarily have to accept your honest mistakes. All in all, life was good for me, and I was grateful for what my relationship with Ms. J taught me. But a new chapter was beginning, as well as a new me. My shoulder had been healing up nicely, and in the middle of October, almost seven weeks after surgery, I was back on the grind and getting better.

With shoulder surgery, you can't fully use the shoulder until the tissue adapts to the pins and wires and slightly tears to allow movement. I didn't experience this for a couple of weeks, but once I did, there absolutely was no stopping me then. As a team, the AUC Flames were dealt a major blow when our starting center had a knee injury and had to sit out for a few months; we really struggled and never recovered. He had to sit out from November until February, and trying be competitive without him was an ugly learning curve for us. In sports, just like in life, people usually only learn when they lose something or someone.

During my senior year, I learned so much, not only about losing but how to reinvent myself on the court. Without our starting center, I was double- and triple-teamed. To be a leader on the team, I had to be smarter, faster, and still try and put in work. During this period, my resolve, patience, and everything were tested. I never quit, but there were times when I felt like it didn't matter if I did or not. Luckily for me, my pride would never allow me to let my standards to drop like that. I had a mantra back then, which I still have to this day: "I hate losing more than I like to win." It's that defiant voice or attitude I gained to never quit and to find a way to make my dream a reality.

Needless to say, even when our big man came back, we still couldn't find our rhythm as a team. We were so close, but it never happened. Unfortunately, we lost a tough road game in the first round of the playoffs, and the season and my basketball career at AUC was over. My stats were solid, and I had played well. But with sports, winning is what ultimately defines you; and at that level, I didn't measure up.

In my personal life, I was having fun, playing the field and just enjoying life with no responsibilities or expectations surrounding me. On the low, I was sizing up someone I will call *Shelly*. She was a cool sister, and we shared the same major. But most importantly, she was a challenge. To this day, I can say I've never dated a woman who did not present a challenge to me. If there's no challenge, I would lose interest quickly, like most guys. On the other hand, I was mingling with another girl who also was a cool sister and seemed so down-to-earth that I kicked it with her as well but used her emotionally and, eventually, physically as well.

I lent my car to the girl I was friends with and went to my soccer games. We were really cool, but you never really know someone until you have drama with them. When you play games with a woman's heart, there are consequences to pay. When you're young and dumb, you don't think about that; you only care about your own fun. As the school year came to a close, I didn't have a plan, but the Bulldogs reached out to me again to play, and I figured, why not play again? It wouldn't hurt and could be fun. On the flip side, I still hadn't decided what would happen with basketball; but I got in contact with the coach, Mr. Smith, and began to ponder a move to the DC area. Soon my girl had left, but little did I know my reckless behavior would leave her pregnant with my firstborn, Ja'hnniah.

To this day, I'm appalled by my attitude upon finding out about the pregnancy. But I'm writing to keep it 100 percent organic and show the truth that people, especially Christians, don't often share. Our phone calls were simple. I told her, "Get rid of the baby. You're going to ruin our lives." Honestly, I really only meant my life. I knew that I wasn't going to be around because I was going to play soccer or basketball somewhere and she'd have to raise the kid alone. I used every technique possible, but thank God she ignored me and followed through to have our daughter. During the summer, I was devastated, angry, confused, and most of all, worried about how others would view me after this.

What worries you, masters you.

- John Locke

Whether I was ready or not, reality had dealt me a child, and there was no running from that responsibility. Being on the field was my oasis from the issues plaguing my personal life. For two hours a day, I didn't worry about anything; all I had to do was focus and play. I would even stay after practice and work on my game just to stay away from the drama longer. This drama really had me in a zone, and on the field, I was on fire, scoring goals and setting up goals left, right, and center. Coach Stevo could sense something was wrong and approached me on the sidelines and asked if I was okay. I said yeah with a sly smirk, but he looked at me and said, "Nah, you're not, but I'll never force you to talk. But if you ever want to, my door is open."

The pain and disgust I felt with myself was propelling me to success, but I had no avenues to let out my thoughts and feelings, so they were bottled up in me all summer. On the personal front, during this time, I had two run-ins with the law; and since my hair was braided, it made me an easy target for harassment. The first arrest came after a night in Boston messing around with a young lady. I entered my city, and the siren lights lit up. Supposedly it was a routine check, but there had been a drive-by where a man was assaulted, so I was made to stand on a corner in handcuffs and be viewed by a gentleman whom I couldn't see to determine if he would identify me as the attacker. If he had positively identified me, I would have been jailed on his word. Looking back on that situation, it was supersad and crazy. In the end, they said my car registration tags were expired, and I had to go to jail for the night because I didn't have cash on me, and I couldn't use my debit card in the station; nor would they stop at an ATM so I could get cash. And of course, they wouldn't let me call anyone. I was in jail from 2:00 a.m. until 8:00 a.m., when I could leave on my own cognizance. But this is what I had to deal with in my town. The next morning, I walked home. My teammates were like, "Dude, are you okay?" I explained the story and just caught a ride to practice.

That afternoon was spent in the Registry of Motor Vehicles (RMVA), checking to make sure my car was registered, which it was, and getting a letter to take to the court and would allow me to drive around after I got my car from the tow shop. Two weeks later, I was arrested again for the same offense by the same cops. This time, I had twenty-five dollars on me, but I still wasn't granted bail, so I spent another night in the slammer. This time, I was pissed and let it be known. At the RMVA, they had spelled my name in the system as S-u-l-l-i-v-a-i-n Phillips instead of S-u-l-l-i-v-a-n. It was a simple matter of a misspelling, but they were so hell-bent on bothering me.

Finally things got sorted out, and the police were off my back, I was free to get back on the field. We were a tough group to deal with, and we remained in the top three for the entire year, as did my teammate and I in the points system for the league (you received two points for a goal and one point for every assist you made per game).

Statistically, by midseason, I was in the top five among all players, but I couldn't shake the off-the-field worries. A road trip came with two games in North Carolina and Wilmington, and I simply played marvelously in both games with two goals and one assist, and an A-League team and an MLS scout were there to talk to me. Was this my daybreak after my summer nightmare? Could this be the positive news I needed to end my most miserable summer to date?

No chance. The Bulldogs knew my value and wouldn't sell my contract to either team. I was so mad I wouldn't talk with anyone. Coach Stevo made his way over to me, and we had our first heart-to-heart conversation, even though at first I wasn't trying to hear a word from him or anyone. He sat me down and explained why they wouldn't let me go. It made sense. If they won the league, the club could go back to a better league, get more sponsors with endorsements for the players, which meant more money. They wanted to win and keep me as a player to hopefully build a team around me if I kept growing in stature on the field. He also asked me what I wanted to do with my life. Was I going to go for the NBA or play soccer and utilize my talent? He saw that I loved soccer to no end, but at the time, the money was in basketball. At some point, I'd have to choose because both were very demanding, and I couldn't realistically play both of them professionally. I would have to choose one. After our long talk, I walked away knowing that although I loved soccer, because of the money, I knew I would pursue basketball. But I didn't tell anyone that, especially not Coach Stevo.

On field, I was his pupil, and he demanded more and more from me. We ended the season as the division champs and were heading into the postseason. The playoffs finally came around, and we won our first round game 2–0, and I had an assist. Then we were on to the semifinals, and it was another home game, where all the marbles were on the table. After a close game, we lost 2–1. I couldn't believe it. We killed this team in the regular season, and we dominated this game, but a lucky own goal ten minutes from time sealed our fate. We felt gutted, but the truth is, anyone can be beaten if they're off their game; even the best can be beaten. As a team, we got to play exhibition games against top Brazilian players from times past; and in my first year, I got to play against the legendary Blanco, a powerful left-back, and the popular Jairzinho as well. This last year, I played against Careca (Antonio de Oliveira Fiho), as well as the famous Dunga (Carlos Caetano Bledorn Verri), two legendary world cup winners. It was unbelievable experience who would have ever thought this could happen.

I had been in contact with Coach Smith throughout the summer, but toward the end of summer, I reluctantly let him know my personal situation. To my surprise, he was nonjudgmental and was 150 percent supportive of me. This really was the deciding factor for me: his response to my situation as well as his genuine care for my well-being, not just how valuable I was to our basketball team either. Finally, two weeks before registration, I had my transcripts sent over to Columbia Union College (CUC) and found out I was accepted in good standing to finish my basketball and college careers there. Everything wasn't smooth sailing all the way; they had just started their social-work program and were correlating it with Andrews University's program, so it was going to be a bit bumpy, especially since I only had my upper-division classes left to complete.

Nevertheless, I wasn't afraid of the road not traveled. To be quite honest, I often shunned away from things that were straightforward and easy. During this time, I began dating a lady I will call *Ms. Mills*, a highly sophisticated, intelligent lady whom I pursued heavily throughout my senior year, but to no avail—until when the end of the year came, and she found time and space for me. She attended my soccer games, and we had a good rapport. It was not the same as I had with Ms. J, but it was cool, and most importantly, there was no stress of labels or demands; we just had fun. We both were quite interested in seeing if our relationship could flourish, but in truth, it never could. My mind was overwhelmed with thoughts of my newborn baby, school, and the whole nine, and I wasn't emotionally available. Finally, after a nice weekend with Ms. Mills that summer, I was on an airplane to DC to start a new chapter in my life.

CUC's campus was small, but definitely not too far from the city, so I loved that. Unfortunately, upon arrival, half the team hated me. Coach Smith spoke highly of me, but the response I received when I finally entered the gym just for open recreational time was crazy. All eyes on the new guy, and everyone wanted to show they were better than me. All wasn't lost. Two of the guys were very cool to me and embraced me; and to this date, I'm still cool with one of them. Big Bo was my Canadian homie, and we had so much fun together. From Thursday through Sunday night, we had a blast and totally drowned ourselves in the best of DC's nightlife—unless we had a game, we were out on the town. My other homie was Michael (a.k.a. ATL, may he rest in peace). He was definitely one of the coolest brothers I've ever met and was a true friend from day one. He had a deep Southern drawl and was always so positive; but on court, man, he had the sweetest jumper ever. This brother could pull up and shoot the ball from the parking lot, and it would go in.

The preseason was going well, and in the first few days of classes, I met three women who would have a lasting positive impact on my life, and I call them my sisters: Larissa Straker, Gwen Marie Davis-Hicks, and Christina Stanley. Although I always avoided being in a clique or being defined by a group of people, these sisters and I became inseparable, and they became my crew. These three women couldn't have been more different from each other, but we bonded and have remained close through the years. They have been very inspirational to me, and my love for them has never wavered over time. I was truly blessed to meet them during my first days at CUC.

When the basketball season began, we won two huge games and started off 2–0; this was big news for a team that had only won six games the previous season. I was superamped about the prospect of really doing something special. However, after the first two games, we split the next ten games, and we were heading into the Thanksgiving break with a big win. I can honestly say that game was one of my best college showings: twenty-seven points, sixteen rebounds, and eleven assists. Hands down, it was my best triple-double ever on the road. This game ignited my professional career. An agent was there watching the predicted preseason player of the year, and I destroyed him from start to finish. Unfortunately, we lost in overtime. I'll never forget what happened after the game. The agent came to me and said, "Man, don't sweat it. You're going to play pro one day." I looked him dead in the eye and asked, "Do I look like I care that I just lost? That's the most pressing thing to me, here and now, not what the future holds." He took my information, and a week later, he began to write and keep in touch with me. He insisted that with my attitude and skill set, I could get a few NBA look-ins and, worse case, get a contract to play in Europe. I took what he said simply as empty words, but I was polite and kept it moving.

Thanksgiving break came, and it was the absolute worse. I had to break the news to Ms. Mills on the trip that I was having a baby, and believe you me, it was a truly ugly break. She cried the whole trip, and I felt bad. But during one of our arguments, her attack went too far. I snapped, and all my frustration came out. I asked her, "How do you think I feel? You think I want a kid with someone who I thought was trying to trap me and make me get married, ultimately ruining my life and my relationship with her?" Ms. Mills was taken aback because never in two years of knowing me had she ever seen me with an attitude. No matter what, I was always upbeat around her; but in this instance, she saw the real me. To her credit, she embraced it and said she'd try to work through this situation with me. This argument pissed me off so much that during the whole Thanksgiving break, I was in a mood and couldn't wait to get back to DC.

I still hadn't told my mom about the baby, but seeing that the baby would be born soon, I knew I had to come clean with my mom and let her know. This was by far the hardest thing I would have to do, especially knowing how frustrated and disappointed she would be. One cold December evening, I made the dreadful call to my mom. The conversation was cool at first. We talked about Thanksgiving and how it went, but she could tell something was bothering me. I just cut to the chase and told her my predicament—that I was expecting a baby and that I was hoping that it wouldn't happen, or that my child's mother would change her mind, have an abortion, and we'd never have to mention it again. My mom, being the typical warrior she is, just prayed with me and spoke the phrase that ends every conversation I have with her to date, "Watch your back!" Man, it was like the world had been lifted off my shoulders, but at the same time, the reality was I was going to be a father in about two and a half months. My daughter was due on February 9, the same day as my birthday. Talk about a coincidence, but that's life. There are no accidents.

During the long-awaited Christmas holiday, my mom and I really connected, not just as mother to son, but she began to talk to me as a woman teaching me things from a woman's perspective; and to this day, they have helped me to no end. With her spiritually discerning eyes, she began to warn me about a lot of things going on in my life, especially my nightlife antics, getting back into church, and accepting my role and responsibility in the making and rearing of my child, who would soon enter the world. As angry as I was, she calmly reminded me of what was right and wrong and that no child ever asks for the situation they are bought into. She also reminded me that I should do right by my daughter. At this point in my life, no one but my mom could tell me off and let me know where I stood without me going through the roof. She handled the situation with class and style, the same way any real woman would do. Other than my mother, I hadn't told anyone that I was having a kid, not even the trinity crew. Truthfully, I just wasn't ready for the commitment and responsibility that was before me.

The trinity crew was still in effect, and they have loved me during far worse periods in my life. But it wasn't until much later that my daughter would get to meet and enjoy any of my true friends, and that was all on me. After the break, it was back to business as usual, except there was some big drama brewing. My boy Big Bo moved to Oakwood, leaving me with just my sisters and ATL, or so I thought. Soon my best homie Shel would come on down to hang and attend school with me. Believe me, when he came, things got pretty bad. There were some wannabe gangstas on the team who had tried to jump him the year before. I didn't know this until he explained it to me. Once I found that out, it was official. There was no love lost between us and no words spoken from that point on; we only ran plays together. Heck, I wouldn't even shower in the locker room with them, especially since it had been confirmed how shady these dudes were. On the court, it was obvious we didn't get along. It was blatant when certain people wouldn't pass the ball to others or would make comments or facial expressions to one another. There was a bad vibe on the court for a few games until Coach Smith shut that foolishness down.

He sat us in the locker room and straight ripped into us. He said that we all were embarrassing the school and, most importantly, shaming our family names. He made it clear that we didn't have to send one another Christmas cards or be buddies off the court, but when we practiced and played together, we had better be, or he would cut everyone's scholarship just like that. It was a tough but memorable lesson that you can apply to your life:

Lesson 13: There's a reason why the team's name is on the front of the jerseys and the individual player's name is on the back. The team comes first. However, if you play well, no one will ever forget the name on the back of the jersey either. But the team comes first.

Talk about tough pill to swallow, but it's a true saying and can apply to all facets and walks of life. I can honestly say this lecture truly changed the mood on court, and we began to compete better, making extra passes, and the whole nine yards. We began to win a few tough games and a few games we weren't expected to win as well.

During this period, February 9 was soon approaching. After attending church one day with my sisters, I got a call from my daughter's grandmother announcing her arrival. She was actually born on February 8, 2002, and it was official: an extension of me was on earth. But how would I step up and make this work?

I will be 150 percent honest. For the first two and a half years of my daughter's life, I was just a sperm donor. Don't get me wrong, I did send money for diapers, but the most important thing a child needs is to spend quality time with his or her parents. This is especially true for a little girl and her father. If you're reading this and if you have the opportunity to step up and affect a child's life as a parent, I implore you to do it. You see, not only does God hold you accountable, your child does too. The worse thing in the world has to be when your child dismisses you, even while you beg for forgiveness and for a place in his or her life. Your child always suffers from your absence. But truthfully, if you're a parent who doesn't have your child's best interest at heart, your presence will cause your child to suffer as well. Basically, I can sum it up in this lesson:

> *Lesson 14: If your absence doesn't make a difference, neither will your presence. In whatever you do, if it's not organic and from the heart, it's for nothing. This was especially true in my case when it came to my daughter.*

On the school front, life was cool. I decided to take a few classes of independent study to improve my graduation status, but that was a huge mistake. As the season came to a close, I had so much work to do it was ridiculous. Again, when you don't plan strategically, your outcome is usually negative. On the basketball court, things weren't great, to put it nicely. We lost five guys on the team due to academic ineligibility, so it was tough. But to be fair, we did quite well with what we had. We ended the season with a 11–15 record, and compared to the previous season's record, it was a great start to a previously struggling program, and hopefully, the basketball program would improve with time.

Personally, I received a few awards that season, including Male Athlete of the Year for CUC. This award is one that I hold dear to my heart even now, as well as a few others. But just like that, my college basketball, and soon my school career, would be over. What would I do? The agent who approached me after that road game earlier had kept in contact and pointed me to an NBA/Euro exposure camp in Salt Lake City, where players go to work on their craft and get an early showing before the draft camp in Chicago. Salt Lake City was a name-making camp where a lot of big-name players went, and I just went into the camp with a strategic approach: do what most people wouldn't do to impress coaches, agents, and teams. Most of the guys there were scorers and "the man" on their respective teams, like I was, but I was a great defender as well. That was going to be my selling point for the trip. I hounded the best players and frustrated the heck out of them to no end, just playing as unselfishly as I could but scoring when necessary. This plan worked like a charm. In three days, I went from a no-name number 147 to "Good morning, two face," as a few agents referred to me (meaning I could play both offense and defense effectively); and I knew basketball-wise, this trip had propelled me into a different stratosphere.

Excited after the camp, I went out with all the guys before flying back to DC, and once again, trouble came hunting me down. A gentleman who was drunk and acting crazy found his way to me and called me *nigger* and threw his drink all on me. In this moment, a more focused, visionary man would have laughed as I would today and say, "Ignorance is contagious to many, but luckily, I'm vaccinated against it." Unfortunately, I was driven by image and still not at the point where I could just ignore foolishness, and I proceeded to let him know exactly where he and his *nigger* rants could go. I got thrown out of the bar and thought nothing of it, but the next morning, those same agents who loved me pulled me aside and were like, "We know the discipline just isn't there." From that point on, I had a negative reputation among the camp personnel.

I went to the administration and explained the incident and that it was an honest mistake, but I'll never forget how one famous black NBA agent took me aside and broke it down to me. I learned one of the most valuable lessons, and that was with greatness comes responsibility. I should have been at home just relaxing, but the demons which would haunt me throughout my career had now put me in place were now my dream to play in the NBA would be in jeopardy. Its super crazy to sit back and reflect, how we make choices and the choices turn right around and make us.

The price of greatness is responsibility!

-Winston Churchill

This was so not fair, and I was so mad at myself for losing my cool. This situation was going to cost me big-time, and I had no idea how much until later in the summer. This really pressed on me over the next few months as I worked out and tried to get connections. To my dismay, I never even got in the door, not because I wasn't good enough but because of my one mistake. Unfortunately due to my immature actions and inability to control myself, the dream was vastly slipping away from me. One of the scariest things in life is to have a dream or goal in your grasps, and then have it snatched away from you just as fast as you got it.

School was out, and I really didn't have much going on or any income to support my child or fund my endeavors to travel to NBA functions or camps—what would I do? During this time of anxiety, I got a call from another D3 soccer team, the Connecticut Wolves, that wanted my services and were willing to not only employ me but be patient with my basketball tryouts in the event something came up. This was the perfect gig: I'd have money, I could play the game I loved, and I could stay in great shape. Seeing as I was being some-what blacklisted from NBA functions, I began to look into European options, and I'm so glad I opened my eyes to that experience. The big camp of the summer was the ACB League camp hosted by Madrid, Spain. Man, you know I was hyped to participate; it was about to be on. In my personal life, I still hadn't come to grips with being a father and was actually scared to be around my daughter, as funny as it sounds. I really just wanted the whole situation with my daughter to be on the back burner and for me to excel in sports, and maybe the two paths would meet later.

The previous year in Boston, soccer was my safe haven, and I used it as a stress reliever from all the outside drama and unwanted negativity in my life. This summer, it was a job! I was literally forcing myself to maintain interested. I played well, but not at the same level as I did the year before. It's amazing, though, that when someone calls your bluff, the competitive nature of a winner shows up and your talents propel you. For the first five games, I played okay; but in truth, I just wanted the money. The coach was a very smart man and called me out in front of the team and said, "Man, do you know how many MLS teams want to sign you? But I tell them all the time, he doesn't care. He just wants to play soccer to get money." I had learned from my past to keep my mouth shut, so I humbly took this verbal slap in my face. He continued, "If Sulli actually cared as much about soccer as he does about going out and chilling, we'd not only be the best team, he wouldn't be able to play with us to the end of the year because an MLS team would pick him up. But again, he doesn't care." The coach put me on blast and challenged me to play better and to be committed where I was, not where I eventually wanted to be.

Like I've said before, you only had to tell me once for me to get it, especially seeing I was blacklisted in basketball. I went on a mean tear of ten games where I played out of sight. In this period, I was named Player of the Week four times and Player of the Month. I was beyond focused, but at the same time, I was also working on my basketball skills, getting up shots, and working on my game at the local gyms. I was so focused I didn't have time for anything except hitting the club. I used to lie to myself and say that was my reward for my diligence, but in truth, I just couldn't get away from chasing women. Even when I had Ms. Mills, who wanted to be with me, I just couldn't stay out of the clubs. Not only was I out partying, but I constantly put myself in harm's way in some thuggish West Indian clubs. Shots being fired were an every-night thing. I could have been killed, hurt, or anything, but it was an adrenaline rush. For me, hearing that reggae music and seeing girls grinding up and down—man, I was addicted. But soon I would learn that nightlife and early mornings on the job don't mix.

After helping the Wolves move from eighth to third place during this time, my long-awaited trip to Madrid had arrived, and not a moment too soon, if you had asked me. The camp was amazing. My hotel was next to the famous Real Madrid stadium, the Santiago Bernabéu (one of the most famous soccer stadiums in the world), so I was in heaven, to say the least. Our team was randomly pulled together by numbers and given to a coach to go out and play together to impress GMs, coaches, and agents. To be fair, there were a lot of big-name players at the camp, so again I looked at my squad to see what I could do to stand apart from everyone else. It was clear after a practice together that I was the only one who could defend nine-ty-four feet (the length of a basketball court) and offensively create and score. My strategy was to defend first, and the rest would follow. We played seven games in seven days, and we went 5–2, earning the right to play for first place on the last day of the camp. My stats were so solid. I was averaging ten points, five rebounds, and six assists in twenty-five minutes on the court (mind you, the games consisted of four ten-minute quarters). Unfortunately, in the last game, I pulled my groin, and it concerned a lot of people. They were thinking, *If he can't handle seven days of playing, then what will happen when he practices hard all week and, on the weekend, breaks down in a game?*

It was yet another hard and tough pill to swallow. I didn't have the push or lift to be my normal self, and we lost by four points. Needless to say, I definitely showed I could play at that level. Now the question was, could my agent market me to the teams? After a week of sobriety, with our only excitement being a visit to Real's sta-dium, we went out to celebrate and relax. We had defied the odds, and with no noteworthy professionals on our team, we straight anni-hilated teams. That evening, we went all over Madrid club-hopping and barhopping. Toward the latter part of the evening, the guys started getting horny and asked the cab driver where they could find some ladies to please their needs.

No lie, we drove out to the city zoo. I was sure we were about to get robbed, thinking the dude had set us up for real. To my amazement, out of the woods walked these guys—I guess they were pimps—and presented their girls in a group. It was like shopping for a girl, just that there was no store and you were outside. It was a long strip. I'm sure it went on for at least two miles, and every few hun-dred feet were women of different races. I was astonished as was; this was nuts to me. Personally, I never have and never will pay for sex; but this night, the dudes I was with paid for everyone to get some action outside on a breezy night in Madrid. I couldn't believe what I saw. Literally every race had a spot for men or women to choose. That was the kind of world I was stepping into, and that was just the tip of the iceberg.

After an absolutely bananas night, I met briefly with my agent to discuss the feedback from the coaches, GMs, and other important people at camp regarding me. Everything was good, except I got hurt and that was a big question mark over my head, I was told. But he reassured me that I'd get a great job and to go home and keep working on my game. Eight hours later, I was back in Hartford, ready to go back to work for the Wolves, except my groin needed to heal, so I had to sit out for ten days. But during this time, I was doing pool work, so I wouldn't lose my edge or my stamina on court. I also didn't go out or drink, so I was more than ready to come back in ten days. Once healthy, I was like a lion released from a cage. I regained the form I had the season before, and the highlight of the season came one breezy evening in New Hampshire. In this game, I literally ran two left-back defenders (left-side defense players) off the field. During the first half, I scored and set up a goal. Not only that, I tormented the defender to the point that he was substituted. His replacement fared no better. In fact, he would be sent off the field with two yellow cards: one for kicking me and another for holding me as I blew by him in pursuit of the ball.

With this intense performance, on the next game, a few MLS teams came by to watch me play, and I never knew until much later that two of them wanted to buy out my contract. However, the Wolves didn't want to sell me. This tore me apart and made me so disinterested when I found out three weeks before the playoffs. I did to the coach what he had done to me, and I was put on blast one day. He was so shocked that I had found out. He openly confessed to the team what they did as a club and apologized to me, saying, "We needed you to win, so we kept you instead of taking the payout." It's safe to say I immediately cooled toward him, but I would be professional and respect my contract.

Weeks later in the semifinals in Long Island, New York, we gracefully bowed out again. It was another semifinal exit, but in truth, I wasn't mad about this one. My sister, Larissa, was there, and she was so shocked that my attitude was okay. Usually I'm the biggest sore loser on earth, but I explained the predicament with the coach, and she understood where I was emotionally. This would be my last professional soccer game ever, and I truthfully played very well. I set up our only goal and created many chances for others, but it wasn't our day. Another chapter was closing in my life, but soon new adventures would arise, and I'd begin another phase of finding the best ME!

CHAPTER 5

European Life: Take 1

History will be kind to me, for I intend to write it.

—Winston Churchill

The summer had come and gone, and several offers had come to the forefront, but one hot summer afternoon would change the way the next twelve years of my life would evolve. I can honestly say that after going to many camps and flirting with the NBA, I came to the cruel realization that it's not how good you are or what you can do; sometimes it's who you know who can help you get to the right place and time to embrace your dreams. This summer was a big learning experience for me. I didn't have the knowledge, but I was too proud and, most of all, too ignorant to go and seek that connection to make life better for me. Playing soccer and looking to begin a professional basketball career, this is one things I had to learn on the fly:

> *Lesson 15: In the professional realm, everyone's good at something or can do a few things well. However, the great ones do everything well all the time and never take days off.*

With soccer, it was my speed and strength on the ball that made me a great player; combining both and fine-tuning them made it tough to mark me. In basketball, I will be the first to admit there's not one thing I can say about my game that's so great, but what I can say is there are a few things I do very well, and I do them all the time and every day. Let's be real, in this life, there's always someone who has more money or is better-looking or has a better car; but what can set you apart from them and anyone else is your ability to creatively use your God–given, cultivated talents. If you allow them to be fine-tuned, there's a point where your quality can separate you from others. This is one of the hardest things I had to come to understand, but I'll get more into that later in this chapter.

Back to this life-changing hot summer afternoon in Connecticut. I worked out on an outdoor court in ninety-five-degree weather for my soon-to-be first coach in the British Basketball League (BBL). There were many moments when I felt like giving up and just quitting. I had to go out in faith and make this money because in my mind at that point, playing sports was the only thing I was good at doing. Drill after drill, I saw the look on his face: *This kid won't stop, and he won't quit.* And he was right. My life depended on this, so I had to go for broke, but not in a desperate manner.

After a long two-hour workout, we spoke at length; and to his surprise, I was quite more eloquent than he expected. I didn't use slang, and I didn't sound like an idiot. He told me that he wanted to sign me to play for his team and would if I was interested. With a big smile on my face, I said yes, I was interested. I didn't go overboard and think, *Yeah, I'm going to be rich!* I pushed the immature thoughts to the side until I had contract in hand, and I knew it was official. You see, when you count your chickens before they hatch or get ahead of yourself, if things don't work out then you're left disappointed. That's what I believed at this point in my life, so I remained extremely even-keeled. Finally paperwork was put to rest, and we struck a deal. Not only would I be playing in England but also in European competition; meaning we would travel to other countries to compete and play as well. This was amazing. Free travel and free exposure to all these markets was very cool. I was beyond psyched.

Before signing, a huge surprise was unveiled to me. I had a Bermuda passport that I obtained while living in Bermuda for many years with my parents. This allowed the team to sign me as a citizen and not as a foreigner. For the next few years, this would be a huge advantage for Europe to have an American playing as a citizen and not as a foreign player. It's funny how back then, when I moved to Bermuda, I had no idea about the impact of having a passport or the advantages it would afford me later; but again, when God has a plan, it usually makes sense to us later. At this point in my life, it was helping me out in a major way and was another prime example that there are no accidents in life. Everything happens for a reason. As a professional athlete and as a person, I began to realize something that summer, which really helped me get through that year:

> *Lesson 16: There are always temptations in life, but if you want to be successful in whatever you decide to do with your life, you have to be willing to let go of certain things or even people. That's the only way you can be the best you.*

You see at this point in my life, it was all about going out, getting wasted, and having fun, but this yielded no success. The NBA was now off limits because of going out, having fun, and didn't protect myself by being mature and ignoring a silly remark made to me. Because of that, I told myself the day I left that I wouldn't drink alcohol for the entire season. Believe me, the worst commitment to break is the one you make to yourself. It was my first commitment to make myself better and allow my talents to take the lead in my life. On the personal front, I had a mouth to feed and attend to, so what was I willing to sacrifice to keep her financially secure? They say as a man, when you have a daughter, you pay for all the bad you've done. Well, when I heard I was having a girl, my heart sank as I knew the sins of her father could come back and haunt her badly. Diapers, formula, anything else she needed cost money, and it was real now. In college, you're allowed mistakes. In the professional ranks, when you mess up, it's your job, the coach's job, or the management's job.

The time for games was long gone, and this job would prove that loyalty in sports goes as far as you win, but not a step further. The preseason was superhard—believe me, you have no idea. Our coaches wanted us to have the identity of an excellent defensive team, and we had to be in tip-top shape to execute this. I spent many days on the track and had long fitness sessions in the gym. Looking back, they were so boring and hard; and as a rookie, I was made to do extra of everything. We started our season in Europe with a horrible start, to say the least. We were 0–12, and combined in those twelve losses, we only lost by five points or less each loss. Talk about misery beyond belief. I must say we were the most unlucky bunch at that point. There were three games I can remember where a magical shot beat us. The guys who made those shots couldn't have made those same shots again if their lives depended on it. That's just the way it goes—when it rains, it pours. In basketball terminology, we were choking, and we would need some veteran firepower to help us get through this tough patch in England.

In our European play, we were excellent, which was crazy because in Europe, there were better teams, budgets, and players. We started off 3–1, but to be fair, with the level of competition we faced, that was no easy task. We started out in Portugal against the Portuguese champions, Oliveirense. It was a great opener, but inexperience caused us to lose by four points. We fought hard and played well, and I even got a huge highlight by dunking on their seven-foot center after just two minutes into the game. I was playing well in England as well as in Europe, scoring and defensively making my mark. I was told that my play was far better than that of a rookie was expected to play, which was a major testament to the work I was forced to put in.

The most fun part of it all was the travel, getting to see so many places for free. Even though we only got a little free time to explore, I was twenty-two. I didn't take naps before games, and game day, I would always walk the streets and get souvenirs for my family and postcards to send to my mom. In this particular competition, I had the pleasure of going to Spain, France, Belgium, Portugal, and Israel, so imagine the joy of getting at least three hours to explore each city—it was amazing. Back on the home front in England, we finally started to get a few wins, but we never had a long winning streak, and we struggled so much. Defensively, we were the best team; but offensively, we weren't far from being the worst.

Our European dream came to a halt one Tuesday evening in Birmingham, UK, with our team facing the French team Dijon. The game was poised between two teams with 6–3 records, and it was winner take all. You can't ask for a better situation. We were on our home court, where we had only lost one game in European play, so this would be the game that could send us to the next round, with the perks and prestige of being one of the first British clubs to qualify for the next round. As expected, it was a tight game, and I was having a good game on both ends of the floor. As the game went down to the wire, they hit a few tough shots, and we found ourselves in a tight situation with seven seconds remaining. They had the ball, and we were down by one point. The referee gave their player the ball, and he began to survey the court. But everyone was covered (bear in mind the team only had five seconds to get the ball in, or they would lose possession), so he took a risk.

As a defender, my strategy was to leave the passing lane open until the last second then shoot the gap and steal the ball. He fell for the trick, and as soon as he threw the ball in, I jumped in front of his teammate and stole the ball. The clock was ticking: seven…six… five…I was pushing ever closer to the basket…four…three…at this moment, I jumped in the air only to be mobbed by a Dijon player. The ball looked like it was going in, but it rimmed out. There were three seconds left on the clock. We were down by one, and I had two free throws. What more could I ask for? This is what I had always dreamed of, and now it was my time to shine.

Stepping to the line, I felt so good and confident I just knew this was money as the referee handed me the ball. I took a deep breath and shot. It felt good and had good rotation, but it just rimmed in and out. In those situations, you began to think of the pressure and all the things that could go wrong in this scenario. To make matters worse, their coach called a time-out to ice me. Bonus money, prestige for making or keeping us in the game, and many other thoughts ran through my mind. I can honestly say I didn't hear a word said in the time-out. With the second shot, there was no chance of missing it—wrong. I bricked it, and they got the ball, and time ran out. The European dream was brutally over, but there's always a lesson in losing:

> *Lesson 17: Leaders aren't made when all is well and things are in perfect condition. They are defined and made during tough, difficult times, when the weak-minded would shy away. True leaders accept consequences in the same way they accept praise for the good they may have done. As a leader, you also have to know that, at times, you might have to follow. Just make sure that what you're following doesn't compromise what you stand for and make you lose sight of the best person you can be.*

After most European games, you have to do press conferences; and reporters ask questions, the whole nine, just like what you see on TV. Of course, the questions were standard: how do you feel, and what were you thinking? I was brief but nonevasive, as I've always tried to be, and I answered, "We lost because I missed two free throws at the end. I'm to blame, and I'll play as hard as I can to try and make up for it." People were somewhat shocked that I took total blame. To be fair, I had seventeen points, seven rebounds, and five assists, so it wasn't like I didn't play well for the majority of the game. However, when you don't come through in the clutch, no one cares. Unfortunately, this is the same in life. When you can't execute on the job, in the classroom, or wherever life throws challenges at you, then you're considered a choke artist, or better yet, someone who will never maximize his or her full potential. I vowed that day to never fold under pressure again and to always be there, ready to be held accountable even when others aren't man enough to be.

*Leaders are like eagles, they don't run in packs, they
are only with a select few who share the same visionary qualities to succeed at all cost.*

Off the court, I had to find a way to balance my life. I wasn't
drinking, so I needed some other form of distraction to occupy the
mind. So of course, I found women. The first European encounter
was with a woman I'll call *Regina*. She was a sexy redhead with an
hourglass figure to die for and the cutest dimples ever. She worked in
a place I frequented, and one day we just started talking about soccer,
and it was on from there. One thing I can say at this juncture in my
life is that I was definitely in a "don't ask then I won't tell" state of
mind; so if a girl didn't ask, I wouldn't say anything about what was
going on in my life. Having said that, I did have a firm policy that if
you did ask, I would tell you the truth because everyone has the right
to decide if they can handle what's going on in your world or if they
want nothing to do with it. It was somewhat a cowardly thing to do,
but it was safe for me and prevented any hurt or harm from coming
my way. Hence, it was a plan that worked for me.

I began to filter women in and out of my life and started a dangerous pattern of finding and using women for various needs. And
when their purpose played out, their importance to my life was gone,
and they were too. It was cold, cruel, and definitely not how I would
like a man to treat either of my girls today. But when your mental
status is programmed for self, that's what you do—totally focused
and living within those parameters of self. Now I understand and
get the importance of being connected through more than physical
intercourse or for just a short time, but back then, living like this was
my safe haven from reality and kept me from facing the truth:

*F and F (friends and family in your life) set the
standard or guidelines for your life and always create and promote balance at all times. I didn't allow
my F and F to have influence in my life, so I was left
with a void and was looking for virtually anything
and anyone to bridge the gap.*

I was distant from the trinity crew at this time. They all had successful relationships, and although things weren't perfect, they were solid. Renzo was finishing school, and he and Nae were looking toward marriage. Our bond couldn't grow because he was pursuing a wife and family whereas I was chasing girls, fame, and things that had no substance! Our relationship couldn't grow and fill that void in my life. My boy Shel was dating a girl, and they would beef because of me, point-blank. He was with her, and they were forging something long-term, but I was the wedge between them because I wanted to go out and hang and she wanted quality time with her man, and rightfully so. But again, when your motivation isn't properly placed, it tears down things and relationships for real! I'm telling you, every weekend I was out and wanted my boy with me. I would tell him, "Shoot, man, she needs to loosen up and let you live." In truth, my actions suggested hate in the highest degree in her eyes; it was as if I didn't want them to be together. Basically, my actions were causing strain in another relationship, and would a true friend do this?

My sisters all had things going on. Gwen was with a decent dude, but I will never utter his name again for what he did to her. I didn't trust him at all, and I made it clear that there was something shady about him even though, on the surface, he looked squeaky-clean and the best thing since sliced bread. But dogs can always smell another dog, and I was adamant, almost overbearing, about him. LaLa was going to get married, and we beefed *superhard*. I thought in my heart that she wasn't ready and he wasn't the one for her, and with tears in my eyes, I regret to admit I didn't even attend her wedding. That's how much against it I was. Chrissy was with a guy who, in truth, fooled the heck out of me and all of us—well, not Gwen. But the fact that everyone was stable and I wasn't is the point I'm trying to make.

To this day, if I had a wish, it would be to have a true bond with my biological sister, Lori. We have never shared a genuine brother-and-sister bond. To be honest, we just had moments in passing. At this juncture of my life, aside from the Christmas holiday or summer break, I wasn't available and wanted to do my own thing. She was married, and that wasn't a world I was interested in, nor did it make sense to me. Why be with one person when you could have many? Then there was my mom, the spiritual soldier who has prayed for me throughout my life, who has cried and begged God to hold me in his care. Her spiritual influence was second to none, but I wasn't ready to fully commit to God, nor did I want to hear the spiritual lectures all the time, so conversations with Mom were cut down and kept to a minimal. I was in a foreign country, and yeah, I was kind of dating Ms. Mills. But in truth, I was chilling, enjoying the best of both worlds; and consequently, I was isolated from all the love that could save me from myself.

Lesson 18: If anything holds more importance than your F and F (family and friends), even success, chances are you'll never be the best you can possibly be because they are the balance and guidance that lead you along your quest.

The more I got to know my daughter, to love her, and be the father I should be to her, the easier it was to put things in their proper place. The same can be said as I've gotten closer to friends, family, and the God-kids over the years. You don't have time to waste on silly things and people because there's a new sense of purpose in your life.

On the court, to be honest, we were just not good enough. We played hard, and the stats were great for me, but we didn't have enough talent on the team to get across the finish line because we lacked experience. The team had changed about six players, and the last batch included the most selfish, greedy, and egotistical Americans I've ever played with to date. They really cost us making it to the playoffs (translation: messed with my money because postseason means more bonuses). We had a center who wanted the ball every time down the court, and he wouldn't pass the ball, and the shooting guard was the same way. Until one day, I had enough.

Man! I laid into both of them in the locker room and let them know how selfish and greedy they were. The center wanted to fight me, but I was no small puppy, and he had been warned that I had a bad temper upon arrival, so he backed off. However, the shooting guard was like, "I don't care, man. Just take the ball and do you." The coach was shocked because usually I'd say things in a way to be positive, but this instance, I just let it out. The frustration of the season had gotten to me. A short time after their arrival, I broke a bone in my hand (great, another chink in the armor), and we had actually started to play together as a team. It was four weeks from hell as I sat out, but it was around carnival time in Brazil, so I devised a sneaky plan to get the most out of the short break. I booked a ticket to Rio for eight days (six days on land and two days for travel) of fun in the sun and told the team I was going home for personal reasons. They asked if I needed help to arrange travel. I told them I was good, and I used Regina and swore her to silence not to tell a soul what I was doing because if word got out, I would be fired.

Regina was a good woman, smart, and physically, she was definitely my type, and she was Caucasian. What you have to understand is I had really only messed around or had sex with two Caucasian women in my life, and one of them was a snake who tried to set me up big-time, so my relationship with her was foreign. I proceeded very cautiously, but in truth, her loyalty and kindness were second to none, and this was the first time I had really opened up to a white person in my life without thinking, *What's their ulterior motive?* I'm sure your eyes must be wide open, like, *Wow, I know he didn't just say that*, but let's keep it 150 percent organic. That's how I felt, and because of some shady dealings in soccer and in life, I was on edge and guarded. I was not going to be taken for a fool again, and I can be honest about my thoughts at this point in my life.

Brazil-bound, I was so excited and hyped. I didn't even tell my partner in crime Rikki what I was going to do; only Regina knew my plan, and what a plan it was. I was heading to Rio de Janeiro for fun in the sun and enjoyment of the carnival. My twelve-hour business-class flight was courtesy of another jump-off from the club, whom we shall call *Emma*. What a long flight, but there was a flight attendant on the plane I wanted so badly. I talked her up and down until finally she just broke down. The last three hours of my flight were quite exciting, to say the least, and got me a free upgrade to World Traveller Plus for my return flight. At this point in my life, my mouth literally could get me anywhere I wanted, from a club that was full to a woman's thighs, where she would, in turn, give me emotional power during our encounter.

Getting back to the flight attendant, she had an amazing figure, was brown-skinned, and had curly hair. Man, I thought she was the best-looking woman I had ever seen. She warned me throughout the flight that when I got to Rio, I wouldn't pay her much attention, but I surely couldn't believe her (I'll call her *Ms. Lucy*). As I previously said, there were many women; and believe me, whenever I had sex with someone, there was always a purpose in mind, and I could gain an advantage or unexpected fringe benefit in my life. Ms. Lucy was no different.

After a long flight and pleasurable company, I went through customs; and then it was on to the hotel, which I got for a steal, so I was going to live it up. Unlike London, things in Rio were crazy cheap. Food, souvenirs, etc., were easy to come by for the right price. Lucy was wrong about one thing, that I'd forget her. For her three-day layover, she basically stayed in my hotel room the whole time. She took me around to famous football stadiums and arranged a day trip for us to São Paulo to see some sights and experience another major city.

The downside, however, was that Lucy was in a serious relationship (which I found out later), but she began to catch major feelings for me on the trip. I knew that wasn't going to work, so on her last day, we kind of distanced ourselves from each other, with me suggesting she go see her family and hang with them on a surprise trip while I partied and just enjoyed the sights and sounds of the city. To my great pleasure, I ran into some Brazilians who were living in the States. They drank nonstop, but my drinking sabbatical was still on. I wasn't going to drink for the entire season, and Rio was no exception, but the twenty-four pack of Magnum condoms had to be used. There was no question about that.

Ms. Marianna, Ms. Thatianna, Ms. Isabel, Ms. Silvia, and Ms. Renata all were down from California for the festivities, and of course, they were all hot as heck. So my last three days, I schemed to have sex with all of them and others. It was crazy how, even being sober, I plotted and successfully ran through their whole crew, as well as many others along the way. I only had sex with Westerners, meaning those who lived in Europe and America out of fear of the high STD rate in Brazil, which at the time plagued 35 percent of the population, or so I had been told. Renata, Silvia, and I went to the beach, and they began to take shots and open up to me about their desire for a threesome. Smiling ear to ear, you couldn't tell me I wasn't the man. Forty-five minutes later on a nude beach, it was going down. I was with two ladies whom men would hold ever so tightly and keep. Me? Never. I just wanted the here and now, and I blatantly ignored the truth that I needed help and love to bring me closer to a better me.

Our last three days finally ended with a night party in the heart of one of Rio's finest clubs, and let's just say I'm glad I packed my bags before we left because we partied until 7:00 a.m., and I had to be at the airport by 9:00 a.m. for an 11:00 a.m. flight back to London. In all my years, this trip by far was the biggest "hoeing" (sleeping with a lot of women) exhibition I had ever ventured on, and I thought it was over until I looked up to see that Ms. Lucy was the head flight attendant on my return flight to London.

In six days, I had slept for maybe twenty-four hours total. To stay up, I would get catnaps and drink Mountain Dew (I took two twelve-packs with me to ensure I didn't waste a moment). I was totally drained, so out of the twelve hours on the flight, I'm sure I slept for a minimum eight hours. The lovely Ms. Lucy and I talked and just chilled. She revealed her relationship and how she was torn and having second thoughts. She was really sweet, but it was just the wrong flight, wrong-day kind of thing, and it went down.

I was back at work in England, and I had six days until my hand could be evaluated by doctors and the cast possibly removed. Knowing this, I began to look for new excitement, and my first hookup was Ms. Emma. She was a well-known fan (more importantly, she was a flight attendant, the reason for my flight to Brazil) or what we call in the business a *jump-off*. This is someone who will do anything to be around basketball players, and I do mean anything. Her purpose was simple: I wanted to get free flights or pay next to nothing, and she was my connection. She would meet me at three o'clock in the morning, have sex with me in the back of a car, or give me oral on a sidewalk—that's just how ruthless and uncaring I was at this point. It didn't matter as long as I was happy and pleased. I even convinced her to have a threesome with her sister, just wrong on all levels on my part, but this was caused by my isolated state and not wanting to man up and be a better person. Shoot, in Birmingham, England, I was a straight pimp, for lack of a better word. Believe me, there was more to come, and sooner than I thought.

The team doctor's office called and said the day had come to evaluate my hand. Little did I know his niece was a fan and was of age to express her admiration in a sexual way. We had a few words for a few minutes before the doctor ushered me into his office. The x-rays were good, and the bone around my thumb had fused back together, so I was cleared to resume training on Wednesday. Unbeknownst to me, they really intended for me to play on the weekend against fellow basement dwellers in the table for the coveted eighth spot for the playoffs.

Literally not even forty-eight hours after my cast was removed, I was involved in the match, and quite heavily, to say the least. I played twenty-five minutes and defensively stifled their best player and helped us get a vital road win. But my hand was so sore, and for sure, it was definitely not fully healed. I would find out later through the grapevine that I was a week premature in my return, and my x-ray results weren't honestly presented to me. Welcome to the business of sports, where, if they need you immediately, they will do whatever they have to just to get you on the court. That evening after the Sunday afternoon game, I found myself in the hood in the West Indian section of town attending a reggae party. Little did I know that someone would lose their life not too far from where I was standing within forty-five minutes of my arrival.

My teammate was Jamaican, so he was well-known in that neighborhood. Since I was frequently with him, they knew me as well as a friend of his. Like always in West Indian spots, there is music, weed, and usually altercations because dudes just don't know how to act. While dancing with a redbone (brown-skinned ladies have always been my weakness) who would be my next victim, I heard, "Move!" She pulled me deep into the corner, and the next thing I saw was a dude dropping to the floor after an unbelievably loud bang. Man, we ran out as fast as we could. I was a little bit shaken up but was excited that Ms. Beth had accompanied me out of the club. Sorry, got to recap this: gunshots had just been fired, a man was killed next to me, and my first thought was, *I can't wait to have sex with this woman*. Forget that I had a newborn, friends, and family who would be so distraught if I'd been caught in harm's way, or that I could be hurt and my professional career would be done. I still only had one thing on my mind.

One veteran player on the team named Big Mart would always take me to the side and break down the business to me and off-the-court life as well. He told me about the x-ray and how people knew I wasn't completely healed, but they wanted me to play, so they didn't tell me (management didn't explain this to me). He also told me, "Everyone knows you like to party. They don't mind because you do your job and much more. Your motive is to win more than anything else, so they accept that here. However, when you go to bigger teams and places, that's not going to fly." I was shocked, but at the same time, I knew his words were true. And if I was in the business to make money, then I'd better start making proper sacrifices to ensure that I'd be ready to take what I rightfully deserved.

Lesson 19: Timing is everything. When your time comes, it's usually a once-in-a-lifetime chance; and when it's missed, rarely do you get a second chance.

For basketball and life in general, this is so true. Some people are lucky and fall in and out of great situations en route to finding their best selves. However, for the majority of people, there aren't many chances, and you usually only get one. During my first season, I heard of different salaries; and even in European play, I heard of astronomical figures for salaries. I wondered what separated me from them and what I could do to bridge this gap in my financial earnings. In basketball, they have a thing called a fast break. In soccer, it's referred to as a counterattack. With both the time in which you can turn defense to offense and execute is usually defined by the first few seconds of play. It took me four years professionally to really grasp and understand this concept. I hadn't mastered my craft, nor had I put the time in yet to be better, but I wanted to reap flowers without planting seeds.

It saddens me to see the mental process of our youth in today's society, with their divine-right mentality of "I deserve anything I want." In truth, nothing has more value than something earned, and I don't care what it is. A person who wins one million dollars will never respect and cherish that money more than a man who earns every penny of it. That's where I was professionally. Even after my conversation with Big Mart, I thought I had a divine right to play for big money, and I really hadn't done enough to truly earn the large salary and the job that could bring it to me. Finally, as summer came to a close, with maybe four weeks left, Ms. Regina just cut me off cold turkey. She wouldn't see me, talk to me, hang out, or nothing. It was just "It's best we don't talk anymore." I was perplexed and quite dumbfounded by this; and to be fair, I did like her, but I played it off and just found replacements to keep my mind at ease.

Six weeks later, I found out the true reason why she cut me off: she was pregnant. Mind you, I always tried to use protection, but it's not always 100 percent. Needless to say, she knew that my daughter's mom and I had begun to beef really badly, and I often said I didn't want any kids. At this time in my life, it's safe to say that I wore my emotions on my sleeve much more than I do now. How I wish God himself would have come down from heaven and changed my thought process. Regina went out and got an abortion, risking her own life, and possibly the chance of having future kids, to ensure my life remained the same.

It's so sad now as I reminisce to see just how far people would go just so I would be happy when I all I needed to do was let go of my past and face the demons that haunted me. At this point, my life was like a giant puzzle, but there were so many pieces missing. The demons that hounded me would continue to do so and make it increasingly hard to be around me and to deal with me, even without the alcohol. But I didn't know how to deal with my demons, so I ignored them, hoping I would get better. But let's face it; they only grow in power when you don't confront them!

On the court, we shuffled to the finish line and luckily won a close game in the end to give the fans a little something to be happy about. But we were one game out of a playoff spot, and thus my first and only professional year of not making it to the playoffs had come to a halt. This is when it would become tiresome. We had a cheap and very stingy owner who tried to nickel and dime us at every turn. He was so cheap it was unreal. I lived in a hotel for the season with very meager accommodations. Breakfast was free, but he tried to fine me $2000 for meal orders that I clearly didn't make. I was never in the hotel and definitely never ate there. Because of the acquaintances I had made, food was never far from my mouth or belly. Then with my car, he tried to fine me for a supposed dent. It was ugly and took two weeks to finally get everything in order, and it wasn't a second too soon for me get out of there.

Before I left, I went to get a haircut at this little spot in the ghetto where the infamous Burger Boys and Johnson Crews (two gangs from Birmingham, mostly West Indian crews) had had many altercations. I just wanted to look fresh since I had negotiated with Ms. Lucy to hook me up with a six-day getaway to Buenos Aries, Argentina, before I headed to Boston. Oh my goodness, as soon as I got in the chair and the dude started lining me up, the door opened, and all I heard was, "Everyone stay put!"

My heart was in my mouth! I knew what time it was when I saw that 9 mm gun in the dude's hand. Man, every scripture about safety went through my head. I also thought that because of all the girls I'd had sex with, maybe this beef could be for me. I just prayed and prayed, *Lord, just get me out of here, please!* As I kept my head down, the gunmen proceeded to take a gentleman in the chair next to me and drag him into the street. While doing this, he warned everyone that we'd better be quiet and don't say anything to the police. They proceeded to slice and dice the dude with their machetes, not to kill him but to injure and hurt him severely. It was like a scene from a movie, but even more so on that side of town. The CCTV (closed circuit television and surveillance in the highest form) was not working, and they knew this. After my haircut, I was so shaken I went home, gathered my things, and just waited for my ride to come take me to the airport. Those type of scenarios just remind you of what's important, but my selfish ego was more interested in getting to Argentina. Also, and since I was flying first-class both ways, it was going to be a blast for sure.

In reality, it was absolutely the opposite of everything I'd hoped for; everything that could go wrong did in the first three days of my trip. The plane was overbooked, so they thought I might have to fly coach. Luckily, I got my seat, but I had a mother and her newborn next to me, and that baby cried for at least nine hours, so no sleep at all for me. Upon arrival, my luggage was lost, but they thought it would be in later that day—wrong. It didn't come for three days, so I had to buy some things and just wing it. The hotel where I was booked apparently sold my room in fear I wasn't coming because my flight was late, and I had to stay at the airport to make a claim for my bag. So the first night, I stayed in not-so-nice accommodations. Anyone who knows me personally knows I don't take situations like this very well, and on top of all that, I have the worst sinus problems due to the change of climate. For the first three days, I hated my trip and was so close to just leaving.

The third day was cool, and I finally got to go out and explore a few places. I got hammered (my season was over, so the alcohol sabbatical was over too), and things started to pick up. Of course, with the sights and the beautiful women, I would have fun. Ms. Maria found me in a great spot downtown in the club. I had my diamond earrings in, and boy, she saw the bling-bling and went crazy envisioning a better life. I, on the other hand, envisioned her in my hotel and then on to the next. After a wild night of fun, I bid her good-night and placed her in a cab home. I had a firm policy: **no sleepovers**. I figured there was too much attachment with the cuddling and all of that, so it was better for the ladies to just leave after our fun. She was slightly distraught, but I promised to see her the next day, and she was gone, never to be seen again. But as she left at 7:00 a.m., I went to the bar just to get a drink and chill and ran into

Ms. Isabella, a wealthy Spaniard visiting on business who ventured down for breakfast.

As fate would have it, we were both there, and she came over and just started talking with me, totally random. The conversation was good, and we just kept drinking until the conversation turned to sex, and I challenged her to a game of truth, dare, promise, or repeat. Here are the rules: For *truth*, basically you have to say if something's true about you or your feelings. *Dare*, you have to do what someone dares you to do, and usually it's kind of crazy, like running outside naked or something like that. *Promise*, you give your word to do something; and if you renege, then a dare is your punishment. *Repeat*, you make someone repeat what you tell them to say in public, and it's usually something stupid, which will embarrass the heck out of him or her.

After dying from laughing at the idea of the game, she agreed, and we headed to her penthouse suite. I can honestly say financially and physically, I was treated like a king for what I thought would be my last couple of days there. However, after a day of shopping and me physically enticing her, she paid to book another day for me so I would stay an extra day with her. Shoot, I was thinking, *Why not? If she wants to pay, then I'm good to go.* Gucci and Louis Vuitton stores were foreign to me before this trip, but soon I had a few belts and wallets to match, and she created a demon for fashion and a love for nice things in me. The sad thing was the price of one belt could have fed my daughter and pay day care as well, but I didn't think about this. I just wanted what I could gain from her. When evening came, we went out, had a blast; but as all good things must come to an end, I was out. This wouldn't be the last I'd see of Ms. Isabella for sure. We were definitely going to keep in touch, and Madrid would definitely be a stop in future adventures.

I landed in Birmingham, England, at 7:00 p.m. and knew the next day, at 7:00 a.m., I would be headed back to Boston for a bit to chill and try to patch things up with Ms. Mills. Upon arrival in the city, I found a cheap apartment for us to keep my shoes in and just lay low, but soon drama would find us. I wasn't really responsive to her needs, nor was I emotionally interested in being romantic and affectionate, and I drove her away from me. Combine that with the fact that I really wasn't doing much to be a part of my daughter's life, Ms. Mills came to the conclusion that if I'd treat my own flesh and blood like that, I would do it to her as well, and she dumped me. Boy, I was so pissed off; but looking back, it was very obvious that I wasn't man enough to be with her at that point in my life. I couldn't be the man she needed to get her where she needed to be in life or help her be her best, so it was over.

Days after receiving this news, I called my mom to just vent about how mad and hurt I was when it happened. Some seven years after I shed my last tear at my father's funeral, I broke down and wept. It was so shocking that even Ms. Mills came to see about me, and I didn't try and spin it; I just said I was sorry about whatever bad things I had done to her and that I was leaving for DC that night to go see my sisters and Shel so I could party and drink her far from my thoughts and mind. Upon arrival at my sister Gwen's house, I told her what happened and vowed not to date again. I vowed never to feel like that again and walked out. Later, she told me that the hurt in my eyes scared the life out of her because she could hear that I would make many feel the pain Ms. Mills had inflicted on me; but in truth, I was the mastermind of my own pain and suffering. Until I faced the demons that wished to destroy me, I would spiral toward destruction, and I figured I might as well enjoy the ride and have fun on that path if it was my destiny. Stay tuned for how a Godly mother's prayers would finally reach me, but not before I went buck wild the rest of the summer!

CHAPTER 6

LEARNING TO OPEN AND CLOSE DOORS OF THE PAST

*In attempts to improve your character, know
what is in your power, and what's beyond it.*

—Francis Thompson

As summer began to draw to an end, my agent hit me up with the prospect of playing in Europe again, but this time, in a better European league. The catch was there would be no certainty like the previous year; it would be a twelve-man team built for European and domestic dominance. I needed this challenge. I wanted to ensure that I got better, and if everyone on the team was experienced, then I couldn't slip up at all. I had to be solid, especially in Europe. I agreed, and I was headed to Brighton on the coast of England. I can honestly say that when I arrived, I realized how different this place would be from Birmingham in every aspect of the word. Birmingham catered more to the things I was used to, but that wasn't the same in Brighton. It was not even close, to say it nicely. It was a very difficult transition, but like always, you make new friends, and you find a way to survive. I opted for another year in a hotel. I liked my privacy and getting my room cleaned by maids as well, so it was a no-brainer.

In the first few practices, I began to see what making the next step in my career required and that I would have to be way more disciplined. Our coach had very strict rules on offense and defense, and if you deterred from the rules and weren't successful, you might not play again in a game—it was just that simple. We had a great tandem of big men and guards, but we had two guys for each position, so you could be replaced in a heartbeat, and this coach wasn't playing. The season finally came, and we breezed through the initial rounds. We went 10–0 before we lost a game, and that was a fluke because we got cheated, but things happen like that in life. Our European group was quite diverse. We would travel to France by way of Cholet; Poland by way of Asseco Prokom; Greece by way of Aris; Croatia by way of Split; Lithuania by way of Rytas. They were all good teams, and playing against them was the best way to gain exposure to get into those leagues and, ultimately, earn more money.

We started off the first half of the group 2–2, winning a home game versus the Aris Greek team and winning a huge game in Lithuania. The Aris game basically went as scripted: I missed a defensive assignment and hit a shot, but at the next whistle, I was out of the game. The coach cursed me out so badly. I just stood there and didn't say a word, and my two minutes out of twenty in the first half were done. This was foreign to me. I'd never had to play a role and have no guaranteed minutes or time on court, so I had to make every second count and matter. During the second half, I made no mistakes when I entered the game in the third quarter, and I hounded their best player. I locked in and was in tune with my teammates, and we just blitzed them. As a result, I played fourteen minutes in the second half. I began to realize that once again, my niche was to defensively hound the best payers from the other team and offensively get the ball to the guys who were designated to score for us. We beat Aris by fifteen points, but our next challenge would be an away game in France against Cholet.

Off the court, I had formed a relationship with another guy from the previous year. My man Phil was in Brighton with me, and my other road dog was my main man Rico. We went everywhere together, literally. Imagine it, we played two times a week in the league regularly and then once a week in Europe, sometimes even flying elsewhere, but I still managed to go out Wednesday through Saturday night to the club. It didn't make any sense at all, but I was addicted to the life. This lack of restraint was my effort to fill the void of positive influences in my life and kept me far away from all the good that basketball and life had to offer me.

Because of my inconsistent play in Cholet, I was on the bench for the whole first half, but once again, I pretty much played the whole second half of the game. They hit a few tough shots in the final quarter to win by six points, but soon we would be heralded for getting the first major European road win by any British team in Eurocup action. After the game that night in Cholet, I managed to find a techno club that was jumping and full of students on one side and classy professionals on the other side for the midweek party.

I started at midnight and didn't make it back to my hotel until 5:00 a.m., and we were leaving to head the airport at 7:00 a.m. After some sex and water, it was time to head out back to Britain, but the oddest thing happened. On the flight, the coach changed seats and made me sit with him so he could talk with me. During the two-hour flight, he basically told me, "If we're going to be successful, you're going to have to be consistent both on and off the court to help us." He broke down the Cholet game to me. Their American scored thirty points, twenty-two of them on me. That was huge because, in my career, never has a guy scored more than twenty points on me except for in this game and one other time because I took great pride in my defensive play. The coach told me about my irresponsible behavior, how I was getting tickets for parking my car in wrong places, and other dumb stuff that big teams wouldn't tolerate.

It hit me hard because he was right. I was just listening and took what I thought needed from the talk to heart. For me, I figured that if I played well and consistently at all times, then that would get me over the hump, and a big team will come calling. For two whole hours, he basically challenged me; and I needed this to refocus, especially since, by Christmastime, we were so far ahead in the league it wasn't even funny. The first half of the season was basically over, and everyone else was playing for second place. Just before the break, Rico and I hit up a nice spot in another town in our quest for alcohol and women. We knew we would find new victims to misuse. He found a businesswoman, and I found the lovely Ms. Melody, head flight attendant for Virgin Airlines—jackpot. For me, this meant I was flying somewhere for free when the season was over. It was crazy! We just walked in the spot and saw them sitting alone with their drinks. Of course, we just walked on up to them and began to chat. Ms. Melody and I took a walk to the bar for a refill for her and a start-up for me, and we really hit it off, and I liked her as a person from the jump.

We might have stayed for forty-five minutes or so and then left to go to her spot for a nightcap, but then she would have had to drive me home because I had practice in the morning, and there was no way to miss it. So we compromised, and she took me home in the wee hours of the morning and spent the day in Brighton with me. After a hard practice and some extra coaching, I was back at the hotel having some fun, of course, before Ms. Melody left. She had a long flight to the States the next day, so she had to go rest up, but not without my wish list of Frosted Flakes, gummy bears, and Krispy Kreme doughnuts, which she gladly obliged to get for me.

No sooner had she left when Rico called and said we were hitting a local spot later. However, we were flying to Croatia the next day, and I thought that perhaps it was better for me to stay in that night. But of course, the nightlife was calling me, so me being so mentally weak, I went out. This night, though, I did chill on the alcohol; but I was on the hawk, and to my surprise, a Brazilian delight would be my new evening companion. Ms. Hevy had the typical Brazilian body, very sexy and sensual, with a beautiful face, and she just wanted fun sex with me. Wow, the world couldn't be better, I thought, and I just had to oblige her wants and desires. This was life for me in Brighton: basketball, girls, and nights out. It was just crazy how it never got old to me, or better yet, I never grew up!

The flight to Croatia was quite interesting. I had to sit with Coach again and got another talking-to about what I needed to do.

This time was different as he offered praise for my play in the last games and said I had been improving. He said he was interested to see how I would play in a tough environment against a very established playmaker or point guard and a shooting guard who both were American. It was another huge opportunity to defensively make a name for myself, but as fate would have it, our starting point guard got in foul trouble, and the opportunity to shift things around came to me. As a professional, this was the first time I had taken over a game. In my mind, everything was like a video. However, I controlled the pace and speed of the game, and man, did I make the most of it. I played twenty-seven minutes and had thirteen points, six rebounds, six assists, and four steals. Even the newspaper there in Split, Croatia, showed me immense respect, hailing me as one of the most versatile players of the group.

Before I entered the game, we were down by six points with five minutes to go in the third quarter. I played the rest of the game, and we won by nine points. I think the shocking thing was how I manhandled their guards and used my size to foil them. On offense, we had a play where we posted the point guard if he had an advantage, and I scored six points off this in the fourth quarter to seal the deal. The funniest thing is I wasn't nervous or shaken; I was extremely calm. That's been my demeanor for as long as I can remember, but on that freezing winter evening, I displayed discipline and maturity on the court, and from then, I continued to show qualities and strengths I possessed. After the game, because the night was young, as a group, we decided to head to downtown to a strip club just to chill because the city was dead during the week. That night, some dudes would get robbed in there, but not me, of course.

We proceeded to a strip club where we found some very scandalous women, to say the least. If you're not familiar with strip clubs in Europe, then the rules are simple: you must buy drinks in order to converse with the women in the establishment. Unfortunately, no one told my teammates these rules. They began to interact with the girls, and the Croatian bouncers came to them with an ultimatum: "Either you buy the girls drinks, or you get out." To be fair, I don't think they even looked at the prices before they decided to just buy the girls drinks. There was no chance I was buying any girl a drink. My motive was to interact with women, not pay for their time. As the night wore on, hormones began to rise as well; but before anything could escalate, tabs had to be paid. When the bill came around, my teammates had accumulated over 7,500 euros ($10,000 USD), and three very huge bouncers stood in front of the table with guns letting them know that the tab would be paid before they left the premises. They had 9 mms and .38 pistols locked, loaded, and absolutely unforgiving.

Of course, being the slick-talker young boy, I stood in the corner with one very astute young lady named Ms. Tatyana. She claimed she was only working as a stripper to put herself through school, but hey, who was I to judge? I only wanted to use her for sex. My teammates began to argue back and forth with the bouncers while I began to make my way to the door after paying my bill of €70. Luckily for me, I had enticed Ms. Tatyana to accompany me back to my hotel; but to my surprise, things got even more exciting when she told me she was a lesbian and invited her partner to join us. We got to the hotel at 3:00 a.m., and let's just say we had a great time up until our departure from the hotel at 7:00 a.m. It was another great European night, but this one was different because I was allowed to show my maturity on the court, and I began to evolve into the leader that I needed to become.

Our next trip was to Vilinus, Lithuania, to play against the best team from their country. At the time, the Rytas team had an American big man named Dickey Simpkins (he won three championships with the Chicago Bulls in the early '90s) and were expected to win. However, on this night, they would be totally outplayed and outworked. Defensively, I hounded one of the best guards in Europe at the time and totally blanked him. With more time on the court, I began to see the flow of the game, be more vocal, and most importantly, take on more responsibility scoring and assisting others.

Off the court, there were two women who left lasting impressions on me. One was Ms. Tony, a beautiful South African queen who saw my potential. Unfortunately, I wasn't ready to be the man she saw I could be. Ms. Tony was a good woman who made me check myself and make certain decisions in regard to what was important in my life. She made me reevaluate how I was dealing with the situation with my daughter and not really being in contact with her, as well as coming to grips with the demons facing me for so long and seeking professional help.

The other young lady was dear to me and haunts me to this day; I'll call her *Ms. Pinky*. She was a beautiful British African queen. When I first laid eyes on her, I can honestly say I knew I had to talk to her or had to be a part of her life. On a cold winter evening right outside South London, I saw her with her beautifully long flowing hair and beautiful smile. I was shaking just thinking of talking to her. Finally I got the courage to walk up and talk to her, and just as I was about to make my move, who would be standing in front of me but her? We shared a few words. I got her a drink, and we exchanged numbers. To be honest with you, those first few days with her were by far the kindest I had been to her; but then I turned so rude and disrespectful to her you couldn't even imagine. Beautiful souls were drowned by my bitterness and evil ways, and one day she just left me and cut me off, leaving me with no one. This prompted me to really begin to search my soul and seek help for my anger and the troubling issues within me.

The crazy thing about these women is that later on in life, I found out that, unbeknownst to me, both of them had gotten pregnant by me and had abortions. I guarantee that at least 95 percent to 98 percent of the time, I used condoms with any lady I had sex with, but it only takes one time to slip up and potentially bring a child into the world. It's a scary thing to know that you may think you have your life in control, but others can see that you aren't mentally, physically, and most importantly, emotionally able to handle this type of situation. Unfortunately, this was becoming a recurring situation in my life because I was continuing the same destructive behavior, making the same mistakes, and damaging people along the way.

As for basketball, domestically, we ran straight through the league. In the regular season, we were beating teams by an average of twenty points or more. To be honest, it was becoming a bit of a landslide. No one wanted to play us, and rightly so because we would beat them into submission. On the European front, soon we would face our toughest challenge, traveling to a very difficult and tough environment to play in Warsaw, Poland, against Sopot Prokom. This was a talented team with many international Polish players as well as a couple of former NBA players on the roster. The game was a very tight contest in the first half. There were many lead changes, and it was very heated between both sides. Many, many times, the referees would have to come in and try to keep the peace because we both would play for that last European spot to go on to the next round of sixteen. The game was scheduled for Tuesday evening, so we flew out from London on Monday afternoon, but little did we know we wouldn't arrive in Warsaw until the wee hours of Tuesday morning. There was an absolutely horrible snowstorm, and it had us trapped in the Czech Republic.

We sat in the airport virtually all day; it was a snowy, wet, and miserable experience. Most importantly, we didn't get much time in their gym to shoot around or just to get a feel for the floor. Our flight there would be one I'd never forget. Flying us into a Warsaw airport with runways covered with seven inches of snow was a dumb and selfish move by the airlines, but we took the risk—and man, it almost cost the lives of all twenty-five of us on the plane. In our initial descent, we went from fifteen thousand feet to ten thousand feet in a matter of ninety seconds; it was like we were about to nosedive to the ground. Everyone on the plane began to panic and scream, but I just remained calm and just closed my eyes.

As we got down to five thousand feet, my teammates began to scream at me, "Man, we [are] about to die! How can you be chilling?" I smiled and said, "God has a plan for me. I won't die in Poland, and neither will you." Fifteen minutes later, after a slippery landing, we were on the ground, safe and sound. Everyone onboard just looked at me incredulously as if to ask, *How in the world did you know we would be okay?* I just smiled and tried to play it off, but my teammates never looked at me the same after that. The crazy thing is they wanted to sit with me on every flight from then on. It was crazy. Even when I tried to ignore God, he still managed to show up and show out in my life.

Let's get on to the game where we had an improbable 42–40 lead at halftime. The second half would be a total brawl, leading to a slew of technical fouls and their assistant coach getting ejected for disputing the referees' calls. As the game wore down and went into the final stages, we trailed by two points with two minutes to go. A sweet crossover from right to left, baiting the defense into helping me, led to me finding my teammate wide open on the court for a shot that would take us over the edge and keep Sopot from advancing to the next round. Unfortunately, that would be the closest we ever got that night. Not only did we miss that shot, we didn't score again for the rest of the game and ended up losing by ten points. A tough lesson learned on the road: when playing great teams, the margin for error is almost next to none. With this loss, we were almost certain we were out of the round of sixteen. We would need a virtual miracle in order to qualify for the next round. Going into the last game of the round, we knew we had to win by a certain number of points and hope that the other teams that had a better position would lose in the point spread, which would work to our advantage.

Our next opponent was the French Cholet team, and they needed to win as well, so this was going to be a very tight and close affair. We won the game and lost our starting point guard to a hernia in the process, but not before he scored a record fifty-two points against them. This injury totally changed my role on the team, as well as my leadership position in helping the team successful. His hernia would have him out for the next two months, which would ultimately take us right into the playoffs. This was critical for us because now we were weak in one position, or so they thought. Little did they know I could fill in more than adequately in pursuit of the championship as well as the domestic title. During the stretch, I personally began to lead the league in assists and began to show that I could lead a veteran team to success, commanding respect in every aspect of the word.

The season finally drew to an end, and we clinched the regular season championship with four games still remaining with an impressive fifty-point win at home. It was almost as if the trophy loss pissed us off to no end and fueled us to success. So I had a cup title, a trophy, a second-place medal, and the regular-season championship under my belt—that season absolutely couldn't have gone any better in my imagination, aside from winning everything, of course. Now the real season began with the playoffs: one game, win or go home each round. Although we were the top seed, our first home game started off slightly slow. We were only up by four at halftime, but we knew that eventually, we would kick it in gear and break them down. Sure enough, in the latter quarter, we did exactly that. The last five minutes of the third quarter, they didn't score, and we went on a 20–5 run to break the game open. After this, it was simply a formality of getting to the finish line. At the end, we won by twenty-two points, 99–77, and were headed to the semifinals of the playoffs.

Of course, drama was with me no matter where I went. At the time, I was dating a nice young lady whom I thought had my best interests at heart, but I found out later that clearly wasn't the case. I'll call her *Ms. RieRie*, a brown-skinned, caramel cutie whom I happened to meet at my favorite spot in DC one summer evening. We had maintained contact, and I invited her over to spend the last part of the playoffs with me. Unfortunately, this didn't sit too well with my coach. He wanted no one to come on the bus with us, nor did he want anyone to stay in the hotels. But she was my guest, and I really didn't care at that point in my life. And I knew they couldn't win without me, so I brought her, and boy, did I get cussed out for it. In truth, the coach allowed so many things for other players, and I never really questioned it, nor did I ever try to do anything contrary to what the plan was for the team. However, in this instance, I became selfish and decided to do my own thing to make sure my guest was taken care of, and I had a blast, as did she.

Semifinal number one had us up against our nemesis Chester, and again, we ran them into the ground. Honestly, I can say professionally, I had very solid game. I had ten points, five rebounds, and eight assists, and we won comfortably by sixteen points. After the game, my coach cussed me out and basically chewed into me about the situation and how he was disappointed in my attitude and my actions in regard to bringing my friend on the trip. My response was,

"Am I not doing what you want me to do on the court, Coach?" He just looked at me and smiled, and that settled it.

The playoff finals would again see us competing against a tough opponent, the Sheffield Sharks, a very well-coached team with good experience and great guard play. From start to finish, it was a seesaw battle that saw both teams fighting tooth and nail to win. In the final five minutes of the game, two very huge mistakes by me cost us the game. One mistake was a gamble on a steal that led to a three-point shot for the Sharks, and then there was a turnover on offense. Instead of making a simple play, I did something stupid, and we were punished by them executing and hitting another three-pointer. We would end up losing by 2 points 86-84 and just like that, the season was over—no more do-overs, just the reality that we lost when it really counted.

This was really when the drama began. My inability to be a professional off the basketball court had caught up to me, and it was time to pay up. Basically, I had accumulated an outrageous amount of tickets on my car. (Living in the hotel, I had the option of paying a flat fee per month for a parking spot, but I didn't want to do this, which, in hindsight, was quite stupid because this was how I received all of my tickets.) With the hotel, I had accumulated some considerable costs for food, especially when I had guests stay over; and to top it all off, there were damages (small dents and scratches really) on my car from me driving around the city while drunk. All these costs left me with no money on my last paycheck! I was so pissed off, so mad, but in truth, I had no one to blame but myself. The funny thing about it is that the choices we make turn right back around and ultimately make us, and my life at this point was a prime example of this situation—bad decisions that led to me being without. I was broke, had no job, no extra income, and had just a bunch of chicks who were giving me money and holding me down. How pathetic was that?

One of the hardest things in the world is when you look in the mirror and see who you really are and what you have become. Don't get me wrong, I had a little bit of money in the bank, but I had to leave it, and I didn't want to tap into my savings to actually live, especially when I had banked on this last check to get me through the summer and support me. I actually ended up staying with a good friend of mine for about a month, trying to recover some funds from the team. I was also trying to go to another team just to make a month's salary because our season was over, and a lot of the other leagues were still playing. Unfortunately, nothing panned out; and after a month, I just realized it was better for me to head back home and work.

That's right, the professional basketball player who had a little bit of money came back to my lovely island home of Bermuda and worked construction for half a summer to compensate for the funds I wasted during the year. Most people didn't know what I was doing there, but my true friends knew I had wasted my funds and that working construction was my way of getting things back in order and finding financial stability. You can say whatever you want, but there is nothing more humbling than having to turn around and live with your mother and adjust to her lifestyle and rules. Just adhering to a working schedule was absolutely brutal in itself.

From 7:30 a.m. to 5:00 p.m. every day, I was in the hot sun, moving block and slate all day. This summer humbled me; it also got me back into grind mode. But with every situation and place, if you're not careful, you will fall back into the same habits of old. Flanagan's Pub on Friday and Saturday nights became my place to let all things go that bothered and stressed me throughout the week. I had a hookup at the bar, and make no mistake about it, I used it every single weekend. It was almost like I ran the bar, real talk. I gave my homie $150–$250 as a tip in return for whatever I wanted as far as alcohol was concerned. It helped that he was a drunk, to say it in the kindest way.

But again, if your priorities are not straight, you'll fall into anything that presents fun but doesn't promote better living or better growth for you all the time. Alcohol was, and if I'm not careful, always will be a downfall or pit stop in my life's journey. At this point in time in my life, alcohol was not only my truth serum, it took me to a place where I always felt in control, untouchable. And most importantly, it was where I could forget all the bad in my life and the responsibilities that I should have been taking care of but was neglecting.

The one good thing about this summer was that two of my closest friends were getting married. After seemingly an eternity of dating, Renzo and Nae would stand before God, friends, and family to commemorate their love for each other. I can honestly say I looked up to Renzo so much. He was in a place in life where he knew what he wanted, and he would drop any and everything to make sure Nae was happy. Regardless of the fact that I spent a significant part of my life engaging in promiscuous behavior, with flings here and there, deep down, I wanted the same thing that they had but was too afraid to step out of what I enjoyed to find it. The wedding was absolutely marvelous. I couldn't have been happier to see two friends completely give their lives to each other in the church that we grew up together in and forged our bonds as friends (and as lovers for Rezo and Nae). People don't understand, but I watched him go from Pathfinder camporees, to music clinics, to college days, and even to graduate school, and nothing could separate them or the love they shared. And it was awesome to see and to be a part of.

Renzo and Nae had a unique relationship. It started when they were young, and it just blossomed into a beautiful, unbreakable bond. Like any relationship, there were spots and places that they could have given up on each other; but again, like any great relationship, their love forged through those obstacles and situations. For me, they were the perfect object lesson in our modern day of what love could be. We all came from great stock. Most of our parents had been together for pretty much most of their lives, so it was the norm to find someone good, keep them, and build a relationship together that would last. I always looked up to Renzo and Nae, not in the envious way but more like an object lesson for what could be in my life. So many people in the world spend their whole lives searching for true love, or just someone to accept them for who they are and maybe help them to be better. These two dear friends stayed with each other, helped each other grow and, against all odds, completed each other. For me, this was huge because I knew I had flaws; but looking at their relationship and their bond made me think, pray, and hope that someday someone would accept me for who I was, good or bad, and just love me for me.

As the summer drew to a close, the partying, the drinking, and the hanging out got old. I found myself in a position where I wanted to grow into a better person but couldn't find a way to break out of the mold of being in the same situation (chasing women, drinking alcohol, being angry for no apparent reason). Truthfully, I didn't know how to break from the mold at this point in my life. I could say I was scared of what I was becoming, a person with so much talent and potential but wasting it away. I was presented with an opportunity to play in Germany, but me being the silly drunk-womanizer I was at the time, I declined the offer and ended up going back to London to play for another season in the BBL.

In the midst of all this, God still had a plan for my life, and my mother's prayers kept me safe from the stupidity with which I surrounded myself over and over again. That upcoming season, not only would I start to make changes, I would be forced to open up and seek professional one-on-one help to find a better me. The funny thing with life is when you're afraid to break the mold and find a way to make yourself into a better person, you simply will fall right back into the old situations and habits that you have developed over the years. Would I do the same thing again? Surely, I had learned my lesson, or will I make the same mistake again? Stay tuned. Only time will tell what would become a priority in my life and if I had truly learned the lessons necessary to move forward and be successful.

CHAPTER 7

WHEN REALITY
AND REAL MEET

*The greatest discovery of my genera-
tion is that a human being can alter
his life by altering his attitude.*

—William James

When it rains, it pours; where there is thunder, there is lightning; and unfortunately, where there is a disco music and beautiful women, there was Sullivan once again. A year and a half in London had changed me and really made me wake up and understand what I needed to be and how I was going to get to that point or place where I could be the best possible me. Looking back on it signing on to play in London again, it put my career back in ways that you couldn't even imagine, especially knowing that I had offers from other noted countries—this really hindered me beyond belief. Yet when you are chasing an illusion instead of following a visionary path, chances are, you will make bad decisions, and they will keep you from being your best you.

Lesson 20: To obtain greatness, you have to be willing to sacrifice all to attain, to gain, and to be the best in whatever they choose to be.

Physically, I was at an all-time high. There was nothing I couldn't do with my body on and off the court. But some demons still lingered, and that's what usually defeats most athletes or people in general, the mental struggles in life. We started our preseason in Ireland. The competition wasn't the greatest, but it was good enough for us to see where we stood and how we should play to gain somewhat of an identity. Offensively and defensively on this trip, because they had not expected me to be such a steady force on the team. That guy was my buddy, and shortly thereafter, he totally turned on me out of anger and disgust at management's decision to keep me employed and to fire him. However, that's the business. And to be fair, his love and desire for women and clubbing was so high that he made it very easy for management to decide because I was beyond focused at this point. I was very mellow with going out and meeting girls and things of that nature at this time. I wanted to establish myself and make a name for myself on both ends of the court, and I always knew the nightlife, the girls, and the women would always be there, so I could put all that on the back burner.

It's safe to say that while we were in Ireland, the coaching staff, as well as my teammates, saw that I wasn't the same player as previous years and that I would prove to be remarkably important throughout the course of the year. In Killarney, Ireland, the excitement of the nightlife enticed us. We went from club to club, bar to bar, looking for women to fulfill our sexual desires. The craziest thing was some of the coaches were out with us, and everyone was on the prowl. The coolest thing was that we came across a hen party (a bachelorette party) where all the girls, including the bride-to-be, were single and good-looking.

Back in London, we practiced for another week before the regular season started. It was quite intense as a lot was expected of our team, especially considering the money that they were putting out for this particular squad. The regular season began with the first home game at Crystal Palace arena, and we got off with a bang. In this game, I played well on both ends of the court with fourteen points, five rebounds, and five assists in a convincing twenty-point win. After a win like that, the one thing you have to do is go out and celebrate, but I held off from going out for the first five games. I just really wanted to master my craft and improve to show people that I wasn't just about the partying rock-star life.

As the season wore on, my commitment to not going out slowly disappeared, and I began to loosen up and have fun in every aspect and sense of the word—I truly had a blast. To be honest, playing as a big fish in a little pond (because England really wasn't considered a great league to play in, though I competed in European competition there) was getting old, and I wanted to try my hand at something new and more challenging. You have to understand, not being focused, we would go out every night from Monday to Monday. The only day we really didn't go out was Wednesday, and it was strictly because the place that we would go to was shut down because someone was shot and killed there. So aside from Wednesday, every night was a party, every day was a new girl. It was really a rock-star lifestyle, and I say that with no hesitation because that's literally how it was. To be honest with you, in two seasons in London, I can almost guarantee you that I had sex with 75 to 150 women. At one point in time, I had sex with 25 girls 3 to 4 days—that's just how crazy it was. (Please don't think this is boasting. I was a lost boy searching to find himself, and I'm not proud of how I behaved.)

You may look at the numbers and ask, "How could you be so reckless?" Well, when you stay as drunk as we were and had access to the number of girls we did, in every city we played through over and over again, it was easy. In London, there was the curse of women of every race available; there was no loyalty for me. Any girl who looked exotic, or from another race or culture, was a go. There was one woman who impacted my life, and I'll have to use a fake name because she asked me not use her real name, so we will call her *Ms. Jazz*. She was highly educated, had an incredible job, and most of all, she was absolutely beautiful inside and out. And she was one of the few women I was in contact with on a regular basis, not just for sex but because she made me look deeper than what I portrayed on the surface.

One day, after consuming an eighth of Jack Daniel's (JD), we had a very deep heart-to-heart. In that conversation, I allowed her to see beyond the coldhearted gangster I pretended to be to mask the pain that I held so close to my heart. She gave me a number to a therapist she had seen after she was raped when she was younger, and she told me I should go speak to this lady and get some things off my chest. I laughed uncontrollably at her and responded, "You so are crazy. Why would I go share my innermost feelings with a stranger?" She looked at me and said, "Who better to share your pain with than someone who will never judge you for anything you say?" That stuck with me, and it wouldn't leave me alone. It made me stop and think that maybe it was time for me to open up those wounds and address the pain, sorrow, and agony that I had been dealing with for so long. Maybe taking this step would free me. I thought it long and hard for a while. The beauty of Ms. Jazz was she knew how to get my attention without making me feel threatened. That's exactly what I needed, and her gentle influence set me on the path that would ulti-mately save me from myself.

On court, everything was going fine. We were a very good team. We knew our roles, we played together well, and ultimately we won. Coming down to the last weekend of the season, it was a basically a three-way tie for the championship. We had to win a very tough game on the road in order to secure the championship, but before the game, other little dramas were going on. One night, my teammate parked his car on the street; and while he was sleeping, an eighteen-wheeler came by and smashed the back of his car, leaving his car halfway on the street. Apparently, the club only had minimal insurance on the car, so it was a possibility that he would have to pay for the damages to the car. As a result, there was a five-game stretch where he really didn't play because he was mad and was worried that his pay would be affected because of the damage to his car. Because he didn't really play, it cost us the championship. We lost those five games, and that was the only five-game losing streak we ever had. To be fair, the first season I was there was a bust. We were runners-up in three out of four competitions, which was not good in the eyes of management, so changes were going be made at the end of the year.

At the end of the day, in this business, there is no trophy for second place. No one is trying to finish second; everyone's trying to win. That was the harsh reality for this group. Some had never won, whereas I had been lucky to win the year before, so I knew jobs would be lost behind this loss. Initially, the team had meetings with players and basically told other people that I was the main cause for our loss, but my contract would be the only one that would be renewed. It's funny how fate would have it that I would be the only one to return the following year, but with a whole different focus and purpose. This particular summer, I would have the privilege of playing for Bermuda's national team in the NatWest Island Games, and they were held on the beautiful island of Gibraltar. However, before I went to those games, more drama found me.

During the year, I had been reaching out to my daughter's mom to try to be a better man and be a part of my daughter's life. I had planned to take her to Gibraltar with me and spend all my free time with her just so that she could get to know me. Unfortunately, things didn't work out as planned, and I didn't get to see her at all during the summer. To be honest, that pissed me off to no end; but at the end of the day, I truly commend her mother for not allowing her to come stay with me, especially since I wasn't someone who was stable in her life. I can see that now, but at the time, I was beyond furious for having already purchased her tickets and not being able to see her.

Nevertheless, the summer went on, and the tournament in Gibraltar was an opportunity for me to play for the national team and help them make history by winning a major tournament outside of Bermuda soil. The first game of the tournament was against the home team from Gibraltar. It was a very scrappy team, but luckily for me and my team, I had experience in this type of situations, and that experience helped us get through the first game safely. We actually went through the whole tournament undefeated, so it looked good for us to actually get into the medal round again. Being that we were the top seed, we got the easy draw to the gold-medal game, but we would soon learn that just because you get the easy ride doesn't necessarily mean you'll win in the end. Coverage for the whole game was a tight affair. We went into the last five minutes of the game down by four points when, finally, my drunk self woke up and began to play.

You see, the night before the final game, I went down to the city to partake in the nightlife but didn't arrive back at the hotel until six or seven o'clock in the morning, and our game was at three o'clock in the afternoon. Drunk out of my mind, I just lay there in the bed, listening to the monkeys running around outside my window making some crazy noises. I remember pondering, *What's going on with my life?* In truth, I was spiraling out of control, constantly finding myself in the same destructive situations over and over again. Finally I fell asleep, and boy, did I sleep. The game was at three o'clock; I woke up at 2:45 p.m. I jumped out of the bed, got my mouthwash in hand and gum as well, grabbed my things, and ran toward the gym. I didn't have time to wait on a taxi to take me down to the arena. To my surprise, when I arrived, it was fifteen minutes until tip-off because the previous game had gone longer than expected. I could see the look on my teammates' eyes. They had no idea if I could perform or if I even cared. In my heart, I knew I cared; however, my actions certainly didn't show it.

With five minutes to go in the game, I had only one chance to prove that I did care and had come to win because up to this point, it seemed like I was on vacation. Since I've always loved pressure, I've been able to perform well in clutch situations. It was the last five minutes of the game that was my masterpiece of this tournament. They played a diamond two set (when three opposing players stay in a diamond set close to the basket and try to keep you from scoring inside the key while the other two players play man-to-man), which allowed me to play a lot of one-on-one and get right to the basket and ultimately win the game for us. The final seconds finally came, and the celebrations could begin. We were the 2005 NatWest Island games' gold medalists, making history, and I was one of the main architects behind this—what an honor. It's something I can always show so my kids, friends, and loved ones know that this group of Bermudans walked out of Gibraltar with an historic, monumental achievement.

The excitement within our team was unbelievable. We had accomplished something no other team from Bermuda had accomplished in basketball. To a certain degree, we felt as if we had established a new standard of excellence. What was amazing was I was selected MVP. If you had asked me, the MVP would have stood for something totally different (most valuable prick) because the whole time I was there, that's exactly what I acted like. Reluctantly, I accepted the award; but to be 150 percent organic with you, deep in my heart, even the smiles and laughter of everyone's congratulations did nothing to alleviate the pain I was in. I was in so much pain, so much hurt, and all I wanted do was run back to my hotel room, grab a bottle of Jack Daniel's, and cry myself to sleep. This prompted me to make changes, not huge ones, but truthfully, it led to me making the biggest decision I had ever made in my life. After returning to the States from Gibraltar, I sought out a psychologist with whom I'd test the theory of speaking with a complete stranger about my issues to resolve them.

If you are of West Indian descent, then you're familiar with the tendencies. You already go in thinking you're okay and usually won't give therapy a fair shot. In our communities, psychologists have never been viewed in a positive way. When someone seeks professional help, it usually means that person is losing control of himself or herself, and no one likes to admit this within our community—that's just how it is. Knowing this obviously didn't help in my decision to seek help to figure out what demons were plaguing me so I could be released from the misery I had held on to for so long.

I had the sessions with a particular psychologist. She was very nice and polite, but truthfully, I didn't feel comfortable opening up to her or being honest with myself. After the second session, she told me not to come back and waste my money because, clearly, if I wasn't willing to open up and be honest with her or myself—and until I was ready to do that—I would never leave the place where I was stuck in my life, miserable and causing others misery. Her words cut deeper than the sharpest samurai sword. She saw through the charm and my admittance to having slight issues and saw the man who would remain a boy until he opened up and allowed her or someone else to help with the pain and demons that daily destroyed me more and more. I walked out of her office, and I just lied to myself, saying I tried and she couldn't help me. But in the back of my mind, I knew that the true reason it wasn't successful was because I did not want to open up and be truthful about my past. This led me to this lesson of truth:

> *Lesson 21: It is one thing to con or lie to another person (this is wrong and not a practice anyone should have), but lying to yourself is a sad and very hazardous road to travel, and people are usually lost on this road and are never found!*

> You see, I was lying to myself, and it was so bad I had almost gotten to a point after therapy where I started to believe the lie was real and that I was doing fine.

> Above all don't lie to yourself. The man who lies to himself and listens to his own lies comes to a point that he can't distinguish the truth within him, or around him, and so he loses respect from himself and for others.

> -Fyodor Dostoyevsky

When everything seems fake, and alcohol and a new woman every night are true and calming influences in your life, that's a scary thing. It was a terrifying point in my life; I was consuming an eighth of Jack Daniel's daily just to cope and feel safe. Truthfully, outside of the friends I knew had my back and my mom, I was isolated for the rest of the summer. Hell, I was so scared I even thought of ending my life. I never had the guts to try, but I thought about it all the time during these months. The only thing that kept me from doing it was Ja'hnniah. I didn't want her life to be damaged because of another one of my selfish choices.

One afternoon in the middle of August, I sat on the floor in my place alone and just sipped Jack and cried. It was like in a movie where you see a girl crying and mad because she was dumped by the guy she loved so much. It's the whole sloppy tears and snot running from my nose that I need you to envision. I prayed, cried, drank, and talked to myself from 3:00 p.m. until around 9:00 p.m. and realized that I needed to go to my last appointment and open up. I called the psychologist and made my final appointment for the next morning. To my surprise, she had an available spot that day around 4:00 p.m., and she said, "I'm going to give you a free hour, and you'll be the last client" (there are no accidents with God). I apologized and promised to be more open, but only if she permitted me to bring my flask of JD because I just couldn't open up normally without some liquid courage. She reluctantly agreed, knowing I wouldn't drive to or from the appointment and forced me to write and fax a letter to cover her if anything went wrong.

Four o'clock came so fast as time usually flies when you don't want to do something. But this "something" changed my life completely, and I haven't been the same after this day. We sat and talked on an array of things, and she revisited my past and my resentments of being a preacher's kid. Deep down, I hated my parents for me not being able to play sports competitively as a kid and hated the stereotypes that unfortunately followed me because of my dad's position. The hardest part for me was talking about my dad dying. Up to this point, I had never spoken of his death or visited his grave, so all the emotions came out like a free-flowing ocean current. I was mad that God took my dad, a good man whom I needed in my life; mad that my dad didn't leave us with anything to help us out financially; and even mad at my mom for not allowing me to choose my own path. I could have been in the NBA had I been allowed to chose a different school.

Then we addressed the other huge failure in my life up to this point: my daughter. I told the psychologist how I had used my daughter's mother and how, when it was time to be a man, I constantly ran away from having to deal with her, and when I finally reached out to her, she basically dismissed me. She had every right to dismiss me. I hadn't made proper strides and efforts to reach out to my daughter, but now that I wanted to be there and couldn't be, I was mad—it all came out. You see, for the rest of my life as a man, I have to live with the fact that for the first three years of my daughter's life, I wasn't really her dad. Other than sending monetary offerings here and there, I was just a sperm donor! That's the biggest regret I have ever had in my life, but I thank God that things don't always have to stay the same and later changes would be made to ensure this. But on that day in the psychologist's office, I boohooed and cried it all out and, as a result, opened and cleaned out a few things from my closet. However, the psychologist referred me to a colleague of hers in London with whom I could follow up when I got to London and continue the journey to find that inner peace. That night was one of the first nights in a superlong time I prayed and fell asleep without a bottle of JD to assist me. It's so sad, but at the end of the day, we all have to start from somewhere to get to our desired destination, and this was my starting point.

The last few weeks of summer, I even went to church and took a trip out to Florida to see my sister and her family so I could spend more time with my nephews and draw from their spiritual influence because they went to church all the time. No matter what was going on, they always made me laugh and forget the drama of my life. Their world was so simple and easy, and they just wanted to be happy. My nephews Jereme and Jaelen were my medication until I left. They made me feel as if I wasn't a failure. To them I was a hero who did what I loved and got paid for it. I was their legendary uncle. In a weird way, I needed this getaway to get me through this juncture of my life. Hell, I needed anything to keep me from that JD because every day it called me back to that comfort zone. But I had to resist, or I would be its slave for the rest of my life. It's crazy, looking back at that point in my life. I can honestly say I was so lost, but it was entirely my fault. I had the power not only to change where I was and where my life was going but resurrect it into purpose and create a better life for myself.

My second year in London, I was on a quite different path, and I had a different focus. Financially, I realized that I wasn't going to be broke from wasting my money on drinking and acting the fool all week in the streets. I also knew that entertaining many women from all walks of life and diverse races also drained my resources, so this diversion would have to take a backseat! It's crazy how a little music and a redbone (a lady with caramel-colored skin) could command my attention at a glance and have me on the prowl, so I knew I was going out only once a week maximum. But this was a dangerous game to play, simply because old habits die hard, and I would again learn the hard way that good intentions don't trump strong morals and ethics that guide your life. There couldn't be a more profound truth in this whole book; that's why I'm going to say it again to make sure you grasp this pivotal lesson:

> Lesson 22: It's a very dangerous game to play with demons or weaknesses from your past. Good intentions are trumped by strong moral convictions and mental fortitude any day. Make sure yours are firmly in place.

I knew that I wanted to make changes and actually wrote them down and began to put them into effect. However, I knew all it would take was one slipup, and I'd be right back where I was the previous year. Everything in this year actually started well, and on the court, I began to flourish and show much more control and leadership potential. I had one teammate who loved to party and have fun. He was the one guy I could call at 2:00 a.m. and say, "Man, let's hit them streets and see what's good"; and ten minutes later, we would be ready to go. So I avoided heading out a lot with him big-time in the beginning of the season. Shoot, the first month, I didn't go out, not even once. I even managed to stay away from the bottle as well. On the female front, most of the girls I had been with the year before didn't take me seriously because of how I left just abruptly. Either way, most of them weren't trying to mess with me anymore. With the few who did entertain me, it was like revisiting the candy store, but they were extremely shocked that I wasn't going out as much at that point.

On court, we were playing well and had reached the finals of the first domestic competition, the BBL Cup, crawling up to third place in the league, so things were going well, and my stats were great as well. I started talking with a lady I will call *Ms. Suga*, who was in the military and was deployed when we began to chat and correspond. To be quite frank and honest, she was a cool woman and began to hold a lot of my attention and kept me quite the more intrigued. I really liked the idea of being with her, but around this time, I began to slip and start feeling myself and our team's success. I started hitting up promoters and club people to get on guest lists, poetry readings—you name it, and my main man and I were there. It's crazy, but we won the cup final by four points, and he and I had gone out the night before and had a blast with some chicks. I was at my glorious rock-star status again, the life everyone thinks they want and need.

Back to Ms. Suga, she had been through a lot in life, and had I not been so eager to get in her underwear, I would have seen the signs to be careful and to approach with caution. Again, she was a good woman. However, at the time I met her, I was dealing with many other women, and we never really had the talk about monogamy. But I guess she assumed from our deep conversations that I was different. I, on the other hand, assumed the "don't ask, and I won't tell" role and kept it moving. This time, though, I would really find out how bad things could get when your words and actions don't mirror each other when dealing with a woman who has been burned in the past. She came back from deployment, and we began to hang out and chill, and eventually sex came along. After our first encounter, she cried, and I was so scared. Even after she told me it was okay and that she enjoyed my company, we weren't the same from that point on because I knew that it was very deep for her and just a sexual pleasure for me. After seeing each other here and there, she came over for a weekend, and that's when it hit the fan big-time.

While I was sleeping, one of my jump-offs hit me up, wanting to come by after the club to hang out and have some sex before she headed home, and Shorty (Ms. Suga) was on my phone in the bathroom. I woke up to use the bathroom, and Shorty had my phone in her hand, demanding to know, "Who is this?" I thought she was joking, so I bust out laughing, thinking, *This chick is bananas. She really ain't going through my phone.* But she was, and it would happen again too. Luckily, I hit the jump-off up and let her know the deal, and she was cool. In fact, everyone else except Ms. Suga was cool with being a mistress. She and I had a war of words until I lied and appeased her with meaningless promises and sex.

However, when a situation is not right, the wrong eventually manages to rise up and present itself in the worse way. Another evening, I was just chilling with Shorty, and my phone rang. It was someone from the States I was cool with, and we talked, and I hung up and thought nothing of it. The next day, I received e-mails and some other crazy stuff sent to me. Apparently, Shorty had hacked into my e-mail and sent messages to people. I was so mad, but I politely asked her to leave and that we had to take a break because she was wilding out. She argued for a minute, and after crying and all of that, she finally left. But that wouldn't be the end. We will get back to that in a bit. During this time, the basketball side of things was fading down, and the playoffs were near. We had successfully made it through to another semifinals round and were making a final push for the playoffs.

Before that, my boy Shel came to town to hang out and experience the European summer I had told him about, and I let him witness it personally. His first night there, I took him out and put him on to a cool spot, and we had a blast. He was there for a week, and we got it in every day (LOL). While he was there, I began to let him know what had been going down and what was new on the chick front, especially with Ms. Suga. When I told him of the drama she had created, he was like, "Man, you had better cut her off. She's no good for you."

Unfortunately, we lost in the finals of the playoffs after a crazy quarterfinal overtime win. The game was remarkable. Our opponents were on an eight-game winning streak, and we straight fought until the final whistle, when I hit game-winning free throws with four seconds left to finish off a valiant effort from the other team. The semifinals saw us literally destroy the opposition by twenty points.

It was a whitewash from wire to wire, and this would set up an epic final. In the final, it was a seesaw battle going back and forth, but unfortunately, we lost by six points. We played with a six-man rotation, so it was quite tough. But in the end, we did lose, and another season had come to an end.

Even going through the playoffs, my boy's words kept ringing through my head about how I was trying to prove something to myself as opposed to accepting what space and place in life I truly was. You see, he was in a relationship, and I thought that I needed to be where he was, not living the bachelor life where anything and everything goes. However, that's the funny thing about lie: you're where you need to be, but that doesn't mean you have to stay in that place forever. Understanding where you are, striving to be better, and making your life better and more fulfilling is your true purpose.

The other scandal that occurred with Ms. Suga involved the few ladies I was talking to from the States, three of them to be exact. Ms. Suga got wind of this, contacted the ladies, and basically, they all got in cahoots to devise a plan to teach me a lesson. Needless to say, after a few days of conversation with each of them, I sniffed out that something was up. Man, she had been e-mailing these ladies via my e-mail account and just erasing the evidence of sent and received messages between all of them. I might have been upset, but at the end of the day, I couldn't be mad because I wasn't forthcoming and right in my approach with her, so I had no one to blame but myself.

They comprised a plan to try and call me one after the other and ask about my loyalty and then call back on three-way to confront me, with Ms. Suga there as well. Dude, all I can say is, looking back, I should have run beyond the moon and just accepted that I had been caught and leave this woman alone—but no, I had to prove to myself that I was not a dog and that there was a good man in me. Around this time, I also began to get messages from friends, saying reckless things were being posted on the Internet (on MySpace, what a throwback) of how I had HIV and warning women if they even had minimal contact with me to go get tested and stay clear of me. Of course, I reached out to all my peoples and let them know that was a vicious prank and not to pay any attention to that foolishness.

The good I gained from this little incident was that it really made me stop and think, *What if this was my daughter in this triangle. How would I feel?* This was the clincher, the mental check, or even better, the player card check, if you will. You see, up until this incident, fatherhood was just a monthly fee to me, not the God-given joy to be a role model in a little person's life and help mold a child into the best person he or she could be. I'd heard other women cry over me for different reasons, but this time, hearing three women cry and express so much pain and hurt really struck home.

While in London that year, I had been referred to a new psychologist to share my problems and pain. Well, I met with the first one, and let's just say there was way too much attraction between us. Walking into her office, we caught eyes, and the physical attraction that shouldn't be seen, definitely not in a business context, was there. After an hour of totally controlling the session and showing her vulnerability to entice her, I invited her out for a drink. She declined the first few times I asked, but eventually, as our two-hour session ended, she obliged and went out with me.

Yeah, it was about 5:00 a.m. when she left my apartment the next morning. She was upset and like, "Oh my goodness, I'm going to lose my job." I quickly calmed her down and told her to just pass me off to another psychologist/therapist so we could continue seeing each other. I told her as a joke, "Just don't give me a sexy one like you," and she turned to me and politely said, "I'll make sure it's someone to whom you'll really open up and not just on the surface. She will help you." I stopped her and asked what she meant, and she smiled and responded, "As charming as you might think you are, I totally see the insecurities, and you came to me because you want to clean out your closet and live a healthy, happy life." Just like that, I was dumbfounded; she really saw through the BS. But she just liked me, and man, would she ever bless me with the best help on earth.

Ms. Diana was a literal thug psychologist/therapist who wouldn't take no for an answer, and she was spiritually grounded. The first session was crazy. She asked if I were religious, and I told her yes, somewhat, and that I grew up in religious home. She said, "Well then, your mom would appreciate that every session, we start with a word of prayer, and we both will pray." My first reaction was, *Oh hell no, I ain't having no spiritual psychologist. I just want an objective one*, but I said, "Nah, I'm good, Ms. Diana. I'll look for someone else." She smiled and said, "Walk out, and you can kiss that peace, love, and happiness good-bye. Or you can sit down, have a prayer, and begin navigating to your happiness." Her words pierced my soul. I wanted happiness and to be in my daughter's life; I just needed things to be right in my life.

We met three times a week in her South London office, and it was always intense. It was as if God himself gave a breakdown of my week and correlated it to my life because, man, she broke me down like a book. I remember one week I met a girl, and we had sex just before my appointment. I had showered, the whole nine, but Ms. Diana was like my mother at the front door, asking what I had been doing. She challenged me to keep my penis in my pants and see women for who they were and treat them how I'd want a man to treat my daughter. That particular day, she made me so mad when she replayed the events in my life but used Ja'hnniah's name as the victim of the drama I had created in my life. Man, I cussed her out so bad and threatened to leave. She calmly reminded me that whatsoever you do, that's what you are going to reap. Maybe not me, but my daughter may reap the drama I had sown.

Time flew, and after an epic journey of soul-searching for months, we were at our last session. I'll never forget our last session. She sat down with me from 5:00 p.m. to 10:00 p.m. to really counsel me from a spiritual woman's perspective. She told me how she was played and raped by an ex and almost gave up on all men, until her husband helped her get past the sin and shame to be the best person she could be. She challenged me to reach out and be in my daughter's life as a dad and a good example and not just as a financial or sperm donor. But the most important thing she did for me was give me a book that to this day has a special place in my heart, *The Purpose Driven Life* by Rick Warren. She told me, "This book will guide you when you can't reach me." After prayer and hugs, I left, but that day, as well as the other sessions, changed me as a man. Could this be the turning point, I thought, or was I just fooling myself and would the real me show up again?

CHAPTER 8

IT's A BRAND-NEW DAY, OR IS IT?

*Any change, even change for the better is always
accompanied by drawbacks and discomforts.*

—Arnold Bennett

Summer was here, but there was a sense of urgency and determination for me to prove to myself that I could and would be
better. I decided not to return to the States to stay and see if I
could be a good man to Ms. Suga and possibly create a union with
her. Looking back on my thought process, I can only laugh at how
naive I was. Truth be told, I didn't even have the most important
piece of my life in order, so there was no way I could create happiness with anyone else! Yet I was still there, and things were okay for
the most part. But we were not having sex, so that definitely was on
my mind and all the easy encounters I could have instead of trying
to play house with this lady. After a minivacation with her, I really
began to delve heavily into the book Ms. Diana had given me; it was
my sanity pill. Because I had been so devious and shady with Ms.
Suga, she would often hound me like a police officer, checking who
I was talking to and what e-mails I was sending—it was crazy. I put
up with it because I knew what I had done, so I just turned my head

away and endured the situation. But it wouldn't be long before my true personality would show up. I wouldn't just stand there and just take being treated like a little boy.

The other issue with Ms. Suga was that, as time went on, I was spending crazy money living with this woman, and I soon found myself in a situation that I vowed not to be in again, and that was lacking finances. One thing was for sure: when my finances become low or I'm in a situation where my back is against the wall, I've never been afraid to do anything necessary to make sure I survived. That's exactly what I had to do. When I recognized the position I was facing, I began to look for work; but to be honest with you, that wasn't cutting it. The finances of the house were drowning me because I was also putting funds away in an account I couldn't touch. Yes, the money was there, but it was like it wasn't because I couldn't and wouldn't touch it. Instead of pouting and complaining, I went and got a job at *Burger King*. That's right, I went and got a job at Burger King to make sure I didn't go totally broke. You see, it's quite simple. Pressure can either cause pipes to bust or can create diamonds. It all depends on how you deal with the pressure. After such an amazing year where I had come of age and began to show such potential in my field, it seemed as if I had been knocked on my back. *This is crazy* is all I could think. However, I'm a firm believer that there are no accidents and you are where you are in life for a reason. During this time in my life, I needed to understand this:

Lesson 23: God allows you to fall on your back in life so you can remember to look up and focus on what's important—Him!

Here in my Burger King era, I once again began to reach out to my daughter's mom and apologize for my behavior and my failure to be in my child's life. Of course, at first, there was a lot of resentment there because I hadn't shown a sincere interest or that I cared in the past, and I had to prove that my interest was there and that I was for real. Ms. Suga was lightweight jealous. I guess she thought I was going to try to go back and make things right by forming a relationship with my daughter's mom when, in actuality, I had finally come to myself and was reaching out to be a part of my daughter's life. This negativity took me over the edge and made me revert to my old ways, and I let her know I was not a little boy and that she could not treat or act as if I were a piece of property that she owned. After a huge argument, I called a friend of mine who lived in London and let him know I was going to stay with her because I needed to get away and clear my head.

During this time from a professional standpoint, I had done the whole Burger King thing, but I also managed to find a new agent and secure a new job in Hungary. So knowing I had a job and was in a good financial position, I wasn't interested in what Ms. Suga was talking about anymore. Basically, I didn't need to prove anything to her or anyone really; it was all about the new me. For the first time in a long time, all the guilt of the different issues that had held me back for so long was lifted.

Seeing me get up and leave made her realize I was not taking crap from her anymore, and she wanted to mend things before I left for Hungary. I can honestly say that I gave it 150 percent, and after a long talk with my boy Renzo, I knew it was time to move on and begin my life as the new me without any baggage from my past. While in London, staying with my homie Mousey, I sought out all the women I had dealt with and met with them face-to-face to apologize for any wrong I might have done to them, whether knowingly or unknowingly. Of the visits, 50 percent were extremely uncomfortable. Hell, one lady spit in my face as soon as she saw me then slammed the door behind her. Behind the door, I heard her crying, and something deep within urged me to knock again and say the words I needed say to her. So I did. As I knocked, she opened the door and screamed, "Do you know what you did to me!" I replied humbly, "No, but I want to apologize to you." She looked puzzled because the old me never apologized. I would have just said, "Screw you" and move on to the next with no emotional ties.

After the initial anger died down and a few more apologies, she invited me in for a cup of tea. And as we sat there for an hour, she led me down the nine-month path where I totally stripped her of her worth and dignity and how I used my insecurities and shortcomings as a man and father to break her down. She made me face the painful images of me dissing her in front of her friends and making her do things that God himself—if he didn't already know, I wouldn't tell. But at that phase and point in my life, I was just an experimenting sexual scientist and needed as many test subjects I could find.

After she finished, I just looked her in the face and began to explain my life, about my daughter, and the void I needed to fill. I just broke it down with no BS. "This is me, and I'm sorry for what I did to you. I hope that one day you can find it in your heart to forgive me." We hugged and have remained in touch, but that conversation really opened my eyes and helped me understand the effects of my actions more clearly, so vulnerability isn't always a bad thing. After almost one hundred visits throughout the week—some ugly, some informative, but most importantly, they were real encounters where I asked for forgiveness—I was ready to open a new chapter in my life.

I arrived in Hungary on a hot humid summer day, and upon arrival, they sent a gentleman named Guba who only spoke in the third person (I couldn't make this up, I swear). But in fairness, Guba was always kind and helped me while I was there. Before leaving London for Kaposvár, Hungary, the last official act of the changing of the guard was my spiritual acknowledgement and commitment to do better spiritually by paying tithes and offering, as well as committing more of my energy to attending church. With that at the forefront of my mind, every morning and evening, I started and ended my day with *The Purpose Driven Life* (which I read about six times while there) and using it as well as the Bible to add spiritual awareness to my life. After being there a few weeks, Ms. Suga and I broke up and decided to lead our own lives. And to be honest, it was certainly for the best because, in truth, this was a totally different job than before, and the new work ethic began immediately upon my arrival.

We practiced two times a day, and it was not easy. We went hard from start to finish, and after a certain number of days, we had to shoot before going to lunch. I committed every day to shooting and free throws, as well as a strict regime of push-ups and sit-ups. For the first two months, I was so focused it was crazy. I was like a machine literally and metaphorically. Over the first five preseason games, I was playing about thirty-seven out of forty minutes; but because we practiced so hard, the games were easy for me. Our practices were straight bananas. We started from go at 150 percent and ended two hours later at 150 percent, or we would keep going. The day before a game would be the only day we slowed down to receive technical instructions about the game. Up to this point, I hadn't met any girls or done anything really because four hours were allocated for practice, and the evenings were strictly used for sleep and PlayStation because I didn't have the energy to do anything else. However, when the season began, I finally went out and met a few people; but even with that, I never stopped my routine, and my play on court showed that I was putting in the work on and off the court.

> *Lesson 24: No success that is found or obtained ever comes without pain, sacrifice, or ultimate dedication.*

The pain can be physically and even mentally draining to no end, but you've got to continuously envision the goal even in the middle of hardship. I endured the physical pain of running the pyramid (a fast-paced interval workout that focuses on improving running economy) in a ninety-degree weather. We ran suicides before and after practice for cardio to take the extra steps to ensure that I could be at my best to help this team. That was my intention as well as my goal. Our coach was the best coach I ever worked with in the twelve years of playing professionally. He simply brought out the best in me on both sides of the court and made me work harder than anyone else had been able to do. Defense, defense, defense was all we heard from one of the greatest scorers in that league, and this: "If you're not in shape physically, you'll break down and give up."

There are no shortcuts to any place
worth going in this life!

-Beverly Sills

The pain can be mental as well. Losing is the most agonizing thing for me personally. The thoughts that come with losing are that you're not good enough, or you're never going to achieve your ultimate goals. At this point in life, I had a coach who would curse me out to no end and put immense pressure on me, and even fans would spit at me, saying they wanted to kill me. It could all get to be too much if you're not grounded or don't have an outlet for your frustration. This is what separates pretenders from the real deal and winners from participants. Leaders and winners in life and sports can physically and mentally will themselves to a place where the pain and mental agony are placed in the temporary section. The success and the prosperity that's achieved after passing the temporary remains at the forefront, and success can be achieved. That's what I was training myself for in this phase of life. I had won in life but wasn't a winner because it wasn't a habit for me; it was just a want or desire. Success is a habitual way of living, from proper diet to good rest, no sex on day of games, or simply studying for a test—whatever helps you zone in and focus. And finally, I was learning how to do this and be successful.

Overcoming these mental and physical barriers enables greatness to surge through you and your life. The season finally started, and to be honest, in the first games, you could see the confidence I had gained under my coach's tutelage in stats in points, assists, and steals. My physical stamina was also amazing. In the first five games, I played every second on the court. That's forty minutes each night, which, for most, was extremely tough; but like I said previously, I had begun to turn my body into a machine. And at 3–2 after a tough first five games, things were going well. I had slowly allowed myself to go out and hang with the team, but on a short leash, of course, not just because of the rigorous schedule but just to keep the nature of the beast under control as well. In our city, there were a few no-nos that you just didn't do. You didn't mess with Mafia guys (muscle-bound guys with huge gold chains and had the best girls and money) and didn't mess with other sports teams and their girls. These rules were made very clear to me when I arrived. These rules had been broken in the past and caused huge problems and almost death for some foreigners.

Seeing that those barriers were up, I clearly had to find fun in other arenas; but like always, trouble will find you even when you're just minding your own business. One night, one of the Mafia guys just happened to leave the club with another fling, and his girl began to come on to me. I was a bit skeptical as to why this sexy woman was chasing after me and spoke English well enough to hold a full-on conversation. What saved my life was I was very distant until I was sure who she was. While talking with her at the bar from a good, safe distance, he came across the room like a bolt of lightning. Imagine 350 people just freezing in place and watching. But this wasn't a game; this was a huge man as hairy as a wolf, and I was a baby lamb for dinner. My teammate came over and began to explain and reason with him, but he wasn't having it or listening at all. He spoke English, so he said to me, "I'll give you one chance to explain very well what's going on. If you don't explain to me honestly what's up, you won't be leaving here alive." The words came out slowly, and it seemed like it took forever; but after they left his lips, it was my turn to respond or die, literally.

The best thing about my personality is that I'm not one to panic under any circumstance. I always try to be objective, and panic is never an option. I moved close to him and said, "Look, man, as you saw, I stood at a distance from her because I'm a big black basketball player, and no one ever wants to talk to me here. So I wondered what this hot girl wanted from me. Clearly, she was using me to get you mad, and it worked." I continued, "We never got further than the general, her name and who she was with, and she said she was alone but didn't want to be. Then you came over. That's it, man. I told him I'm never gonna stick my head in a lions mouth and sneeze on his tonsils no way!"

Surprised by me being so forward, he began to laugh and introduced me to his boys and their girls so no more mishaps would occur. But what's crazy is that I spoke with my mother like I did every Sunday, and she told me she had an urge to pray for me around the same time of this event (that would have been 6:00 a.m. Bermuda time). Here I was, thinking my slick-talking self had gotten me out of a life-threatening jam when, in truth, my mother's prayers had once again come to my aid in the time of need. Genesis 46:1 (KJV) says, "God is our refuge and strength, a very present help in trouble."

While reading this the next day during my daily devotional, I had to smile at the obvious help God had sent my way. I had found some friends to pass the time with, but unfortunately, I broke the rules when I allowed Ms. Petra into my hotel room for an evening of fun. I was driving down the street after practice, and I just happened to see this sexy tall blonde walking on the opposite side of the street. I looked, and she saw and just began to grin, so you know I had to do a U-turn and go say what's up. We began to talk and found common interests and decided to meet up later that evening just to chill in my hotel room. She was a very famous volleyball player and was hounded by many men. She said she only came to b-ball games to see me and wanted to know me better. Well, she didn't have to say more, but it could only be an evening thing and nothing during the day because of the club's very strict stipulations. Again, I would not only break the team's rules but also my only strict rule of no company the night before a game. That was a no-nonsense rule I've had over the years: no company of any sort other than teammates before a game to ensure that my mental and physical awareness were at their highest and that my complete concentration was there.

My other rule of no sleepovers was also broken. I had a firm policy that no one sleeps over, but Ms. Petra broke the rules and managed to spend many nights over because when you break the rule repeatedly, the rule can no longer stand as a principle for your life. That night before the game, I can't even lie, I went to bed smiling. I didn't really care if she enjoyed herself, but I knew I did, and that was all that mattered—until the morning, when two officials from the team came by to check on me out of the blue to make sure the hotel was up to par. Man, what a shock. I was like, "Are you kidding me, dude?" I had to shove shorty and all her clothes into my walk-in closet and then let the team sponsors come in and chill, and they stayed for thirty minutes. After they left, I finally opened the closet to see Ms. Petra sleeping on the floor naked. I just burst out laughing as

I woke her up and told her she had to go because we both had games that Saturday on the road. Luckily for both of us, we won our games. Basketball was back in the city, and we were definitely a tough team to beat, which was highly unexpected by the media and the other teams in the league.

We ended the first half of the season by winning six out of eight games, leaving us with a 10–4 record going into the Christmas break, which was going to be an amazing time. Going into the break, I was in the top ten in scoring, assists, and steals. So the general consensus of the league was that I was the MVP going into the break. This Christmas would be the first time I would actually spend time with my daughter alone, to get to know her one-on-one and see everything that has made and still makes me the proud father I am to this day. Anyone who knows me personally understands my deep dislike for the Christmas holidays because I believe and feel that people only look for the gifts and present; no one ever really remembers why we truly celebrate Christmas anymore. This time, though, it would be special and different with Ja'hnniah, my nephews, and my mom. I decided to truly embrace the holiday season. It's something about seeing a child's face light up with the thought of Santa, food, and all the fun of the holidays. It's almost magical and makes me wish that we could lose all the programmed thoughts and ideas we have learned and just bathe in the ignorance of a child's excitement for a moment.

Sabbath morning came, and as I drove with my mom, nephews, and my daughter, tears just began to run down my face. My mom went into panic mode, asking, "What's wrong? Are you okay?" I told her that, finally, the piece of me that I should never have allowed myself to push away was in its rightful place in my soul and that I was very grateful. The ugly truth was I had used my daughter's mom for sex and abused her friendship to get what I wanted and needed. But to make things right, I had to apologize to her face-to-face. It was hard to do, but I did, and it truly was heartfelt. Thankfully, she forgave me, and things seemed smooth on her end.

Beyond my closest friends, I held Ja'hnniah as a secret to my bosom. I was selfish and didn't want to believe I had a kid. But during this holiday, that all changed, and she was the focus of everything I began to do. There's no way to make up for lost time, but luckily, with second chances, you can make the most of the new times and opportunities presented. Seeing Ja'hnniah and being in her life only led me to believe that God did have a plan for me, and even bigger than being a dad in her life, but I would find these things out later. Those eight days went by so fast, but I was so refreshed and enjoyed every second of the time with my family, and those days really helped me tune in even more and focus on the goal at hand: to be even better and more successful to ensure a better future for my family.

At the beginning of the season, I was doing 250 push-ups a day, 125 in the morning and 125 before bed, but I began to push even harder and went up to 500 a day. I did this because I had a target on my back, and the physical beating I was receiving and the beating I'd continue to receive. The push-ups and sit-ups not only set my body up, but mentally, it made me much more disciplined. And I can't lie, I was in the best shape I'd ever been in, and the added size didn't hurt me either.

> Opportunity is missed by most people because
> it is dressed in overalls and looks like work.
>
> -Thomas A. Edison

Up to this point in my career, I had worked hard enough to fit in, but truly never like this, to stand out from the pack and be successful, and others couldn't help but notice it. I was a machine going into the fifteenth game of the season. I was averaging thirty-eight minutes a game and really had a nice flow in the season, and the team was in the top four out of fourteen teams, so all was well, except from management's perspective. We weren't being paid, or our pay was extremely late. In the sports arena, you can't get the product unless you pay for it. Truthfully, they were paying me late, but the other guys weren't getting paid at all. Seriously, it was a jacked-up situation. I felt so bad for the other guys, but in this matter, it was truly every man for himself, and I wasn't 'bout to wait or just ignore the fact that they were late, and I wanted my money. But then again, these grown men with kids were out there grinding for free. It was crazy and unfortunate.

> *Lesson 25: You have to love what you do so much that if you weren't being paid, no one would ever know based on your effort, energy, and most importantly, the representation of yourself.*

These guys epitomized and embodied this lesson to the highest degree. Professionally, this humbled me and showed me a lot about character and how to be a professional even in tough times. These men were always on time, never late, never rude. They just did their jobs every day and never made excuses. When it came down to it, we loved the game so much we went until March putting up with that crap; but in February, that's when my patience ran out. They owed me a whole heap of money, and I received an offer from another team, offering more money and a better chance at the championship. I jumped at the opportunity without hesitation.

The last game for me in Kaposvár was my best game of the season by far. We won by eight points 78–70, and I had thirty-seven points, eight rebounds, and eight assists. What a way to go out. But I couldn't say or mention to anyone I was leaving, so I was quiet until about midnight when I told my fellow American hero that I was out for more dough and a better opportunity, or so I thought. In truth, my stats and my work habits went downhill when I left Kaposvár. That's the beauty of life: you never know what's around the corner when you make some decisions. This swan song game was a masterpiece and by far one of the most memorable ones of my career personally, and there have been quite a few good nights, if I must say so myself.

All good things must come to an end at some time in life, and a new era begins, with opportunities to create new legacies for ourselves. Unfortunately for me, moving from one team to another was a very bad move. On the court, I was always out of place. Even when we won, I was just the odd man out there. The cohesiveness and team-oriented structure I had left was definitely not a part of the new situation at all; it was a very selfish, every-man-for-himself environment. However, that was what I had chosen, so I had to man up and just deal with it. Speaking with my mom on the phone, I often moaned and complained about the situation. The money was a substantial upgrade, but it wasn't a good look for me.

Off the court, I began to compromise on the push–ups, the sit–ups, and even the rules I had for what I could and couldn't do before games—everything just fell apart. As far as the women, I met a few good women with whom I am still cool today. One was an Italian Romanian beauty who swept my mind away from the moment I saw her in the nightclub. She was a real woman, so it wasn't a quick conversation. We talked for three hours until finally I convinced her to meet me for dinner in my town the following evening. After dinner, she left, and a hug and kiss on the cheek were all I received from her for the next month. She wasn't having sex with me, so I found others.

One lady I encountered was Ms. Nikki, a superfriendly lady who spoke English and was quite familiar with American life, having been married to a US military guy. She was beyond sweet to me and even to my boy Shel and my mom when they came to visit. But emotionally, I'd never commit to her or anyone because of my selfish intentions. Things were always fun with her, and the funny thing is, we have remained friends over the years. During this time, my mind was firmly stuck on this Italian Romanian lady, Ms. E, and how and why she was always on the brain and why I couldn't get with her. I was in constant contact with her and even finding myself at her house for dinner and riding home for morning practices. I was falling for her, but I had to catch myself.

On court, we had made it to the finals of the Hungarian Cup, and I actually had a good game this particular day. Going into the fourth and final quarter, we were poised to beat the host team, but our young coach subbed me out with five minutes to go and never put me back in. Mind you, I had basically carried us up to this point, so I was mentally done with a month left in the season. That night, my reputation, which I had carefully rebuilt without a blemish, would forever remain changed even to this day.

After the loss and long ride home, I decided to head out with my teammate. Usually he would drive, but that night, I was angry and didn't want to wait, so I drove to downtown Budapest to the spot. Banging music and still furious about the game, I had my friend with me, plus JD and Coke as a passenger—and let's be real, I drank an eighth of a bottle in that forty-five-minute ride to Budapest and was like, *I don't care. Tonight, it's whatever happens, happens.* Just to give you an idea of my recklessness that night, Hungary's currency is called forint; and at that time, 100 dollars was like 25,000 forints. Usually, on a night, I never spent more than 4,000 forints to get wasted and get drinks for chicks; but on that night, I spent 10,000 forints on drinks. Ms. E had just come back from business in Italy and told me to come by after to sleep, and I agreed because usually I would park my car and then go back and get it the next day and then go home. But that night, I decided to do it Big Willy–style: have a blast, do it big, and go home alone.

I left the club (to this day, I have no idea how I found my car or got behind the wheel) and basically drove some twenty minutes on the highway before I crashed my car into a huge railing on the highway. It was 3:00 a.m., and there I was, a professional athlete just lying in the car, asleep and drunk out of my mind—what a pathetic sight, especially considering just a few months earlier, I was the toast of the town and was looking as a sure prospect for MVP of the league. But this fast life was the life I had chosen, and it resulted in major penalties for me. After hearing about the incident, management was furious beyond belief with me, for my negligence; but most of all, they were more concerned that we wouldn't make it to the top two for the playoffs. We had five huge games left in the season, and we were still fighting for a regular season championship. From my viewpoint, I never thought at the time how stupid and selfish my actions were; I just wanted to know if I could play that Saturday and help the team. But I could have killed someone, or even worse, I could have killed myself that night. Looking at the pictures from police, you could see the dashboard bent around my knees. The impact should have permanently injured or amputated both of my legs, and my career would have been over.

Lesson 26: God's grace and mercy are constant. Even though we may be undeserving he still covers us.

This lesson struck home with me when I saw the pictures of the accident, and my heart literally stopped. I couldn't believe that I had survived, and the main damage to my body was a huge knot, which I have to this day to serve as a reminder of that day. After seeing the damage to the car and seeing how it could have turned out differently, I picked up the phone for my Sunday dose of truth serum from my mom, and boy, I was beyond shocked at our conversation. After telling her about the accident, explaining what happened and my negligence, she just calmly said, "Thank God you're okay." She began to just break things down to me and referred to a couple of months earlier and how I was going so strong and was spiritually steadfast to a point where I wasn't swayed like I was at this point. She urged me to go back to the basics and get myself together because it wasn't just me who was affected by the moves I made in life. It was weird. As she prayed, it was like she almost expected me to screw up, or she had a hunch it would take something dramatic to happen to me to remind me of my purpose and what's most important in life.

I wasn't really feeling my mom's response, so I called Ms. Diana, my psychologist from London. Well, she gave me what I needed, a good telling off and a reminder of where I wanted to go and that I had more to lose in life than what I had to gain financially from basketball. She was so right, but things would get really ugly soon. My boy Sheldon came over for a week, and with three games left, it was good timing because I wouldn't feel the stress while chilling with him.

Before the first of the last five games, I was notified that I would be fined $5,000 for the car (the car was a piece of junk that wasn't worth $500) and $5,000 in fines, court clearances, and club fines. So all together, I dropped $10,000 for one stupid choice to drive when I had rides, as well as taxis, available to take me to Ms. E's home for a good night's rest or to Ms. Nikki's to relax, but I decided to play Russian roulette with my life.

A man must be big enough to admit his mistakes, smart enough to profit from them,
and strong enough to correct them.

-John C. Maxwell

Financially, I got blasted and had to make an official apology to fans and members of the board for my behavior—it was superhumbling. Hell, it was embarrassing too, but it had to be done. My best friend in the crowd, Ms. E, and many sexual exploits in the crowd watched me beg for forgiveness, and I was told if we didn't win the big game and I didn't play well, I was going home! On the court, I pulled it out and actually had a good game with twenty-two points and ten assists to go with four steals. The fans were happy, but the owner still wasn't happy and was mad and had a stern word with me after game and basically said neither me nor my visitor could drive anywhere. If I wanted to go out, I had to use his car service and pay for it up front. Our owner was one of the biggest mobsters in the country, or at least that's what everyone told me. So when he spoke, it wasn't an option, it was law. Shel, Ms. E, and I went out in Budapest for the night, and it was crazy fun. He got totally wasted, but I really just chilled because I got the message from what had happened previously, and I would make sure it never happened again **ever**!

After a week of relaxation and chilling with Shel, my mom came out to visit me as well, and that week had a different vibe. It was spent just reminding me of the roots instilled and implanted in me from my youth with spiritual examination of my behavior. She challenged me to be better and embrace the opportunity I had because many would die to be where I was financially and job-wise, doing what they love on a daily basis. We walked the streets of downtown Budapest, embracing the sights and sounds that warm Sunday had to offer. But mentally, I had been challenged and forced to think beyond myself and realize the example I was setting for not just my daughter and my nephews, but if word got out in Bermuda about my actions, it would not have been a good look.

Normally, I don't care what others think of me aside from my loved ones. However, when playing and going back home, you see the major influence you have on a lot of people's lives and the kids who look up to you and say, "I'm going to be a pro just like you." That's big. It's a tall task, but I had chosen this life, and with great abilities come great responsibilities. Those words and thoughts gripped me throughout the week, and even on to the final games of the season. As the season drew to an end, we won four out of the five last games, giving us a share of the regular season championship, and it was money time, the playoffs, where one's nerve and resilience are shown and tested.

We breezed through the first round of the playoffs, winning the series three games to one, and I actually played quite well. But the second round was a nightmare, and we ended up playing for third place, which was unacceptable. You see, when people invest a lot into you and you don't fulfill their vision of success, then things will get ugly, and very ugly fast. Not qualifying for the finals was a huge disappointment, especially when our budget was far larger than most other teams. So playing for third, we were warned that if we didn't win the series, then no one was going to get the remainder of the money owed them! That was all they had to say to me. Three straight wins by almost twenty points ensured at least a third-place finish and gave us some breathing room to at least collect our funds in the end.

During this trying time, I met a beautiful woman I had fallen for emotionally but had never seen because we were using the Internet to communicate. Ms. Peaches was a good woman with a spiritual foundation but was also a jack-of-all-trades. It was crazy how we communicated, and she constantly pushed me back to my spiritual foundation and helped me stay on the wagon while in Hungary. I kid you not, my phone bill for the couple of months was like $2,000 to $3,000 easy, but it was so much fun and relaxing that I didn't care.

As the season finally came to a close, I can truly say I was beyond exhausted and decided to head to Italy to visit Ms. E and just unwind for a few days while my funds were being tallied and to wait for my plane ticket home. The trip really was a nightmare. During this trip, I realized how incompatible Ms. E and I were. It's enlightening what a few isolated days of alone time with no distractions can show you. While there, we visited a lot of monuments and attractions, but the vibe between us just wasn't there. When you're introduced to something real, it makes all the fake things and people around you even more obvious. The funniest thing about it was she felt the same way, but she wanted things to work out so badly she went to ridiculous measures to try and make me happy, but it just wasn't happening.

After three *loooong* days, I flew back to Budapest, and it got ugly fast. When it was time for me to get my ticket and pay, they called me into the office for an exit meeting about the season and about fines and other things or, basically, the breakdown of my final payment. I wasn't really interested in talking too much. I just wanted my money and wanted to be out, but they had other plans for me. They basically began to threaten my wages. They told me if I signed for another year, I would get all my money, as well as an extra signing bonus. If I didn't sign, they would smear my name in the mud and see to it that I never got another good job there or anywhere else for that matter. It was alleged—I mean, I'm forced to say *alleged* because I only heard and saw the fear people had of him—but people said that our team's president was a huge mob boss, and truth be told, dude was a thug because everyone feared him. Apparently, he thought that I would just do as another foreigner did: take the offer and back out when I went home or something like that. But I clearly wasn't going to do anything like that, and we went at it for two hours. He didn't speak any English, so my agent was translating everything for me and him. Looking back on it now, it was crazy how I acted because with the power this man had, he could have done anything to me from getting me arrested to, even worse, having someone hurt me and end my career.

In the end, my stance remained the same. I was not going to be blackmailed into signing off on anything. I wanted my money, my ticket, and was out of there. To be honest, the offer wasn't bad at all, but I didn't want to be there any longer, so I stuck to my stance and left. The day I left the country, warrants were issued for my arrest, including a warrant for bogus drug charges saying I was trafficking illegal drugs through Hungary. All and all, warrants for drug trafficking, drunk driving, and a few other bogus allegations were issued for me. Immediately I was blasted job-wise and put behind the eight ball simply for my arrogance and the mistakes I made while I was in Hungary. To this day, I am banned from there and can't return, all because of one very bad and selfish decision. The president of the team (and alleged mob boss) made sure bad press was leaked to the media as well, and my agency threatened to sue if the team didn't recant the story and stop falsely accusing me. However, let's face it. When you hear a story like that in the sports world, no one wants to take the risk of seeing if the stories are true. So there I was in 2007 in the States, behind bogus allegations, trying to get a new job. The stress was superintense, to put it mildly.

The saving grace for me was getting Ja'hnniah for the summer. She made all other things literally not matter and bought so much joy to my heart. Summer was here, but I had to make a pit stop as soon as I got back. I had to see if the connection between Ms. Peaches and me was real or if it was just a fluke. Before that, I had my traditional homecoming and get-faded week with Shel: to hit all the new clubs and have a blast. He had a girl, but I was free as a bird and wilding out like tomorrow wasn't coming. Money wasn't an issue, so I did what I wanted. We wore what we wanted to the club and drank what we wanted unto our heart's content. Thousands and thousands of dollars were spent just to have fun and wild out. Ms. Diana (my psychologist from earlier in the story) would have slapped me silly if she had seen me, but this was what I wanted to do.

Spiritually, I started back reading the Bible and attending church; but shoot, even with progress, at times you take steps back. At church, I found some easy sexual targets, and I did what I knew how to do: get them in bed and excite them physically until I became bored; then it was on to the next. It was crazy, but whenever I began to feel the spiritual connection grow, it seemed like a new girl would enter the scene. Though she would not sway my attention totally, she would stunt my spiritual growth and the bond I was trying to develop and keep me from connecting to the Source.

Well, I finally made it to Detroit to see Ms. Peaches, where I was pleasantly surprised and delighted by what I saw and just everything about her. I can't even lie; I was loving her. Just everything about her was awesome, and she knew the deal that I had a daughter and just was a cool sister. With her, I made a pact of no sex, and trust me when I say it was superhard to keep that going because we were so connected physically, and most of all, she was on point spiritually as well. Five days with her went by extremely fast. But I knew I was still having fun in DC, so I held off on the relationship for a while so I could still have more fun. But I definitely left thinking we had a good thing in the works.

During the next phase of summer, it was time for the Island Games, which would be on the beautiful Greek island of Rhodes. Before the trip, I had to head to Bermuda for a few weeks and work out with the team, and that would give me a few weeks just to hang with my friends and family before we headed to Greece. Two weeks went by superfast, and then we were off. This would be my first Island Games with athletes from all sports there, and I was superexcited about this. Needless to say, before I got to Bermuda, old fling Ms. E wanted to see me and spend time with me. So I told her where I would be, and she booked her flight to come over for three days to hang out with me. Truthfully, we had a blast heading all over Rhodes on our mopeds, just straight cruising and having fun. But the truth of the matter was, she wanted all of me, and I wasn't ready to give that to her, or anyone for that matter, and that hurt her to no end. But that's where I was in life, and she had to accept it. She was such a strong woman, mentally and physically secure, yet she literally broke down and begged to do anything to have me. That was so unattractive to me and was a huge turnoff, but her paying for everything and spoiling me was fun, I can't lie. Our time together for those couple of days was quite good, but I told her about my new friend Ms. Peaches; and although she was pissed off, she could do nothing more than try to win me over from her or just get down with the program.

Rhodes was extremely hot, with sweltering heat beyond belief that had me locked in the air-conditioned hotel room or on the motorbikes we rented, riding around and letting the cool breeze offer me an escape from the furnace of the sun. It was ninety to one hundred degrees every day for a week. Man, it was crazy, but in the evenings, it was extremely nice because it was cool, but not too cold that you can't relax and have fun. On the court, we had three games, and we knew we'd have to win two out of three at least to qualify for the medal rounds to play for another gold medal. We won the first game against Gibraltar by at least fourteen or fifteen points. They fought hard and, in the first half, gave us a good test. However, we had more scoring and experience, which would enable us to pull away later on in the game. The second game of our tourney experience was against Menorca. We didn't know much about them, and they knew little about us, but soon we would understand that these gentlemen would stand in our way of obtaining another championship.

They straight pounded us. The first half was close as we fought back and forth in a heavily contested affair. But during the second half, their organization, speed, crisp passing, and two big men totally destroyed us. We were literally given a clinic on team basketball 101, and believe me, they were quite ruthless in their approach. That night, we humbly shook the hands of Menorca and realized the following night we were in a do-or-die situation where if we lost, we wouldn't have the opportunity to play for a gold medal. It was Bermuda versus the Cayman Islands, and the winner would earn the jackpot prize of facing the hometown boys in the semifinals. It would definitely be a tough, tough road to get to the finals, but we knew it would be a battle.

The game against the Cayman Islands was a straight beatdown from wire to wire. To date, it was by far one of the most dominant performances I've ever been associated with on a Bermuda national team. That was the perfect performance heading into the semifinal game against the host nation. The semis would begin in two days, but the next evening, they had a party for all sports on the other side of the island.

Imagine some fifty motorbikes (like a gang or something, all with Bermuda jackets on) racing across the isle of Rhodes all heading to the big athletes' party being thrown in our honor. Normally, these type of events happen after the games, but this was a prearranged event, so we had to go. We all arrived like it was a serious bikers' convention and totally threw the party for a loop. Of course, we weren't supposed to drink, but that was inevitable at an event with free alcohol and beer flowing. I was definitely going to have a few JD and Cokes just to ease up and relax for tomorrow evening's game. After about six or seven drinks, I was definitely in my element, and a certain lady with whom I had locked eyes throughout the week just happened to be at the party as well. I would find out later that it wasn't a coincidence because she had planned to be there. After exchanging small talk, I offered her a ride back on my bike to the other side of the island, and she willingly and anxiously accepted my invite. As the others sped off, we rode slowly, passing through other spots and stopping along the way by the beach and exploring other places in the night.

By 2:00 a.m., we finally found ourselves back in our village/hotel area where a night of fun and excitement would go on into the early hours of the morning. At the sound of my alarm, I got up, rushed to my place for my shoes, and raced to our mandatory practice where everyone laughed and teased me to no end because I had on the same clothes as the previous night. Even the coach and others were dying laughing at me, but was it really funny? When you build a reputation like this, how else can people take you or expect you to do things any differently? I will never forget when, before we left for lunch, the coach came to me and said, "I usually never worry about you, but tell me you're okay to go." I smiled and told him, "After my nap, I'm good to go, man." The craziest part of the whole encounter of the evening was I didn't know this lady was married. I would see and figure that out that evening after the Rhodes game.

After a three-hour power nap like always to cleanse my mind, I jumped in the shower with a Powerade—this was my drunk routine—and visually mapping out my plan of attack for the upcoming game. The plan is always to keep it at a pace where I would always be in control. Being a good point guard is all about controlling the pace of the game. If the pace isn't to your liking and it's too fast or too slow, then you're not able to play at your best, nor will you be successful. So mentally, I began to replay the previous game I had seen them play, and I identified spots where I could use my abilities and incorporate my teammates so we could be successful. One thing

I can say is that even though I had bad habits, I've always been a student of life and the game of basketball, which are very similar to each other:

> *No one plans to fail in life, but without a visionary map of where you want to go or a blueprint for a plan for your life, you're lost. In life and in basketball, goals, dreams, and aspirations serve as barometers of success to measure how successful you've become. Most successful people always have goals and accomplishments they hope to achieve, and the great ones usually meet and surpass the original goals set.*

As we readied ourselves for the game, there stood another opportunity for me to step up and erase the dreadful memories of Hungary, with the disappointment and shame I brought to my family name and my professional reputation, and end the 2007 season on a great note. The game was a phenomenal one, and the gym was overpacked and superrowdy—just the kind of environment I love. The first two quarters were a very close seesaw affair. We traded baskets, and the game was actually tied at halftime. In the third quarter, they pushed out and went up by seven points before a few timely baskets, which closed the gap some, and we entered the fourth quarter of the game with Rhodes with just a two-point lead. The fourth quarter was all about our defense, and we attacked their best player, causing him to foul out. Toward the end, they were scoring and fouling, but we hit about twelve to thirteen free throws in that quarter and went on to win the game by eight points. I actually had a solid game, especially in the fourth quarter, and I contributed ten points to help us reach our second final in successive years, a huge achievement for our basketball program, to say the least.

After this intense victory against the host, we earned the final prize of facing Menorca in the finals of the 2007 Rhodes IG Final. Many tapped them to win as they crushed us by twenty points in the initial game, but confidence and momentum were with us after a tough win the day before, so we weren't scared at all. Actually, I was excited for the challenge. Clearly, we'd shown we were the best two teams representing basketball at these games, so it would only be fitting we had the opportunity to play again and settle things as to whether the first game was a fluke, or they were just vastly better than us.

Finally the day came for the game, a hot Saturday afternoon game for all the marbles. Prior to our game, Rhodes had won the bronze medal, so now attention was on the final. An epic final it would definitely turn out to be as both teams were definitely on their A game this day. We quickly made it known that there was no chance of a repeat performance; this would be a close game. Up by two points, down by two points, as a fan, this was the kind of game you didn't want to end; but as a player, when your team went up, you wished the clock would stop because it was just too close. The tension in the air from the coaches complaining to referees, to the fans screaming and howling—it was amazing. I think the term is "you could cut the tension with a knife," and that's how it was in the arena. I've always thrived on situations like this. I had an amazing night: twenty-two points, ten rebounds, and seven assists, but we fell short by three points. And if you know me, you know that **I hate losing more than I love winning**! One of the hardest things to do was to be a good sport and congratulate them on their success, especially when, on that day, we were the better team. We just missed some shots we normally hit, and the result was that we lost.

They danced and mocked us to no end, at least that's how we took it, and we vowed that in the next games, we would get our revenge. The image is still clear in my mind of them dancing and laughing in front of us, but as a person, you have to accept the good with the bad and understand that bad can be used as fuel to push you to desired outcomes in life. Disgusted by the loss, I really just sulked the night away with my buddy JD and Coke and walked the infamous strip looking for a victim to relieve my stress and anger on—because I had found out that the lady from the party was married and didn't feel so safe going that route. Even though I did have sex with her after the Rhodes game, I fell back after that. It's bad enough to mess with another man's girl, but messing with someone's wife? That's stepping into a commitment made with God, and that's not something anyone should take lightly. As always, when you're looking hard enough for trouble, you will surely find it, or it will find you.

Trouble came in the form of Ms. Miisa, a blonde from Finland who was looking for a great nightcap. After a few hours of us both drinking heavily, we talked for a bit before we found ourselves on the beach, engaged in some heavy petting and soon having sex. Unfortunately, security for the hotel came down to the beach and asked us to leave. Actually, he demanded we leave and said he was calling the police. We went back to her hotel, where the craziest thing ever happened. As we walked into the room, she and her roommate said something in Finnish, and then they both straight attacked me. It was like a movie, and I was the director of the cast and the action. A couple of hours later, I jumped out of the bed to take a shower and head back to my spot and left the ladies in bed with my e-mail address, just in case they wanted to reach out to me, of course. In truth, I did it because I didn't know where I would be playing, so if I had the opportunity, I would want to see them both again. They both smiled and said they would definitely be in touch. As tempting as it was to jump back in bed, I made my way back to our hotel to pack and get ready to leave. I was leaving Rhodes with a silver medal, and I can say that was not in the cards, but the hunger in my spirit and my game would see to it that I'd taste success again. I was sure of that.

Finally it was time to head back to the States. I said good-bye to my teammates and headed home for a few days of relaxation before getting Ja'hnniah. A father's bond with his daughter is special, and my bond with Ja'hnniah had two levels:

1. *Absolute fun.* Let's go get candy and bubble gum, blow bubbles, visit amusement parks—you name it, and we'll do it.
2. *Absolute respect.* Basically, don't get it twisted. I'm not your friend, I'm your dad, and if you cross the line, you'll wish the devil was next to you instead of me.

She was a great kid. I never had to hit her. I would just give her the stern look, and she would fall back in line very easily. The bonding activities of taking a bath, reading her bedtime stories, playing with dolls, and tea parties were things I was extremely excited about doing with her. However, I was superstrict, almost to a fault, because I knew how I treated women, and I was determined to protect and guard her at all cost.

It's a tough reality, but they say God gives men daughters to remind them of the folly of their youthful days. Clearly, I was being overprotective of Ja'hnniah, but she was my baby, and that's just how it was going to be. As she has gotten older, the dynamics of the bond we share has been altered by my mind-set and no-nonsense approach with her. After a week in DC, we flew down to Philadelphia, where we met my mom, my two nephews, and my aunt for a kid's retreat. The retreat included live plays with animals, going to amusement parks, and much more. We visited an Amish village where they used no electricity, and watching the kids play with goats and sheep was amazing and brought me so much joy. It was a crazy, busy itinerary, but it was with a Christian group from Bermuda.

Even though my life wasn't in perfect harmony with God, I longed for my daughter to have the foundation I had as a kid; and for the six weeks I had her, every week was spent in church in the AJY. (Adventist Junior Youth) program for children. She loved it and longed to go, and most importantly for me, she understood and appreciated the experience. The time flew by so fast, and soon we all were headed back to Florida, where my sister and brother-in-law lived, for the remainder of the summer.

During this break, I received an offer to play in the Czech Republic and took the deal. It was very good to know that I had been given a second chance or, better yet, a clean slate in regard to my career. Having received the news was bittersweet because it was time for Ja'hnniah to return to her mother, so we had a huge feast to celebrate my success. The summer ended perfectly with my time with Ja'hnniah, but unfortunately, things would get extremely rocky between her mother and me. But in this space of time, things were finally coming together, and it was no surprise because my daughter was closer to me.

The best and most beautiful things in the
world cannot be seen or even touched—
they must be felt with the heart.

—Helen Keller

CHAPTER 9

NEW BEGINNING, NEW PROBLEMS

*I can't change the direction of the wind, but I can
adjust my sails to always reach my destination.*

—Jimmy Dean

The drama and the reputation I gained in Hungary pretty much put me behind the eight ball professionally. Many good teams and big money that I could have signed for walked away. Having said that, I did end up with a good-paying and safe job in Pardubice, which was the third largest city in the Czech Republic at the time. I was a bit mad at the pay, especially when I looked at what I had done in Hungary; but once all the big teams heard of my DUI and accident, I was like a black plague; no one would take a risk on me. At the end of the day, I would receive the fruits of my labor. One huge mistake can cost you everything that you've worked so hard to achieve in your life or career up to that point. After the summer, I finally arrived in Prague, one of the most beautiful historical cities in Europe, but I wouldn't be taking in any of the sights because I was headed to training camp. A beautiful office manager who spoke very little English was there to take me to the woods; training camp was literally in the middle of nowhere.

Upon arrival and meeting my new teammates, I was introduced to the harsh reality of boot camp: no hot water, no heaters, and wild-life surrounded us (so at night, it was in our best interest to stay inside). What in the heck was this? Man, I couldn't get a calling card fast enough to call my agent, but he broke down the 150 percent gospel truth to me: "You're there because you screwed up. Deal with it or go home and wait for another gig." Harsh, but it was the truth, so I had to man up and deal with it.

The next morning at breakfast, I could only eat fruit because I'm a vegetarian, and the spread was loaded down with meat. I just sat quietly but fumed with disgust on the inside. On that partic-ular day, our morning activity was a thirty-two-kilometer (twenty-two-mile) bike ride. That's right, thirty-two kilometers, and the first twelve kilometers was all uphill. I couldn't believe what I was hearing, but it had to be done, and we were being timed on top of that. I had no idea why, but later the next day, I found out we would have to ride again, and the kicker was that we couldn't stop. The rebel in me wanted to confront the coach and give him a few choice words. If I had, they would have sent me straight home, so I just held my head down and didn't utter a word.

Excruciating is the best way to describe this three-hour period in my life. The pain, mental agony, disgust, and anger seemed to fuel me on through the ride. My anger got me to the finish line and not positive thinking. The whole ride, I mentally took myself back to Hungary. I was falsely accused for drug abuse and drug traffick-ing and many other slanderous offenses, but that's the entertainment business. People may know you've done nothing remotely close to what's been said about you, but they won't take the chance on finding out or allowing you to prove the critics right at their expense.

Three hours later, I was finally back in the log cabin we called home for the week, and I literally couldn't feel my legs. The exhaus-tion in my voice suggested I was done, but we had another session of weights before dinner. Shoot, by nightfall, I was beyond done, yet I managed to salvage enough energy to call my new boo Ms. Peaches. I walked away from the cabin to have a private conversation without everyone in my face, and she received the full brunt of my disgust and anger. However, it's amazing how a woman can bring things into perspective with her calming spirit and encouragement, which help you maintain your focus. The next day after breakfast, the coach told us that we would lift in the morning and then ride again in the evening, and that's when I lost it and was like, "Nah, bra. I'm not Lance Armstrong, and biking isn't for me. Running or something is cool, but this riding isn't going to cut it."

After I said it, I was so mad at myself because even though everyone felt what I was thinking, I was the one who said it. Surprisingly, the coach was supercool and responded with, "Okay, you can run a few miles through the woods." But he basically made all of us run. After the run, I apologized to the coach and my teammates, telling them that if I had made anyone feel uncomfortable or mad by my actions, I was sorry. The coach was very cool and said it was no sweat. By the way, he spoke no English at all, so communicating with him during games would be hilarious. With his lack of English, my backup plan was to just try to understand the diagrams and, when in doubt, ask the teammate who spoke English and Czech to interpret. Finally the week drew to an end. Ms. E wanted to come and say hello to me, and that's all, so I was cool with it. She caught the train in from Romania just to chill with me.

Yes, I had a new boo, and she was a good lady, and most impressively, we weren't having sex at all. I can honestly say I did really like her, and the true test would be when Ms. E came and how things played out. Ms. E knew me like the back of her hand just as I knew her, and that was dangerous. We chilled for a few days, and nothing physical went down until the last night. Man, she found my weak spot, and it was on like Donkey Kong. Did this mean I didn't like Ms. Peaches, or was I just mentally weak and never should have played with fire, knowing I had gasoline in my hand as well?

On the court, I was pleasantly surprised with the talent we had; but deep within, I knew we had a very small chance of being anything special in the league. But I was up for the challenge. We started the season 5–0, and we were the toast of the town, or so we thought. Reality hit real fast when we lost five games in a row. Management became furious with us, but mainly at the coach. After a nationally televised game that we won, he was fired. The man didn't even know he was fired until we got on the bus and he received the word. That was some shady stuff and made me realize from that point on what type of management I was dealing with. Apparently, before the game, the management had reached an agreement with another coach who I can honestly say taught me the most influential lesson of my career: to just be quiet no matter what and let your play speak over the politics of the game. We had a new coach but the same results. We couldn't beat the top four teams, and we would be stuck in fifth place.

That being said, he decided to take me out of the starting lineup and put a Czech player in so that we would have firepower off the bench, but I knew better. The guy was the captain of the team, and he had been complaining all the time because he wasn't playing as much as he was promised. Unfortunately, I took the hit, and I didn't take it well at all. It made me superfurious. And the way he told me was absolutely priceless; he said, "I'm going to start the other player, but it's not because you're black and he's white or I don't like you. I'm trying this for the team." I couldn't believe what I had heard, so I asked him to repeat it just to make sure I wasn't going crazy. I was the leading scorer, the third leading rebounder, and the leading assist man, but you want me to come off the bench? I agreed to the change, but inside, I was fuming. It was evident to all that I didn't like this guy, and it became even more evident after this. Off the court, I totally ignored him; but on court, I had to maintain my composure and make it seem we were a cohesive group.

Off the court, I found a nice spot in Prague called Radost, which was hot on Thursdays and Saturdays, so you know I had to get it in once a week. But the drive was long, so I couldn't get wasted. I guess that was a blessing in disguise, but shoot, I just had to find a few places closer to me where I could enjoy the liquor. During this time, I had arranged for my daughter and mom to come and visit me in Prague for a week because I wanted Ja'hnniah to see what I did while I was away to understand I did love her but this was my job and how I made a living to support her. You see, during the summer after she had left, she wanted to know when she would see me again as well as when I was coming home. She had a deep desire and need to know this as opposed to my nephews who were just happy to hang out and weren't too bothered about when they would see me next.

As a result, I truly wanted her to see firsthand what I did and let her know that even with my job, I would carve out time to make sure she knew that I loved her no matter what. The void a lot of women have emotionally often is a result of the absence of their fathers or good men in their lives, and I didn't want this for my baby girl, so it was a no-brainer. She would come visit me. Knowing this, I also was moved to bring Ms. Peaches over so she could see Europe and experience my world as well. Unfortunately, the day before she came, Ms. E began to bug out and threatened to come over during the weekend. I couldn't believe this was happening. I told her she could come through, but she wouldn't get in. But I knew her personality and her gangsta mentality, so I booked a hotel in downtown Prague for the weekend to ensure Ms. Peaches had a great view of the city, and I was safe from any drama that might occur. I normally would have just told her to come through and visit, but this time, I told her the truth. She was mad, but I didn't care, and this pissed her off more. That Sunday morning, I went out for food while Ms. Peaches slept. Ms. E. called and told me she wasn't coming but that she did want to come soon and see me. I laughed with her and went back to breathing more easily because that could have been ugly.

On the court, things were still bad. Statistically, I was supersolid; and going into the Christmas break, I was definitely ecstatic about finally winning a game against a top four team and that I would see my darling Ja'hnniah. Tradition had us in Orlando, Florida, with my sister and her family. My brother-in-law's family came down as well, and we had a super time. Ja'hnniah was growing up, and she was clinging to me more, which was weird because I'm not the clingy, emotional type, but she brought it out of me, which was nice. Any athlete, member of the military, or regular working person enjoys seeing family and friends during the break and to spend the holidays around people they love. Being so far away during the rest of the year made it that more special to hear the words *I love you*, and the joyous screams while opening gifts was amazing.

Unfortunately, I had to return to work; and when I did, my dislike for my coach grew like a cancer inside a stricken person's body. It got so bad that the president of the team called me in after a tough loss to the top team in a game that we were winning by four points going into the fourth quarter. It was like the coach played the game to lose, and when we could have won, he didn't let us, and I was superfurious. After the game, the president and I spoke, and he asked what was wrong with me because I didn't look happy, and I told him straight up, "[Playing] with this coach who doesn't want to win, I'm not." I proceeded to basically bash the coach and let the president know how I felt about him. I was, in essence, crucifying myself because when we won, I knew this guy would never bring me back. The president knew I was frustrated and assured me I was good and appreciated my honesty. However, in my haste to complain, I forgot one important thing:

Humans and fish are the same in life. If both mind their business and keep their mouths shut, they'd encounter a lot less drama.

Around the same time this was going down, my mom and daughter were about to arrive. I needed my mom's raw but honest advice to direct me when I would have to make a big decision on the night of her arrival. The top team in the league approached my squad, offering a trade and major financial backing in exchange for me. I was once again in the same boat as the year before. What should I do? It would be great money with European exposure and, most of all, way more cash and a guaranteed championship. But then that would mean bailing out on all the good work I had done in Pardubice. The other factor was that my stats would drop dramatically. This was huge as the same thing happened the year before. I didn't know what to do. Should I leave a coach I wouldn't speak to in public or private and a situation that wasn't that great? My mom just sat me down and told me to pray on it like always and to move slowly. I knew the right answer, and that was to just follow my heart no matter what. Sometimes when you're not in tune with yourself or don't know what you're really worth, you'll just take whatever comes your way and not stand on principles.

> You are always free to change your mind and
> choose a different future, or a different past.

> -Richard Bach

After talking with my mom, I decided to wait and give myself a week to figure things out. In the meantime, I would just enjoy my baby. My teammate Big T had two daughters with whom Ja'hnniah had a blast and bonded with every chance they could. McDonald's, Bratislava, Vienna—we all went everywhere, just enjoying the free time we had. It was truly amazing watching them bond and getting to know my daughter better. Before they left, we had a huge home game where the coach almost caused us to lose because he didn't play me until things got extremely close, and we barely won. I was so furious, and after the game, my mom shared the exact same sentiments as me that it was a bit more politics involved than the naked eye could see. But I had to continue to do my job. That night before I had to make my choice, I almost left the team on impulse, but after a shower and reality check from my mom, I ignored the offer and chose to stick it out. You see, I've always enjoyed challenges on and off the court, and I figured if I played well against them and showed my worth, I would be offered more money and more playing time, and the rest would be history.

The word leaked out before the week ended, and people were asking constantly if I was making the big move, so that Thursday night. I just came out and told my teammates and management what I had decided. I saw the relief in their faces, and even the coach began to act like he cared and needed me to win. He finally realized this when our most experienced player went down with an injury that would keep him out for a month, and the pressure would lie solely on me to hold us down and carry the load with a couple of huge, tough games coming up. As the tough stretch approached, Ja'hnniah and my mom left, but my homie Sheldon came in two days later, so once again, I had a great opportunity to get through a tough patch with a loved one close by.

The next month, we went 6–1, and my stats shot through the roof. I was in a zone again, and they rode me to the moon and played me for forty minutes in three of the five games. Sheldon and I only went out like one night a week, and he was shocked because, in Hungary, by the time he came, I was so through with that place, and we found lots of little corners to skate into. We played two times a week in Czech Republic, so there was not much time for anything outside life other than basketball. It's just the type of situation where discipline is heavily measured and seen.

But don't be mistaken. At the time, we both had girls, but we had fun in Prague hanging out and chilling. In Europe, this usually meant one thing, that girls will want you even more and sweat you even harder than you can imagine. Ms. Peaches was there for two weeks and was seen out with me, and people knew I had a lady, but it didn't stop women from approaching me—and man, it had some fun moments with it. After a tough stretch of two weeks, Sheldon was gone, and March would soon turn to April.

Any hooper or person who is away from home for long stretches at a time knows there are certain months when you begin to miss home and become homesick. For me, it was March; and as the month began to end and we started gearing up for the playoffs, I knew I would fall off the wagon soon. So once again, Ms. Peaches came to Prague, and she came just in time for the first round of playoffs and game one. We were on the road against team Decin, a squad we hadn't beaten all year, so it was going to be interesting. The game was physical as expected, but we handled it and were up comfortably by five points when a freak accident happened. Going for a rebound, I accidently stepped on someone's foot and cracked a bone in my foot. Instantly I knew things weren't right. Knowing I was hurt, I took some pills and just finished the game, hitting some tough baskets to help us off to a 1–0 lead in the series, but it wasn't pretty for me. X-rays revealed a cracked bone in my foot. It was as though my season was over.

There was no chance I was going to quit. I had to find a way to play. In game two, we got smoked at home; they killed us big-time. I was soaking and icing my foot, trying to find a way to play; and somehow, without any injection (which was absolutely nuts), I played. No one knew if I would play or for how long or if I could run, but twenty minutes before the start, I came out and began to warm up, and the other team's faces showed a bit of worry then. The game was a close one that basically went down to the wire. I played about thirty-five minutes, and the doctors told the coach if I wasn't hurting the team and could physically move, then don't take me out. The pain during the halftime and before the start of the third quarter was, at times, unbearable. Imagine a sharp blade slashing your body each time you moved—that's the pain I felt. Unfortunately, we lost by two points, but we definitely showed that we were there to play. The third and fourth games, I miraculously had twenty-three and twenty-one points respectively to lead us to the next round and eventually earn us a third-place medal for the season, the first medal ever in the club's history.

Off the court, my relationship with Ms. Peaches flourished, and the tremendous potential it showed prompted me to take a trip back to Michigan. But this time, I wanted to bring my nephews and my daughter. My ground rules were that we would stay in a hotel and only hang out during the day because I wanted to see how my daughter would react, but not totally put her in a situation where she had to share me with a woman or feel that I was trying to replace her mother. When I explained this to her mom, all hell broke out, and a war began, literally. I look back now, and I can say Ms. Peaches and I were done from that day on because she had subtly alluded that I should bring the kids down, and I mentally, but not verbally, blamed her for the situation. It would be a year and some change later before I would be able to see and have a solo visit with my daughter again because of that. As a man, I can honestly say that I was miserable and heartbroken without her.

I didn't know how to cope. This was such an extremely low point in my life. I didn't know where to turn or what to do. Rain and thunderstorms in life usually precede the appearance of rainbows and times of joy. Again, I'd find myself embracing alcohol and the nightlife to cope with the void of not being able to see my daughter. I was angry because this was some total BS. I was an active father, financially and the whole nine yards; but with one word, I was shut out of my daughter's life. In hindsight, this would be the absolute best thing to happen in regard to my daughter because it made me become much more understanding and knowledgeable of men's rights as fathers and gave me the opportunity to show my baby I would fight for her no matter what and financially support her even when I wasn't allowed to see her.

I can say without a shadow of a doubt that 2009 was the longest summer of my life, and probably one of the angriest and saddest times I've ever experienced. What people didn't understand was that money was nothing. Watches, diamond earrings, VIP sections in the club—I could afford all these things; but without my daughter, I was totally just lost. Emotionally, Ms. Peaches and I just drifted apart that summer, and professionally, I was slacking. I had a job offer with great money and needed to e-mail my agent ASAP to let him know I was down for the gig. I got drunk and wrote back two days later— that's just where I was. I was depressed, but my little sister jumped in and said to me, "Man, bump that. Get a lawyer and go get your baby back. Stop sitting here feeling sorry for yourself and fight for your true love, and trust me, she will never forget what you do." Tears rolled down my face, and my heart was heavy. But I began the search, or I should say, I began wasting my money searching.

Let me explain. **When you're going through situations in life, you can't go in blind, or you'll get blindsided!** I forgot this and just started looking for lawyers and trying to see who could help me the fastest and get me joint custody and the right to see my baby. But I should have done my homework, checked their rates, and see who was best suited for me and my situation. I didn't, and it cost me a pretty penny just fooling around with people who weren't meant to help me. One of the people was a church member who screwed me over quite badly, but I tried to give him and others the benefit of the doubt and not sweat it—wrong move. In business and in pleasure, you have to be smart and do your homework.

As summer came to an end, I was literally in the same boat as I was at the beginning of summer, aside from having lost a whole lot of money to lawyers who couldn't gain me access to my daughter. As September rolled around, I got on the plane to head on over to my new team in Cyprus, but man, they had no idea who they were getting because who they saw on tape was so far from the person who showed up.

When I got Cyprus, I went MIA with everyone except my mom, Ja'hnniah, and Sheldon. No one could find me for like three weeks; I just didn't want to deal with the world or anyone at all. Being so far away, I didn't have to deal with anyone, so I used that excuse to distance myself from Ms. Peaches, and that would eventually kill what we had. I went back to the old days and ways and hung out in the little pubs, bars, and clubs just to maintain my sanity. On the court, I just did my job and did the dirty work because I was too tired to do more of what my reputation had promised in scoring, rebounding, and defending. I couldn't do those things because my lifestyle changed, and so did my game.

Off the court, it was like being a rock star all over again; but in Cyprus, it was summer all year round. I ran into a cool lady named Ms. Ana. She was an older lady who knew life, was quite fun and attractive, and most of all, she wasn't a groupie and understood athletes. We began to hang out, and I'll never forget her words to me one day: "You look so sad and empty sometimes. Are you okay?" I always joked it off and blamed it on my lifestyle, but she saw the true me.

Every man has secret sorrows which the
world knows not; and often times we
call a man cold when he is only sad.

-Henry Wadsworth Longfellow

Lesson 26: The scariest human on this earth is the man (or woman) who just doesn't care.

Drinking and partying were my addictions, and they did nothing but make my body wear down. Until one day in a scrimmage, I pulled my groin, but silly me kept playing until the end of the game. After meeting with the doctor, he said I had pulled it pretty badly and that I would be out for three weeks, and I would miss the free trip to Bulgaria for some additional scrimmages the team had arranged for us. I was really pissed because a homie of mine played for the other team, and I wanted to see him and, of course, hit the nightlife of Bulgaria to see how it was popping off. So I had ten days alone with no practice to go to, only physiotherapy. Shoot, nothing changed aside from me meeting more chicks and having more fun.

On the personal side, Ms. Ana made me open up and tell her about my daughter's situation, and I explained what was happening. Even though I got faded, I was still persistent in my search for new representation to enable me to get closer to my daughter. When I finally explained the situation, she just cried and said, "Now I know why you do what you do." I looked at her like, *What are you talking about?* She smiled through the tears and said, "The pain is all in your eyes, and now I can see why you look so empty at times."

On the court, the season was finally near, and I was healthy and ready to play as was needed of me; but right before the deadline, we signed a veteran, my man I'll call *Big Homie*. We were the true definition of hoop, and we would hit the clubs nightly. We'd sleep after morning practice, eat dinner, go out all night, and practice first thing in the morning. The smell of alcohol is quite strong, especially JD, but our coach was chill. This would be his demise because he didn't draw the line between discipline and fun. By not doing this, it made it impossible to really get the best out of us. If you're reading this right about now, you're probably shaking your head and wondering how in the world can a professional athlete perform at a high level while inflicting so much harm on his body? Truth is, your body is a machine, and machines can be used for good or for bad. It all depends on what you want to do with it.

Our season in a nutshell was helter–skelter, and that's a nice way to put it. We had a great squad, and all the pieces were there, but we traded a combined fifteen players in eight months. That's absolutely crazy for a professional-level sports team, but we did it, and it cost us big-time. During this year, we had one player come in who really was the biggest gunner I've ever seen in my life (he shot the ball every time or always had to have the ball). Unlike in other places, at this point in my career, I was very quiet and didn't really share my opinion unless it really mattered or counted. But one day on the court, this guy and I almost flat out went to war. He was just so selfish, and I had had enough of it.

I went over to the coach and said loudly enough for everyone to hear, "Oh, this BS stops now. Since y'all don't want to stop it, I will." And I proceeded to run point guard and literally not give this guy the ball at all for the rest of the game. Of course, he was irate and came up to me and tried to get loud—wrong move. I almost killed that man. He was about 5'10" tall and I was 6'6" tall and weighed about 230 pounds. Man, he got up in my face, and boy, I couldn't grab him fast enough. Thank God Big Homie grabbed me just as I was about to swing and knock him out dead. He was mad, but as a team, we played better when he didn't have the ball. So when he started the fight at the game, he basically had signed his resignation letter and would be leaving immediately.

Going into the Christmas break, we were tied for second place. With all the personnel changes (they bought in fifteen players in four months), this was a remarkable achievement. Unfortunately, right before I was due to go home, I received an e-mail saying Ja'hnniah wouldn't be coming with my mom on the flight I had booked, so that money was basically wasted. You have no idea how mad I was, but I made sure that I was the one to break the news to her and explain what had happened. It hurt like hell to hear her cry, but my rationale to her at that time was, "I'm gonna tell you and make sure you don't hear any lies about me not wanting to see or be with you." It started a war between her mother and me, I kid you not. I was so mad I went out and found a victim in the club and decided, *Why not do it in the bathroom and totally humiliate this girl?* So I did and had my teammate come and take a picture of her while she pleased me. After removing the condom and flushing it, she asked, "What are we doing after the club, part two?" I laughed and said, "Sure, find me later." But in my head and heart, I knew I would never see her again, and I would make sure of that.

Christmas without my kid meant one thing: going out and getting hammered in Orlando and hanging with my nephews during the day, and that's it! I was devastated by not seeing J, and to be honest, I didn't speak to her that much during the break either. I can honestly say, looking back over her first five or six years, that I wasted too much time not being smart and using the courts, claiming my legal rights and thus giving me more time with Ja'hnniah. It's a tough lesson to learn. Parenting isn't an easy thing, especially when the two parents aren't on the same page. A funny thing my dad used to say was, "Communication is like a choir. All it takes is one person to misinterpret or read from the wrong song sheet, and it messes up the entire choir." That's where I was as a parent, reading from a different song sheet. Hell, I didn't even make the choir; I was just outside trying to get in and join. This Christmas incident would be the last straw that made me financially and mentally cement a relationship with my daughter.

After the break, I flew back to Larnaca, Cyprus, with an even worse attitude about basketball than before. I wrote the following while on the plane, and it will give you an in-depth look into my mental state at the time. I was a very depressed soul who yearned and longed for answers, and this was my venting stage word for word:

WHY?

Why do I dream big and live so small?

Why do we live big to impress people, knowing our budgets are small and the people we seek to impress really couldn't care less?

Why do cars and clothes put you in a certain category in this life, especially when you can't buy class?

Why are gangs and so-called thugs more loyal than churches, church officials, and people who you'd hope would uphold loyalty and set examples?

Why can't any of my friends hear my pain every time I speak, or have I learned to mask the pain so well? Or do they only like me for the money?

Why does everyone think my life's so perfect, and I'm so lucky?

If they only knew fucking girls and getting drunk has made me so emotionally detached. I'm so alone. How can I break this addiction?

Ja'hnniah, will you ever really know me, or will the BS always keep you away from me, even though I long and yearn to be a part of your life, contrary to what you're probably being told?

Can someone tell me where can I turn other than to this paper to air out my pain without the fear of being judged or made to feel even less than I do now?

Tell me please why Jack Daniel's is my best friend? I can't make it without this bottle, it may seem; but as soon as the effects of euphoria wear off, I'm upset, disgruntled, and right back to ground zero.

Why are so many women blinded by my stupid words and don't realize what's between their legs runs the world?

If you close your legs, you'll see who the man really is. If he likes you, he will wait. Is that so hard?

Why is it because I'm black and here in first-class, I have to be an athlete, rapper, or drug dealer? Is there any chance I could just be a middle-class gentleman who decided to splurge?

Why is this lady at thirty-five thousand feet holding her fucking purse when I know my monthly salary is more than she makes for a year?

Why am I so mad, sad, and lost?

God, am I too far to be helped, or do you really have a plan for me?

If happiness heals and stress kills, Lord, how soon before I die? I'm just saying I'm pretty fucking close to death, huh?

After a long flight, I arrived in Cyprus; and as you read above, my heart was heavy, but this was the path I had to tread. In regards to my daughter's situation, I can admit that up to that point, I had looked for lawyers to help me, but not wholeheartedly. But upon my return, I began the serious process of finding the right representation. I didn't spend as many nights out in the streets because now I was researching, reading forums, and doing all I could to resolve this custody issue with my daughter so that I could be in her life on a consistent basis. She needed that in order to be the best she could be in life.

On the court, we made a decent surge, due in part to us keeping a core of players for more than a few weeks at a time. We definitely began to play more as a unit, and life was good. As the season finally came to an end, we had cemented a third-place finish and readied ourselves for a tough playoff run. In the first half of the first game, my teammate threw a fastball at me from three yards away and broke my finger, and it was fractured in the shape of a horseshoe. At halftime, it was diagnosed as broken. But it was a pivotal game, and I decided to stay in the game to ensure a game one victory. You can't imagine the pain running through my body over this broken pinky; it was unbelievable.

Luckily, I made it to the end of the game, but I basically made the fracture deeper, and it would require minor surgery if I wanted to go home, with my money, of course. It's crazy, but I thought my season was over, but they sat me in a room and said, "In seven days, the semifinals start. If you commit to play, we will give you your money. If not, screw you. You go home with nothing." Man, that's a tough place to be professionally and personally, backed up against the ropes. The question was, what would I do? I knew financially I wasn't dying, and I could live without the money, but I was too thirsty for the cash and wanted to ensure I had money for the lawyer I would choose later that summer to represent me.

The surgery commenced at 11:00 a.m., and at 12:30 p.m., I was out of surgery but didn't wake until 2:00 p.m. They drugged me up pretty well, and as soon as I woke up, I needed meds because of the pain. Ms. Maria and Ms. Ana came to visit me and make sure I was okay.

Everyone thought I was crazy to stay and play; most people thought of it as committing professional suicide. I had to utilize every brace possible to protect my pinky and avoid any further injury. Remarkably, five days after surgery, I was back in practice, not full contact but hard enough, considering I just had surgery. Nevertheless, I was trying. Unfortunately for us, the semifinals were as far as we would go, and we would have to settle for third place. Management was furious, and they all left the island within seventy-two hours and only left partial payments for some of the players, and some guys got nothing. Again, that is the nature of the business. I would have to go through the courts to get the funds owed me. After I had risked my career to play for them, management showed me no loyalty at all.

Luckily, my flight was already booked because I was beyond ready to go home, and why not? It was Friday, and I was mad at the team. So you know once I touched down, I told my boy Shel to pick me up, ready to go out. I had spent nine hours on the plane and was full of drinks (thanks to my international flights that offer free liquor, not that you should be trying to get faded on the plane). I landed in DC, and I was lit up and had to get a Red Bull and a Mountain Dew after clearing customs just to keep my eyes open. Believe me when I say we had a ball as always. I was on the prowl and hanging with my boy while he sipped and just chilled. We were popping VIP bottles, and at the end of the night, $2,500 was gone. I can remember finally getting in bed and feeling numb. I couldn't believe I had just spent all that dough; it left me numb, not in a bad way. All of a sudden, it's 8:00 a.m., and I lay there wide awake.

I took this as a sign to go to church, so bright and early, around 9:00 a.m. I called my sister Christina and said, "Let's have a church date with lunch after." I could hear her mouth drop through the phone like, *Huh? You want to go where?* as if I was punking her, so I said it again, "Let's do church and lunch." Amazed and overwhelmed by my invitation, she agreed, and it was on. I went to the gym to sweat out the smell of JD in my body, and forty-five minutes later, I was good. I just needed a long shower, and I would be ready to go. The ride down was fun, and like always, Christina and I just chatted about life and if I had stopped being a playboy. Then it got serious, and she asked, "What's up with you wanting to go to church? And what happened to Ms. Peaches?" I laughed and told her I needed a new girlfriend, but in truth, I needed peace in my soul. I was afraid that even though I was looking and fighting to be a part of Ja'hnniah's life, things weren't working out, and I felt like I would never be close with my child.

We arrived at Miracle City SDA church, and I tell you what, when you're going through something and you head to church and the pastor or speaker seems like he is talking directly to you, it's a powerful thing and very scary. It was as if he and I were the only ones in the church. If he had said my name, it would have felt like a one-on-one counseling session; that's how real that message was to me. He spoke on letting go of the bondages of our past, no matter what they are or how long we have held on to them. He began to make an appeal to the congregation, and I got up and went to the bathroom, not because I needed to use the bathroom but because I was so scared. Scared that, for the first time in a very long time, the service was personal and not professional. Stay with me here: we go to church and master the "Hallelujah, thank you, Jesus" act and go home unchanged without a spiritual connection.

Then there is that time when the service is personal, and it does affect you. It's not a show; it's a relationship and connection that shows in every aspect of your life. I had experienced it somewhat when I was younger, but some twenty years later, that tug on my heart and the spirit to surrender my will to God and let him fix my life straight shook me for real, and I ran away from it. As I came back from the bathroom, I saw people lining up for instant baptism; and truthfully, if I just had the courage, I would have been a part of the baptism myself. As I sat quietly, I couldn't help but think, *If I don't get things right with God, everything else will remain chaotic.* But like the prophet Jonah (a minister in the Bible whom God called to preach, but instead he ran away), I still decided to run.

After a great lunch and chat, I found myself home alone; and the thoughts of the message, the baptism, and the pricking of my conscience was still in the forefront of my mind. The only way I knew how to drown those thoughts was to go out and get wasted again. With a flask and a stiff JD on the metro one hour later, I was in the city, ready to start the evening off early. I met up with someone from the past for dinner and dessert and then left her place, heading into the city for another drinking binge. It was literally the only way I could ease my guilt and quiet my conscience, but it was almost like I couldn't think of anything else that night. Although I did my best to try and drown out his voice, I knew God was tugging on my heart, and it was apparent he wouldn't let me go.

In the next days, I hit up an old fling for professional help with a lawyer she knew, and he broke down the situation for me and, as a result, saved me from wasting more time and money. He told me to get a lawyer in Saint Thomas where my daughter was and that only a lawyer there would have jurisdiction. He also told me to seek out a certain noted and well-respected female lawyer. As a man, I never knew these things, but after he explained in full why he suggested I take these measures, I quickly heeded his advice and followed his recommendations. The search had me on a wild-goose chase for a few weeks until I found the lawyer who would reunite me with my baby girl.

It was quite crazy and a bit ironic how I came to find her. I was looking online and accidently hit a page of lawyers in the US Virgin Islands, but now I know it wasn't by chance. God allowed me to find her. Through doing my homework and connecting all the dots, I had found a good lawyer to help me. To be honest, it took me about four days to finally have a conversation with her after a long game of phone tag. After the first conversation, my spirit was at ease, and I felt like things would turn around for me. She was extremely honest and real with me when we talked, specifically when discussing a time frame for our custody issue to be resolved. She told me it could be over fast and quickly or could be a long and ugly battle, seeing as my daughter's mother and I didn't get along or see eye to eye. She wanted me to prepare for the worse.

I couldn't be mad because her words were true and honest, so I couldn't help but appreciate that and do my best to help when needed to get things resolved. One suggestion she had for me was for me to set up an account and to start putting the child-support funds there, and when an agreement was made, then I would pay it. I refused immediately. For me, this was the perfect opportunity to show my loyalty to Ja'hnniah and let her know I wouldn't just have her back when things were good but also in the bad times even when I couldn't see her. To the gentlemen who think it's cool to just do right by your child when you want to or feel like it, you must remember, if you have a daughter, you're the primary model of the man she will look to for love, and your sons will mirror the man you display for them as they grow up. For this reason, it has always been important for my daughter to know what a good man was, even though I wasn't perfect.

Many people told me I was a fool to keep paying child support because my daughter's mother was playing me and just using Ja'hnniah as a pawn. My response was simple: good men take cow manure and use it to create beautiful gardens. I told them that was all my daughter would see in the end. My mom also stayed in my ear as well: "Don't punish Ja'hnniah financially because you and her mother don't get along. She didn't ask to be a part of your mess, so don't put her in it." And my mom was absolutely right. Priorities overrode preference, and that's a tough lesson that many never learn or simply choose to ignore.

After finally getting a game plan and tentative time frame, it was time for the annual Small Island Games, which that year would take place on the Åland Islands located between Sweden and Finland. I can't say that I was excited with the spot, but I can say that I was looking forward to seeing my boys from the team and getting revenge for the outcome of the last games. I went to Bermuda for a week to see my family and the Trinity Crew just to unwind and relax before my flight to Åland. It's always good to be around true friends and family. Walking in Hamilton SDA church each time brings to mind warm memories of the fun times we had as kids: the trips we took and even memories of burying my father there. It's always emotional, but I thoroughly enjoyed the week back in Bermuda. But it was time to head out in quest of another gold medal.

First of all, let me address the accommodations in Åland. I can honestly say it was the worst location ever. We literally had no Internet except for a small area in the hotel/halfway house we were in. It was a crazy experience, but we were there to compete, even though the diva in me wasn't too happy. Our first game in Åland was against our somewhat new rivals, the Cayman Islands team. They fought hard, but we've always had their number, and this game would be no different. It was a strong shooting display from the team, and some clutch free throws from yours truly helped seal the deal and ensure we got off to a great start. In tournament play like this, it's always important to get off to a good start because you only get three to four maximum group games before you head to the medal round. Our last two games were against two mediocre teams, and we comfortably eased into the medal round, but we'd be facing Rhodes once again. It would be an extremely tough game, especially since we knocked them out of the gold-medal game on their home soil two years earlier.

This game against Rhodes was literally a slugfest from start to finish. They had a few players who were extremely hot and hitting a lot of tough shots, and we had the usual suspects doing what we normally do, and that's winning by committee. As the game entered the final five minutes, we were up by two points, and on a bogus call from the referee, one of our better players fouled out. The look on their faces said, *We got them right where we want them.* My reaction was simple. I knew I would have to do more to put us in a better position to win, that was all. Over the last five minutes of the game, I scored and assisted on our last fourteen points, including a tough fadeaway jumper to beat the shot clock with forty-five seconds remaining. Still, Rhodes wouldn't falter. And with ten seconds left, we were tied, and a spot in the finals was up for the taking. Time was slipping away— ten…nine…eight…seven…the ball was in my hands, just the way you envision it as a young boy in the gym with the opportunity to be the game's hero. At six seconds, I began to make a move crossover from left to right, and my defender bit on the move, so I left him in the dust…five…four…and here comes another defender whom I sidestepped and edged even closer to the rim…three…And with two seconds left, they tried to trap me, but I passed the ball to my man Deano, who went up for the dunk but got clobbered with one second remaining. He hit one of the two free throws, and just like that, we were back playing for another gold medal.

Three times in a row playing for the gold medal, only this time would have more meaning to it as we were playing against the team who previously beat us two years prior in Rhodes. It was Menorca versus Bermuda for the second time, and this would be another game for the ages. Like in previous years, they hosted an athlete's party on a huge ferryboat, which would take us on a three-hour tour. Unlike in years past, our team made sure we had no alcohol. We just chilled, but one thing was for sure, I'd still be on the prowl, looking for some adult fun.

She appeared out of the blue and just hit me with some cool, intelligent convo. It was easy to see this could be a stress reliever right before the final, but I never get too excited and just enjoyed the encounter. After a twenty-minute conversation, we quickly decided that the music was not good and that we would get a playlist of some sort going to change the vibe of the cruise. They provided entertainment, but it was extremely disappointing. So like always, my teammates and I made the party live and took over the music for the last forty-five minutes and made those forty-five minutes amazing. People you'd never imagine were up dancing; old people, all races, just let go and had a blast. Truthfully, people were reluctant to even get off the boat and wanted to stay and party with us; but clearly, the people running the cruise shut that down. They were like, "This is no hip-hop event. Sorry, time to go." We laughed it off and got off the boat and invited people over to party until our curfew kicked in at 11:00 p.m. Luckily for me, my friend whom I just met on the ferry ride decided to come by and hang out, so I would be sure to make an escape and have a bit of fun and still be in bed by curfew. In Åland, there was no real transportation, so we all rented bikes and just pedaled away together.

On this particular night with no alcohol, I found myself riding through the woods on an adventure with my newfound friend, looking for a spot to enjoy each other's company on a more personal level. We found a secluded area and had a little private party in the woods. It's funny, but I saw a competitor as we were leaving, heading to the spot probably to do the same thing. But hey, I had no cares in the world. My new friend was happy, and I was relaxed and ready to finish the tournament in style.

Game day came, and we were well rested and ready to go as a unit like always. We rode our bikes down to the game together. Everyone looked at us as if to say, *There go those crazy Bermudians.* but in truth, we were a close-knit unit, and we always traveled and even partied together. As the game approached, I had a great feeling that we'd win, but I've learned over the years that good feelings don't equate to success. The game was a nail-biter from start to finish. We went back and forth and had a two-point lead of 38–36 at the half-time break. During the break, we just relaxed and discussed how we hadn't really imposed our style on them, yet we still were ahead. They weren't very physical, but they were very organized and smart.

As the second half began, I wish I could tell you a different tale; but we were neck and neck, even heading into the fourth quarter, and they had a two-point lead at 55–53. The intensity at the end of the game was unbelievable. They had a chance to finish off the game with a layup, but they missed; and at the other end of the court, my boy Steven drained a three-pointer as the buzzer sounded to force overtime. Once we got to overtime, we just overpowered them with our athleticism and won our second gold medal in three years.

Gold medals aren't really made of gold.
They're made of sweat, determination,
and a hard-to-find alloy called guts.

-Dan Gable

Island Games champions once again, and the celebrations had begun. But I can honestly say that even after wsinning a few championships, I've never been one to go overboard and crazy with postgame celebrations. Even though two years prior, they straight tormented us to no end and were very tacky in their celebrations, we did have fun, but it wasn't too much or disrespectful. Many asked me why I wasn't over-the-moon-crazy happy. Truthfully, success has been something I've always demanded from myself, so when I win, it's somewhat expected. I'm not cocky, but I expect to win, no matter what it takes to accomplish that. I can honestly say that's why I have been successful.

The afternoon and night would come, and my new friend wanted to hang out at the final ceremony celebrations, but there was no chance of that. I hit the streets with my teammates and enjoyed the night to the fullest and looked for a new friend, whom I did find and got lucky with, and I ended up staying with her for a bit. Afterward, I headed back to the party and ended up with my old friend. What can I say? Winning has its perks.

It was the craziest thing, but the day of the final, I resigned in Cyprus with the champions from the previous season, and we would play in European competition, as well as domestically, in Cyprus. The money was super, and finally I'd have European play experience on my résumé again. Things were shaping up. My life was slowly but surely taking the turn for the better. As I returned home, I began to have videoconference calls with my lawyer, and she began to break down the advantages of me being with her firm. Statistics showed that with a female lawyer with kids, the male had a much greater chance of getting custody, especially a man in my profession. Often a judge might just assume like the rest of the world that the man is just another no-good athlete who wants everything his own way. It was crazy to hear these things and piece together how securing the right to be a part of my baby's life was going to work out for me in the long run.

The only uncertainty was the spiritual side of my life. I constantly pushed it away so I didn't have to deal with it. But the truth can't be hidden, and neither could I hide my upbringing that was deeply rooted in God, whose place in my life would soon become more evident to me.

CHAPTER 10

REUNITED AND IT FEELS SO GOOD

Our greatest weakness lies in giving up. The most certain way to succeed is always to try just one more time.

—Thomas A. Edison

After another intriguing summer, during Labor Day weekend, I found myself being scandalous and seeking revenge on a lady from my past. Okay, I'll give you the condensed version. A certain lady played me big-time during the first few years of my career, and I took the high road and let it go. However, upon seeing her again some years later, she was feeling me, so I told Shel I was going to get her back real good, and so I set it all up. We had sex, and she was on cloud nine. Then late in the evening, I basically rushed her out and was quite rude about it, and I went out with Shel after she left. We laughed about it, and she called me in tears, very upset, and I calmly reminded her of what happened before and said, "Now you know how I felt." She was furious and tried to get loud, and I hung up on her and kept it moving. That's not where it ended. She got crazy on your boy (me), and when I saw her in the club, she tried to come and confront me in the VIP area. She was a hot mess, and Shel and I stood there and laughed. Like the jerk I was, I told the bouncer there was no way she could come near us, and I just yelled out to her, "Bet you're feeling stupid like how you made me feel, huh?"

The next day, she and I spoke, and I apologized and smoothed things out somewhat. She was still salty, and rightfully so, but I kept it moving and was ready to head to Nicosia, Cyprus. I had met plenty of people in the previous city, but in Nicosia, I only had one friend named Ms. Fingers, and we had kept in contact throughout the summer. It was cool to meet her officially because when I had met her initially, I was beyond drunk and didn't really remember her. My first night in Nicosia, we had dinner and just hung out together. Thank God she wasn't ugly or fat as I had thought she might be. Man, I was so shallow, but I was consistent about that and can say that, for the most part, I was on track when it came to the women I liked and slept with. They usually met the same physical requirements I liked.

On the court, before I ever sign, I usually observe the team and envision what I can do to make the team better and ensure I'm a focal part of the plans for the team's success. On this team, like the previous year, I knew I was the best defender, but I also knew I could play more offense as well and wanted to show more versatility for my professional development. We were stacked from top to bottom, and from the first games of preseason, I showed that no one would be a better defender than I was. The only difference now was I would shoot the ball and would score at will. Offensively, now I was at the point (point guard position), scoring and running plays. I had that fine line where I wouldn't overdo it, but I wouldn't be passive about it either.

Finally, after a month there, I decided to go out and experience the nightlife. I must say that I was definitely impressed and was hooked from that night on, except for nights before games. I would be respectful of the court and my job. We started European play, and had a two-game playoff against a good team from Italy. In the first game in Nicosia, I mocked and embarrassed their best player, and as a result, he was on the bench for the most part of the game. We played fast and smart, and defensively, I chased and hounded whoever was in front of me, and we won by fifteen points. We should have won by twenty points, but heading into the second game, we felt quite confident about our chances.

During the second game, the first half was close, and we had them on lock and actually entered the second half up by two points. But they had devised a new plan to change the pace of the game and make us falter and turn the ball over. Unfortunately, we faltered, and with fifteen seconds left in the game, we had a one-point lead over the two games. This was the moment I had been waiting for. One defensive stop meant we were playing on live TV every Tuesday, and I couldn't wait. They in-bounded the ball, and their main player blatantly ran right over me, and we were out of the Eurocup and were doomed to play in the EuroChallenge tournament. I was beyond pissed and was embarrassed by our loss.

> The secret of success is learning how to use pain
> and pleasure instead of having pain and plea-
> sure use you. If you do that, you're in control
> of your life. If you don't, life controls you.
>
> -Tony Robbins

There couldn't be a better saying to phrase how we would approach the remainder of the year from that point on. We let our loss and pain fuel and propel us to success in Europe and domestically in the Cyprus league. The good thing about playing in European play was you get travel to other countries to play; this makes the season go by much faster. We found out our group would be going to France, Ukraine (it would be my first visit there), and Holland. It was groups of four, with six games in the group stage, and the top two teams moved on into the next round. In Cyprus, we straight strangled the league and started out with an 11–0 record, and out of the eleven wins, six were by twenty points or more. We were to be feared, and teams didn't want to play us. In our group in European play, aside from two slipups, we went 4–2.

In the last European game, I pulled my groin, and it looked as if it was torn, but thank God was just a bad pull. I would miss a regular season game for the first time in four years, and it was a firecracker right before the Christmas break. We played the team Big Homie and I had just left the year before, so it was a crazy atmosphere, and we won in overtime by five points. Imagine a gym full of people who hate each other and are bitter rivals. It was like a huge soccer rivalry; there were police and ambulances at the game—smoke bombs, firecrackers, the whole nine. But in Cyprus, this was normal behavior; they were passionate fans.

During Christmas, I had two female friends whom I had met via the Internet, and I invited both down at separate times in Florida. Let me be honest, I invited them both at the same time and split time between both ladies and my family. I was a hot mess, but I liked them both and wanted to see if I had a future missus in either one of them. I had physiotherapy every day of my eight-day vacation, and it was quite intense, to say the least, but I had to do it. I had to take every precaution for my job because if I didn't come back from the break better, I'd be cut from the team for sure. Both ladies knew this and were cool with it, but I would take them around my mom because she has the impeccable ability to discern if someone is compatible with me. Don't get it twisted. I would and did date whomever I wanted, but I'm no dummy. No one knows a person better than God and an attentive mother. Thumbs-down for both was the response, and I knew I should look more closely. Other than some physical fun, one was out the door; but I really did like the other lady, Ms. Yella, and wanted to see if things could work out. However, at the end of the season, things would go south; but this time, it was cool.

After the Christmas break, I began to run again and gear up for our second group stage, where we would be heading to Italy, France, and Montenegro (it would be my first time there). The trip from Montenegro to Cyprus literally took almost twenty-four hours and was no joke. But once again, getting stamps on my passport for free and getting paid to play, there were no complaints from me. Before leaving Montenegro, I had the opportunity to go and take in the sights in Belgrade and see the city, and it was magnificent. Everyone spoke English and was friendly as heck, and the women were amazing-looking, so it was amazing time for me.

Off the court, I was having a blast going out every night, getting hammered, and knocking down women at every turn—what more could I ask for? One particular night, I was out having fun with "Mary" and told her to head to my place and that I would be over in a second. Then I literally stood out in front of the club for two hours with "Lady V," just trying to get her to go home with me. And all of a sudden, Mary showed up out of the blue and started screaming at me, "What are you doing! I'm at home waiting for you, and you're here with this chick!" The crazy thing was, I had honestly forgotten about her. She threw my keys at me and left. How reckless and heartless was I? This all happened in the middle of the street in downtown Nicosia—just craziness, man.

I went right back to the task at hand and finished sealing the deal with Lady V. She and I went to my place and had a blast, laughing all night at the incident. Eventually, like with most women I dealt with, Mary and I patched things up and moved forward because it was just sex to me. She knew I wasn't committed and that she couldn't have me. She had gotten emotionally attached and lost her cool, which is an absolute no-no with me and would never be tolerated.

Around this time, documents had been submitted, and things were in motion for me to see and be with my daughter. I hadn't lost sight of the visionary path that included having my daughter in my life. Also around this crazy time, my team was behind on my payments; and I, like a few other teammates, was threatening to sit out and not play. As fate would have it, our team president fired our coach and hired a new dude whom no one liked and who, before the next round of European play, began to threaten people about their jobs and not paying them. So it was a bit of a chaos, to say the least. Back on the court in Europe, we maintained a stronghold and went 3–3 to secure a final eighth spot where we would face a very tough French outfit for the right to head to the final four of European play.

The first game, I had a friend I had met in Bermuda that summer, Ms. JH, come down to check out the game. Even though we lost by fourteen points, I had a great night. Our team knew all we had to do was win at home, and we would force a final game on their court, but it wasn't meant to be. We were short on players due to the financial inability of the club to pay salaries, and we lost by four points. It left us thinking what could have happened if we had our full squad and we all were mentally there. But in sports, what-if doesn't produce results, and that's what the business is about—results, and we had been eliminated from the competition. Beyond pissed at the results, I did what I was accustomed to do: hit the bar and searched for the high that never seemed to let me down and got me through tough times, JD and Coke. At this particular spot, I had a special friend who always hooked me up with drinks, so I wallowed in disappointment over losing the big game and decided to take the lady behind the bar home and began to seduce her.

The crazy thing was her boss was also into her, and when he saw me working my magic on her, he tried to ban me from the premises and call the cops on me. It was strange. I asked him, "Why are you acting like this? You can't date your employees." He just looked at me with a look like, *I wish you were dead, black boy.* She begged me to go quickly and promised to meet up with me later, but I wasn't ready to head home. I called good old Ms. Fingers to accompany me to our special bar, where I was such a regular that every waiter and waitress knew my drink and face without hesitation. The sad thing was this was the case in many establishments throughout the country. Believe you me, that wasn't a good look at all.

After drinking way too much and being beyond faded, I went home to meet with my waitress friend; but to my surprise, the police were at my doorstep and wanted to speak with me about the incident earlier. They said the bar manager had filed a complaint against me, but they wanted to see and confirm what had happened from my end. As I began to talk to the police, my waitress friend arrived, and they asked if she was involved. I knew her job was at stake and told her to go inside, even after she insisted she wanted to help. I told her I would deal with it. What I told them was that I was having some fun with a waitress when her boss came up and got mad and asked me to leave the premises, not even allowing me to pay my tab. The policemen told me they were fans of my team and wouldn't make a big deal of it, so I had escaped yet another drunken mess. When I told her of what had happened, bless her heart, she wanted to confront her boss, but I told her, "Girl, you better keep your job and get that money. We can always meet on the side."

The next day at practice, everyone was talking about my night adventure more—well, more like laughing at me and calling me crazy. My coach took me aside and said, "Watch yourself. You're a good player, but your reputation can prohibit you from the job you deserve." Unfortunately, I didn't take his words to heart, and I was out again later when I'd meet a special lady, Ms. Bambi. She was an absolutely gorgeous lady, had great body and an exquisite taste in fashion and design. But most of all, she was so exotic-looking it wasn't even funny. We were both at the same spot, and we locked eyes a few times. As she was leaving, she smiled at me and walked out, so you know I straight rolled out after her and her group of seven friends and started speaking to all of them.

In groups this size, when you greet the whole group, you find out who the ringleader is and always put her mind at ease first then proceed. In this case, it was her best friend. She asked me twenty questions, but I answered all calmly and coolly; and five minutes later, I had her number and would see her very soon. This lady and I had amazing sex. Unfortunately, even in our carefulness, she got pregnant. I'll never forget the day she came by to tell me and talk with me; it was like a movie, just crazy. I had just finished morning practice when she called and asked if she could come by. She usually worked her shift until 7:00 p.m., and if she wasn't exhausted, I'd see her after evening practices. She came in and was just very monotone with me, so I was like, "All right, man, cut to it. What's wrong?" And the words came out, followed by tears, "I'm pregnant!"

My face went blank, as did my mind. I couldn't believe I was hearing this again. I consoled her, and she asked what I wanted to do. Man, that's the hardest question to answer as a man, especially because the brutal truth is usually the first thing out of my mouth no matter who is asking! But seeing the tender nature of the situation, I knew I had to be cool. I told her in truth that a baby might not be a good idea (in my head, I was thinking, *Are you crazy? I'm not going to be here forever, and you know you don't want this kid because we spoke about this before*). However, I told her if she wanted to have the baby, I would be there financially and physically as much as I could, but I couldn't nor would I promise her more. Her next words brought the same relief to me as they do to any man who's ever heard them from a woman he's not planning a long-term relationship with. She said, "I'm going to make an appointment."

After she left and I found out the details and knew it was in motion, my heart sank, and I began to feel terrible. What if things didn't go totally as planned? This woman could have complications for the rest of her life just because of this. Then the moral guilt of cheating a life of its existence weighed heavily on me. It's really a selfish thought and action to take, especially knowing that God never gives you more than you could bear. But I didn't want the responsibility, so like a punk, I shut up and just let it happen.

She was blown away by my reaction and didn't want to see me for a while. I understood why. I would send messages to ask if she was okay and if she needed anything. Then one day, I was out and ran into her and her friend, and she emotionally broke down in tears in front of me. It was one of the hardest things I've ever faced as a man, but I listened to her spill out her emotional pain to me. It was so deep to hear her tell me how many nights she cried holding her stomach, how she thought of names and pictured what the kid could have looked like. She went on to tell me how much she liked me and had just wanted me to share her excitement about the gift that she had in her belly, but I didn't give her any of the reassurances she needed.

It was uncomfortable for me, but I listened intently and earnestly to her every word. As her friend came back around, Ms. Bambi asked if I would drive her home. Even though I was due to meet someone, I gladly obliged and texted my other date some excuse but told her I would be there soon. When we got to her place, she asked me to come in, and I did. The crazy thing was, she tried to have sex with me again; I couldn't do it. I told her I did like her as a person, but because of all the pain I had caused her, I wouldn't go there with her and sleep with her. She kept begging, asking me to do this for her so she could have closure, but all I could feel was her words piercing my brain, and soon I was gone. For any woman who has had an abortion, or any man who has been in my shoes, it's a crazy web. More often than not, someone stays tangled in the web even after the abortion is done and time moves on. In this situation, I was the one to move on.

The court was my sanctuary, and we were coming to the end of the year. We began to drop some games and not play so well and lost five out of the last eight games and ended up in second place. But the cool thing about us was that we were confident with playing anyone anywhere, so second place wasn't that big of a deal. However, it was payday time again; and as usual, our president and administrative staff were MIA. We were playing against a depleted team, which we crushed in the first game by seventy points. I sat out the second game and vowed not to play again until I was paid the funds that were due me. Everyone thought I was kidding until I arrived at the game in my polo shirt and had nothing else with me. That's when the owner, president, and committee called me in the next day to try and make things right before the start of the semifinals, and I told them, "No money, no play!"

In this business, if owners and coaches get a sense you will play without being paid, like a lot of players do, then you get screwed. I knew they wanted to win to avoid being blasted as a team that doesn't pay, and I was an important part of the team, so they needed to pay me. Sure enough, I left the meeting with my money in hand, but this wouldn't be the end of the saga between the management and me.

As the semifinals rolled around, we were facing a tough team. In game one, I was basically invisible until the second half, where I scored seventeen points, had six rebounds, and three assists to help us secure a ten-point win. In game two, once again, I came alive in the second half, where I scored twelve points during a critical period where we saw our opponent go up 2–0. I ended up with fifteen points, five rebounds, and three assists. Now the other team had to play me, which honestly freed me up to play my game.

Game three almost produced a season-ending injury for me. As the game progressed, we fought tooth and nail with the other team to get control of the game. As their point guard made a crossover move, he stepped on my finger and ripped it open. Blood was gushing out, and I could see the ligaments and everything just hanging out. It was a supergross sight, and I was run back into the locker room where they gave me pain and numbing injections to help before they came at my finger with a fishhook and thread. Yes, that's right. I had to sit there while they used an actual fishhook to sew my thumb back up. This was quite an adventure for me again. Looking back, it was freaking nuts, but the craziest thing was that the finals would start in seven days, and the team asked me to come back and play. I laughed when they initially said this and said okay, but I thought I wouldn't play again. Luckily for me, I began to soak my hand in saltwater and alternate with ice and heat; and in four days, my hand almost looked normal.

> We gain strength, and courage, and con-
> fidence by each experience in which we
> really stop to look fear in the face…we
> must do that which we think we cannot.
>
> -Eleanor Roosevelt

This was where I was with my finger. I would have to look past the pain and fear and move above and beyond to try and help our team win a championship, but trust me, it would be easier said than done. Be mentally strong and allow my mind to override the natural protective instincts of the body and perform—in a nutshell, that was basically what I had to do to help my team win. It was Russian roulette. You have to understand the potential loss if my thumb got hit during the game. It could possibly lead to all sorts of complications and, as the team doctor so bluntly pointed out, even amputation of my thumb. Off the court, however, I had received great news. I learned I had won my court case and had been granted rights to see my daughter. That was my fuel to get back and be healthy and super-active in her life again.

That day, after a video session and practice, I came home to that message, and it was like a waterfall of tears opened. I cried uncontrollably because the fight was over. The exhaustive searches, the excessive money spent, and the letdowns—all of it was just preparing me for that moment when I could exhale and embrace the reality of finally being reunited with my daughter. Man, the tears are in my eyes even now when I think back to that time. You see, as an athlete, a lot of things are just handed to you. You may fight in the games and to get jobs, but on a whole, your life's pretty easy, and people cater to your needs and wants. This situation took me back to the days when I wasn't being catered to and life was a struggle, to say the least, when fighting for any and everything was just the norm. I will say this: I wouldn't change any of the hardships for anything because I'm telling you that made my love for my daughter grew even stronger and allowed her to see firsthand that real men will fight for the right to be with a good woman (in her case, to be in my daughter's life). The night definitely called for a celebration, but this night, I wanted the solace of Ms. Fingers's company, and that was it. I didn't want to get too drunk; I just wanted to bask in the news. And for the first time in a long time, I had a glow of excitement in my life again.

Finally, after a long seven days of rehab and mental preparation, game one of the finals rolled around, and it was evident from the start that both teams would fight to the death to win. They were the regular-season champions, but we were the runners-up, and heavily motivated to win. Defensively, we swarmed them like bees to honey and forced them to play our style of play, which was very physical. I played maybe fifteen minutes, which was light for me; but defensively, even with one hand, it was known that I wasn't the one to attack. At the end of the game, we had won the crucial first road game by six points.

As I said before, in Cyprus, the fans are crazy, I am not even going to lie. As soon as the final horn sounded, we had to run out of the gym because their team threw lighters (Euro coin note firecrackers) onto the court. Yeah, it was bananas. We couldn't leave the gym for at least an hour after the game, and when we did leave, we had a police escort as well to ensure the crazy fans wouldn't do anything stupid. During the finals, I didn't do much and just stayed home.

This was money time, and I knew I had a lot of *money* on the line, so going out wasn't an option.

Game two was a whitewash from start to finish. We straight ran them off the court. It was a case of all the things that made us so good clicking at the right time, and we beat them by at least twenty points. Again, after the game, and even during game, there was fan drama. One of the other team's players spat at a fan, and our fans began spitting on them each time the ball went out on that side of the court. Talk about disgusting. He wanted to fight and ended up getting ejected, and we would have to play our next home game at another gym as punishment for our fans' bad behavior.

Game three was on their court, and we lost in double overtime. It was a nail-biter, and in truth, we should have won easily, but we shot terribly from the free throw line. As the bus ride home commenced, one crazy bunch of fans threw a boulder on our bus, and of course, whose seat would it land in? Mines. This was way beyond crazy, and thank God no one was sitting there because they would have been killed for sure. In fact, my head was actually against the same window a few minutes prior to the stone being thrown at the window. Even now it makes me quiver at the thought of my head against that window and how I could have been, at best, severely brain damaged or, at worst, could have been killed. Thinking on this incident makes me realize another important lesson:

> *Lesson 27: There are no accidents. Everything happens for a reason. If we choose, these things can act as lessons learned and lead to personal growth. Or we can ignore these situations, and an opportunity for personal growth will be wasted.*

I am not going to lie. This incident shook me up and made me really stop and realize again that life is a gift, and it's not promised to us! The media jumped on it as soon as we arrived back at our gym. Cameras and reporters were all in our faces, especially mine, because I was the one who had been targeted. After speaking to the media for a bit, we all left and thought nothing of it. The next day, it was all over the media, newspapers, and news. Man, it was crazy. The worst part about it was we were the home team next, and our fans would more than likely retaliate, especially if we didn't win or didn't look like we would win. Luckily for us, it would turn out to be the last game of the season; and in a somewhat comfortable fashion, we won the championship, and I played an integral part as we closed out a long season.

For the club, we would repeat as champions. The atmosphere and everyone's reaction to us were insane. People were trying to rip off my shirt, my shooting shirt, and braces—it was nuts. Finally we received the championship medals and the trophy, and that's when it hits you. All the sacrifices made, the bonding, and camaraderie as a team—they all pay off. And the result is a championship, and it all becomes surreal at that point.

On this night, we would drive up to our clubhouse and show off our trophy to our crazy fans, spray champagne at them, and show off the trophy some more. Even in these festive moments, I remained calm and wanted to soak it all in because these moments in sports come few and far in between if you're lucky. One guy on our team had played for fourteen years, and that was his first taste of success. Imagine working on your dream, no matter what it may be, and you only experience some success fourteen years after you started your quest. That's deep to think about and leads to a good question: is your dream worth fighting for?

On this night, I remained somewhat sober, if that makes any sense. I drank, but not enough to forget, just enough to keep things on edge a bit. I had invited a new acquaintance, a Serbian cutie, Ms. Tanya, to come down and celebrate. She had a hell of a body, but most of all, she was such a cutie and quite knowledgeable about life. After exploring all of Nicosia, to my surprise, she gave me a ride home and decided to tuck me in. Needless to say, even with all the fun and games, I still was thinking about the financial headache I would have to deal with to get my final pay from the club. After a weekend of bliss, Monday morning, it was "on your mark, get set, where is my money?" To my surprise, I was receiving the deaf ear from the team, as if I wasn't going to get paid. I had my agent at the time hit them with a nice note, reminding them of their duties and to ask them to reach out to me and let me know what's going on. Finally they proposed to pay me like a one-fourth of what was owed to try and play me. I played ignorant and took the cash. I just worded the paperwork to say I had only received a portion of what I was totally owed, and that Monday, I flew out being owed a lot of money.

As the summer began, unlike my normal routine, I didn't go crazy in the club, spending abnormal amounts of cash. I went home quite mellow and quiet and started attending church weekly, which bought me back to this lesson:

> *Lesson 28: Without God in my life as my founda-*
> *tion and source of strength and refuge, no matter*
> *what my best intentions might be they would never*
> *be the same without divine intervention.*

As the summer began, the fight continued. Even though I had won joint custody, I still was going through it and trying to connect with my baby and fill the void left in my life by her absence. Finally, in the middle of July, I got her, and it was an absolutely joyous occasion. Tears were flowing down my face from relief that the fight had finally paid off. She was so excited to see me, and the feelings were mutual. During the one-and-a-half-hour ride home, we just played catch-up and had a blast. Before I had gotten J, I had a bit more online dating experience. I went online just to find people and look for connections really and, of course, maybe a sexual encounter or two. With online dating, I didn't have to reveal who I really was or how I hurt people or that I even played sports. I just showed the part or image I chose for them to see. I'd be lying if I said it wasn't crazy fun meeting women left, right, and center; but usually we'd meet up, and it wouldn't be about anything but sex.

It was an insane month and a half. I was hooking up with women at church, the club, and online. At one point, it got to a where I literally thought no woman could say no to me. My boy Shel was just looking from the outside like, *Wow, this dude is a crazy chick magnet*; and at this particular point, he couldn't have been more correct. But like everything in life, when reality and the real meet, it might not be the introduction you expect or want. There was Ms. Bubble, an intelligent down-south sister with a body to die for. She could cook like her life depended on it, and she had lips that could make the strongest man melt. Unfortunately, like many good packages, there was one problem, and it was the biggest deal breaker for me at that time: she just showed up to my place on two separate occasions unannounced. There was absolutely no pardon for this in my book. She didn't interrupt or find me in a bad situation, but I made sure I let her know that wasn't going to fly.

The second time she just showed up, I politely met her at the door and was straight rude, like, "What do you want? No, you can't come in. Good-bye." Let's just say that she didn't appreciate my bluntness and basically said, "Screw you." However, one late night at my favorite bar in DC, I happened to stumble across her, and she was on a date, so you know I had to be a straight fool in the sweetest way. I walked to the table and politely said good evening and saw the look on her face. Her date asked if we knew each other, and we responded that we were friends.

He invited me to sit with them, and after a few drinks and convo, I knew I had her interest. So as I was leaving to go to see a new friend who had entered the bar, I whispered in her ear, "Let me know when you're ready to go." I exchanged pleasantries with her friend and moved away. The whole night, I had a blast, and a couple of ballers I knew were in there, so you know I was having a blast for sure. As the night wound down, she came and said, "I'm ready to take you home." I smiled and told her I would meet her at her place in a few as she lived literally fifteen minutes away. Shoot, I closed the club and got a ride with my new friend and didn't make it home until Sunday afternoon. That was how our relationship was, fun but totally superficial and physical, but that was safe for me.

The last lady I will mention is Ms. Rosalynn (yes this is her real name, and I will later refer to as Roz). This is the first real name and last reference of a lady you will read in this book. She was a charismatic, intelligent, attractive woman. I had never been with an Asian, so I thought, why not? Out of the many flings, we hung out for the whole summer, and I even hung out with her after my daughter came. One night, Shel and I went out and got pulled over for a DUI. Of all the flings and people I knew, Rosalynn was the only one who came at the drop of a hat and never complained or anything. That night was the first night I actually said she's more than a fling, someone I want to keep close to me, maybe even grow to love.

If you change the way you look at things,
the things you look at change.

-Wayne Dyer

While Ja'hnniah was here, the summer would be filled with nothing but entertainment, lots of long walks, playing on the playground, kickball—you name it, we did it. Most of all, we went to church every week, and I'll be the first to admit it, going to Sabbath school and being in church all day wasn't that bad. Many times on the weekends, my sisters Gwen, Marie, and Christina offered to take her, but I didn't let her go and kept her close to me for the entire summer.

Toward the end of the summer, Rosalynn's daughter Mei-Lin had a birthday party, and I would be able to see the crop of friends she had. "Show me your company, and I'll tell you who you are" couldn't have been more true a phrase in her case. Her friends were awesome, good women, highly educated and loyal to a fault. In truth, only one spoke with me candidly, but I was supercool with it because that gave me all the more time to evaluate and understand her more through her interactions. Ja'hnniah was having a blast just enjoying the company of other kids, and I just sat back quietly and watched and observed how good a woman Rosalynn truly is.

On the basketball end, I had fired my agent and was desperately looking to go back overseas and finalize legal paperwork for my daughter to ensure there were no more hiccups with our visitations. The agent lied and told me we had a huge offer, and after I signed, I found out he never had a deal and that I was stuck with this guy for a year. He was a loser who couldn't get me a gig, and it would be a frustrating few months chasing after this dude, trying to get him to get me a decent job after having a quite successful year. I had been lied to, and earlier in the summer and close to the end of the summer, I had passed up on two amazing jobs to secure a long-term structure and solidification with my daughter, and soon the summer was over. After spending a few weeks in Florida with my family, I took Ja'hnniah back to Saint Thomas, and time was basically running out on me. My lease was ending, and I had no job. The only real option I had was to move in with Rosalynn or move to New York with my other bro Shurland (Sheldon's brother) and try to coach and work out.

> Your present circumstances don't deter-
> mine where you can go; they merely
> determine where you start.

> -Nido Qubein

In all my years, I had never been at this point of uncertainty. It was like a blur. Not having a job, nowhere to go, and nothing to do was a rude awakening for me, as what a lot of people experience and what, as a professional basketball player, I had never seen. Until Christmastime, I pretty much just lay low and tried to stay ready in the event a good job came up. I just didn't want to let go of my dream, especially knowing I had a great opportunity that I passed on earlier in the summer. Time rolled on, and right before the holidays, I went to Bermuda, and I started to play soccer with my boys J-Money and Ste just to stay in shape and keep out of trouble. Around this time, I had stopped drinking, cold turkey, and playing football (soccer) helped me miss the most dangerous nights because I wanted to make sure I was good to play on Sundays. While home, I had a blast just hanging with my nephews and catching up with family and friends. My mom wanted me to go and look for work, but I was like, "Nah, I'm good." I was waiting for what I knew I rightfully deserved.

Now that I think back, what did I really deserve? I played well, but my off-the-field habits were horrific. I was a functioning alcoholic unless my daughter was near, so what did I really deserve?

At thirty-one years old, I took that ugly look at myself in the mirror, and it was truly scary what I saw: no job, no potential job, and things were just not looking good at all. Around January, I had the court case with my old team in Cyprus. They owed me quite a bit of money, and I had to go to court to try and get what was due me. As expected, they wanted to lowball me; but as always, I stood firm and made them pay everything owed to me, plus compensate for my travel and lawyer's fees. While I was there, another team offered me a job, but I was too high on my horse, so I snubbed the offer and went back home. Around the same time, an offer from France came for decent money, but it was in the second league, and again, my big head full with pride wouldn't let me sign.

During the same month, I moved in with Rosalynn and Mei-Lin. It was weird for me because I had been accustomed to helping others out of jams or providing for others, but here, this woman opened her doors to me and only asked me to respect the space and place she lived in. Things couldn't have been any better. Life really was good for us until one day in February, real and reality met face-to-face when she uttered the words, "I'm pregnant." Anyone who knew me or had close dealings with me knew what I had been through with Ja'hnniah and didn't ever want to experience something like that again or have any kids outside of marriage. So when I found out, I was beyond furious, more at myself for putting myself in that position and ultimately for having to live with her choice. Like my first child's mother, we argued, and I pushed for an abortion because it was best for all parties, I thought, But she didn't try to hear me. I went to Atlanta and broke the news to my mom, and she just looked at me with a blank stare, like, *Are you kidding me right now? After all you've been through, you stuck yourself in the same place again, and for what?*

She was in town to finalize the purchase of her retirement house, and I was helping her out. I said things that I would never repeat. God knows I regret that they even left my mouth, but the anger and fear at the thought of this child being born consumed me daily. My mom was brief but, like always, precise when she said, "You could jump ship or make the best of it and do right by your child.

Complaining and crying ain't going to change a thing." Luckily for me, I eventually chose the latter, although I won't lie; many days, I thought, *Screw this and start over, homie. Don't get locked in again.*

Too often in life, something happens and we
blame other people for us not being happy
or satisfied or fulfilled. So the point is, we all
have choices, and we make the choice to accept
people or situations or to not accept situations.

-Tom Brady

Even though I decided to go ahead with the baby, trust and believe that I was not amused with the idea and was beyond miserable. For the first two and a half months, I was always out every weekend just to run away from the reality of this new life I had helped create and the new responsibilities that would come with it. I'm talking about getting hammered from 7:00 p.m. to 2:00 a.m., stumbling in and just not caring and not talking. I heard the tears drop from her face, but I didn't care because in my head, it was the right thing to do. But this plan only worked out for her because a kid traps or keeps a guy close. One day, I went with her to an ultrasound exam and saw the sonogram of the baby, and it changed my attitude and involvement from that point on. Seeing the growth process, I realized how blessed we were to have a kid on the way. I hung my head in shame because all this time, I only thought about what I'd be losing in my own personal situation instead of realizing what I'd gain from this child, the blessing it would be, and how ultimately it could possibly keep my family name going on.

I know some men can relate, and I'm expressing my true emotions because, in truth, that's how a lot of men feel. We never stop and think of the damage we can cause emotionally and mentally by asking a woman to give up a blessing from God. Knowing it could possibly ruin her chances or the ability to ever have a child again, a man shouldn't ask that of a woman. Rosalynn had medical issues in college, and it had done major damage to her body, putting her at high risk throughout the whole pregnancy. Basically, it was not going to be smooth sailing, and she could encounter complications that could almost take her life. Knowing and understanding this, that she would not have an abortion but would risk her life and be adamant about keeping the baby even though she knew it might be the end of us, was so deep. How many people will go through hell and be in harm's way but will still allow you to choose the easiest way out for you? I don't know many. Hell, I think Rosalynn is one of the few people I know who has these qualities. Knowing this and other things made me lose my selfish attitude, and I began to embrace the blessing that God had bestowed on us.

I was much more positive, but deep down, I wanted my career back and needed my own identity. I didn't want to feel as if my life was over because of the baby, so I was looking to play again and use the upcoming summer tournaments to ensure I got top exposure and got the job I so coveted. I was like a madman on a mission. Hell, I was obsessed, and I wasn't going to be hampered by anything or anyone.

On a spiritual tip, I went to Restoration Praise Center (RPC) for the first time in a while, and I can say without a doubt that the minister had a special word ordained for me that catered to my needs. He spoke on faithfulness even when things aren't going your way, or when you feel like nothing is working out in your life, to hold on to God, and he won't forget you or forsake you or your efforts. I needed to hear that because at that time of the year, I felt like God had given up on me and that my efforts were being ignored.

Time = Life. Therefore waste your
time and waste of your life, or master your time and master your life.

-Alan Lakein

With that being said, a new leaf was turned over, and I found a new home church with a minister who wasn't afraid to be 150 percent honest with the Word.

CHAPTER 11

WHEN ONE DOOR CLOSES, ANOTHER ONE WILL OPEN

A pessimist sees the difficulty in every opportunity;
an optimist sees the opportunity in every difficulty.

—Winston Churchill

A whole season had come and gone, and I didn't play one single game (I did have offers, but I was too headstrong to humble myself and take one), so chances for me to get a job again were slim to none. But that's one thing I've learned over the years: people who usually tell you things are impossible aren't devoted enough or passionate enough to step out and make the hard and tough things of life doable. Old teammates laughed at me; coaches, agents, they all laughed and said I was finished, and I would never win again. But haters are motivators, so the hate began to fuel me. I began to work out like a madman to ensure I was ready and equipped to regain the success I longed for in basketball. The quest involved playing or working out every single day, sometimes up to three times a day. It was literally like I was a machine programmed to make it happen. It's funny how you can want something so badly that no matter what it takes to get it, you will do it. Imagine if I had given this much effort and commitment from the beginning, my disappointments with the NBA surely wouldn't have happened.

Church-wise, I maintained focus and went every week, forging a relationship and seeking guidance in the upcoming months that would ultimately make or break my career. So working out every day and constant communication with God was my daily routine. And I must admit, there were days when I slipped up, but the difference in the days away from God were so drastically bad I made sure they weren't often. On my plate were two huge tournaments that could make or break me, a pregnant girlfriend, and two girls—Mei-Lin (Rosalynn's daughter) and Ja'hnniah (my daughter)—all whom I had to support somehow, some way, so I was so on the grind it wasn't even funny. The first tournament were the Island Games (hosted by the Isle of Wight near England), where we were the defending champs; and then there was the Caribbean Basketball Championships in the Bahamas, where there would be a few NBA players and plenty of European players and coaches as well. Of course, prior to the trips, I had to endure some petty drama surrounding Ja'hnniah and obtaining her passport; but at this phase of life, it was simple for me: let a lawyer handle it and get my baby!

I won't lie. No, a man should never walk away from his responsibilities, but over the years, I can honestly say I see why a lot of fathers walk away. Again, I'll be the first to admit that I'm not the best parent in the world, and I have made many mistakes, so please don't read and think, *Oh, poor guy, he's a victim.* I did contribute a lot of my own drama. Having said that, I grew up and allowed myself to realize and recognize that, at the end, the only one who gets hurt is the child. I didn't want my daughter to make the same mistakes or worse because of my absence from her life, so I made changes instead of expecting them to happen.

She finally arrived, and literally the tears flowed again. If you're a father or parent who has fought to be part of your kid's life and you've truly had a real tough time accepting the distance affecting your communication and emotional bond with your child, then you know what I'm talking about. It kills you mentally day in and day out, especially when your motives are pure and you want the best for your kids and can't make it happen. Luckily, Rosalynn was there for me as a friend, helping me to be a better, patient, and more mature man in every aspect of my life. Her influence changed my approach and helped me continue to fight for my daughter, but this time, with more brains than emotions. When Ja'hnniah came, I must say that I was pleasantly surprised at how well things were going and how the kids got along quite well. Of course, there were bumps along the way, but I can honestly say that things were good.

As things settled down, it was time for me to head to Bermuda and then England for the Island Games. But first, while in Bermuda, I got to relax with my family and friends and just enjoy their company and reminisce on the good times. That's what the Trinity Crew always gave and continues to give me to date on any visit home. After a few days of practicing and just relaxing, we were off to England to defend our crown and go for an unprecedented back-to-back championship. Our first game was a joke. We played a first-entry team and beat them by like eighty points. It was literally the worst game we could get because wins like that make you feel invincible and make it easy to lose focus. We were humbled and beaten in the next game right on cue by a tough Saaremaa team. They weren't better than us, but on that day, they outworked and executed much better; thus, they beat us by like six or seven points. I've always been an advocate of this fact and always will believe that in life and in sports, you learn when you lose. Here, we were humbled and would have to win our final game to make it to the medal round against our archnemesis, the Cayman Islands.

Over the years, we have never lost to them, and once again, we were in position to ruin their chances of making it to the qualifying round for another year, and we were keen on making this reality a tough pill for them to swallow as well. To be fair, they had a new coach and a lot of players, but our experience once again came through when it mattered, and we beat them by nine or ten points to secure another berth to the medal round. Truthfully, we had a safe and quiet round leading up to the finals, beating teams we were supposed to quite easily.

On the other side, an upset in the making was being set up as Saaremaa had amazingly made it to the finals against us. This game was a super grudge match for us, and from the outset, there was no question about it, there would be only one winner! We totally controlled and dominated the game from start to finish. Their best player walked off the court halfway through the second quarter faking an injury, but in truth, he admitted, "We had no chance, so I quit." It was our third final in a row; and this time, like the previous one, we had won it, making history in the process as the first back-to-back champions.

It was another great accomplishment, and I received MVP honors again as well, but the hunger for my career to be reinstated and further success still burned on the inside. I knew that I had more to offer to my legacy in sports to be the best I could possibly be. The night would be long, but first we had closing ceremonies. We never would receive our gold medals on the court, firstly because it's the easiest way and place to lose them. Secondly, we (the Bermuda squad) never liked to flaunt or brag; we just like to win. And if someone asks, then we let them know how we did it, but our goal was to cement our legacy as one of the best teams in competition by our winning on the court.

During the final procession, I gained a new friend, one I had admired from a distance over the years but had never actually spoken with. But during the trip, fate had us around each other and speaking. She was a very cool person, and even though I was tempted, nothing happened. However, I gained a new friend and learned about a new sport. During the final parade to salute the champions, we walked and talked along with other athletes; it was a great time. And to hear our team announced as "the first back-to-back men's champions for the first time in the history of the games" over the microphone was an awesome feeling and an honor I'll hold dear to me, and no one can take that from me.

The night was superfun as well. After going cold turkey the whole week, as was tradition, I bought a special bottle of White Hennessy to commemorate our success and to make sure everyone would be more than relaxed for the evening festivities. After a few shots, we all were relaxed. But I wanted to remember everything, so I made sure the night was fun but in control and that I would be more than functional in the morning. In the previous games, I had a certain encounter; and on this trip, a similar situation fell into my lap like a layup (a very close shot next to the basket) and the opportunity to add another victim to the "hit list." I don't think I've referred to this before, but this was my list of all the women I've had sexual encounters with as a professional athlete. Believe you me, the temptation was so strong. I was away from home, and her attractiveness aroused me, but there was more to lose in this encounter than to gain. Lose a potential wife, family, and friend or gain a number on a list?

Lesson 29: Sometimes you have to recognize what's worthwhile in life and never lose what's important over things and people that aren't worth keeping.

I left the premises alone, gave away my T-shirt as a souvenir, and went back home to pack and get ready to travel home. The old me would have embraced and made sure I ended the night right, but my focus was elsewhere, and soon I would be home and getting ready for the Caribbean Basketball Championships (CBC) in the Bahamas in a few weeks. The CBCs are a prestigious Caribbean tournament to determine which team in the regions can qualify for the next round to possibly make it to the Olympics. For Bermuda, this would be the second appearance after a previous last-place finish and was the perfect chance to set the record straight and show that Bermuda had a good basketball program and the first competitors' play would soon be forgotten.

After a few weeks with the family, I was truly beyond ready to meet up with the fellas and get this tournament started. We met up in Florida for the night, and the next day, we were off to the Bahamas. For a lot of people, it was a basketball trip; for me, it was an interview to show that I still had it and could compete on a high level in an industry that was getting younger and younger by the day. There was a lot of personal pressure being in a tournament again filled with seasoned professionals, and here I was with my boys, the only professional in the ranks. But to whom much is given, much is expected. On this trip, my family would come down and meet me later on, so it would be fun and family and work and more work. But it was all good; those are the sacrifices you make. It can't always be about you in the family dynamics or on the personal front either.

The plane landed, and we were greeted by the unbelievable blazing sunshine of Nassau. Dude, I was so ready for the pool and accommodations as soon as we got out the door. After arriving at the resort and resting, trouble came knocking again. While just minding my own business and chilling with the fellas, I decided to go for a cool bottle of water and virgin piña colada when, out of the blue, a lady came my way and just randomly struck up a conversation with me. She was beautiful and apparently single. I didn't see a ring or tan line (hey, I have to check the fingers because I've been caught like that before) and was as friendly as a puppy who'd just been fed. Ms. Michelle was superexcited and seemed hell-bent on knowing me on a much more personal level than her questions might suggest. Just from talking to her, I would find out about her drama; and I can't lie, it was sad, and I did feel her pain to a certain degree. But I knew what the angle was with her; she wanted some sex and fun before leaving.

Trust when I say I never gave her my room number, but I received flowers, candy, and JD at my room, and even a watch was delivered there (I was tempted to keep it, but I gave it back to her). She stood and looked at me in amazement like, *Dang, I just want to sex you up. I don't care if you're in a relationship and about to have another kid. I just want you for two days, and I'm out of your life.*

> *Lesson 30: If someone shows you who they truly are, make no mistake about it, that's who they are, and you'd better believe them.*

Say what you want, but I respected her all the more after she told me this. She was, in essence, saying, *I'm insecure. I don't think guys like me like that, but I know men like gifts, and if I can get what I need that easy using my ex's money, why not? I lose nothing.* I was like, *Am I really hearing this?* The spiritual person in me began to speak with her on a deeper level to find out the true source of her insecurities, which stemmed from abuse by her dad, mental and physical, and she really just married her ex to be secure financially after growing up dirt poor. She had a plan, and basically she was sticking to what worked for her, and that was buying men's affection and attention. As tempting as it sounded and she made it, I knew that when you compromise one time, you'll always justify the behavior and compromise on everything that matters. I slid her off to a teammate and gave him the layup, and for a while, they stayed in contact and had a bond. But I had to walk away not just for me but for the good. I was trying to build a long-term and secure Christian family home.

Finally the games had come around, and Ms. Michelle happened to come to our first game against Saint Vincent. We played very well and broke the goose egg, earning the first win for Bermuda. I played a solid game—nineteen points, eight rebounds, and eleven assists—and the message was clear: we weren't the previous team that came, and we were a threat. Our next game was against the host team, and I can honestly say I lost my cool from the jump, and my emotions killed us. We lost by fourteen points, but my emotions caused me to foul out, and there went my plans to dominate the tournament host team.

Our next game was for all the marbles to ensure we made it to the medal round, and it would see us playing against British Virgin Islands. It was a close game, and we had them on the ropes. But we had critical turnovers toward the end, and I missed a critical jumper at the end, and we lost by three points. So our next game would be for last place against the Cayman Islands, our archnemesis. This would be a grudge match where we needed to win to play on for, at best, a fifth-place finish out of ten teams, which would be a huge improvement for the sport in Bermuda. For some odd reason, we came out extremely sluggish. Looking back, it was more of an arrogant approach of, *We know we're going to beat you just like we always do*—wrong. They weren't trying to be in last place, and they wanted to get off the goose egg of never beating us. And after the first half and being up by twelve points, it looked like they had found a way to get the monkey off their back. Unfortunately for them, our pride and skill set were better, and we got going and began to show why they had never beaten us.

Five minutes to go in the game, and we were back up by four points. This was and is the time when I usually begin to assert myself more and put the finishing touches on an opponent. This game would be no different. Ending the game on a personal 6–0 run, we walked away winning by twelve points; but most importantly, we could continue playing for at least fifth place. Understand me well when I say I'm all about winning, but in this tournament, there were some NBA players and NBDL (NBA Development League) players and seasoned European professionals, so the competition was a bit harder. Anyone who knows me understands I despise losing, but the reality was that I was the only professional on our team, and we had a superslim chance to get through to the next round and didn't make it.

Off the court, my family was there with me. I would play or practice and drive back over to the resort and just relax and unwind with them.

It was awesome to see Ja'hnniah develop and grow with her new sister Mei-Lin. You see, many men make a huge mistake of thinking that if they get with a woman who has kids, they won't have to interact with the kids much and can just focus one-on-one with the woman. The reality is, when you take her, you take everything that comes with her—bad credit, kids, emotional, mental, and physical baggage, you take it all on. So now I had two beautiful girls and a son on the way. One thing I made sure was to always treat both girls the same way, no matter what. Just because Mei-Lin wasn't my blood kin, it didn't give me the right to treat her as if she wasn't my daughter. I made sure that along all lines, they were equally treated. During this trip, amid all the things going on, I can honestly say that there in the Bahamas, all my questions regarding family life and the dynamics as to how I could cope or deal with them were dismissed.

On the court, physically at age thirty-two, this was an absurd tournament for me to play in, and it was starting to weigh in on me mentally and physically. From the age of twenty-six or twenty-seven, I've had bad tendinitis in my shins; and through the years, it has spread through my right leg. Before our next game against Guyana, let me tell you, I was nothing and was in pain; but Louise, the physiotherapist, kept me playing. Man, I was on the table 24-7. If I wasn't playing or with my kids, I was at physiotherapy. It was supercrazy.

> We must all suffer one of two things:
> the pain of discipline or the pain
> of regret or disappointment.
>
> -Jim Rohn

I have to keep it 150 percent honest when I say physically, I was finished and shouldn't have played because where I was physically was the easiest condition in which to get hurt, but my mental resolve and prayer wouldn't let me quit. Guyana was a good bounce-back game and setup for our final match. They had a very good scorer, and the team was okay. But talent-wise and team-wise, we beat them easily and won by fifteen points. With this win, it was set: we'd play the next day for fifth place against Antigua and their superstar trio, or so we were told.

At the beginning of the game, their best player looked at me and said, "This is going to be an easy triple-double" (this is when you get double figures in points, rebounds, assist, or in steals in one game). I looked at him and asked, "What did you say?" He repeated it, and I just smiled and wished him good luck. He had no idea he had just opened and unleashed hell on his squad. Before I go on, let me list the talent on their team: an ex-NBA draft pick and player and two seasoned professionals. They just knew they were going to beat us, but the good thing is that the game is sold by what you do and not told by what you'd like to do.

In sports and in life, there's no divine right to anything, except God's gift of salvation, and even that comes with sacrifice. In this game, J-Money and I totally annihilated them to bits and pieces; their cockiness killed them from the door. With four minutes to go and up by twelve points, I went through a screen and began to turn the corner only to be clotheslined by one of their players. It was a cheap tactic to provoke me to get kicked out of the game. The old me would still be killing that guy as we speak, or at least I would have ended any chance of him playing basketball again ever. I jumped up from the ground and turned and walked to my bench for water and to relax. Of course, he was thrown out of the game; and in the end, we cruised to a twelve-point win, and I ended with twenty-six points, eleven rebounds, and eight assists to lead Bermuda to a fifth-place finish in the games and gain much respect for the country. As the game ended, my teammates wanted to walk out and not shake hands with the opposing team. For me, this was unacceptable! In sports and life, you always show class in victory or defeat. It's a must for me, and I made the guys go shake their hands. You see, in truth, it's even more humbling when you do wrong to someone or treat them badly, and they just ignore you and keep living their life.

The funny thing is, later that night, I saw the guy again, and he quickly apologized for what happened, and I acted like nothing even happened. He couldn't understand it, but I told him, "It's bigger than me. I can't act the fool because my guys will follow my lead. But when I act like a grown-up, accept the abuse, and still show class and dignity by shaking your hand no matter what, that's a life lesson through actions, not words." After hanging for a while, I headed back to the family for a good night's rest before we left the next day.

The summer was cool and slowly coming to an end. I hadn't obtained employment and didn't have anything concrete in the works, but I wasn't scared. For the first time, I knew that no matter what, it would work out. That's a great feeling and place to be in, especially at that juncture of my life. What was next around the corner, and what new adventures did God have in store for me?

CHAPTER 12

WHEN YOU CAN'T FIND THE RIGHT DOOR, BUILD ONE!

*Success is simple. Do what's right, the
right way, at the right time.*

—Arnold H. Glasow

After a successful tournament play and exciting times throughout the summer, it was crunch time, and I hadn't received any decent offers because my main priority in the negotiations was that I had to be home to see my child born! That was nonnegotiable for me. This would be my last child, and I hadn't been present to see or be somewhat part of the birthing process before. I knew this was most important to be there for Rosalynn and my new child. This rubbed many teams the wrong way, and it didn't help that I had snubbed many of the teams the year before and wouldn't humble myself to get a decent job. If I had, it would have made the process much smoother this season, but I didn't and didn't play for a year. To be honest, in the basketball business, a year off is a major red flag and causes teams to question you as a player. The most humbling position in the world is to go from literally fighting off offers to a position where you're begging for a job.

It was a very low point for me. I received a good offer, and they were basically saying, *We want you now, but no way in hell will we let you go to see your baby born.* This was almost the third week in August, so I knew it wasn't looking good. While sitting at dinner at the National Harbor with Rosalynn, we sat and discussed the one solid offer and with tears in her eyes, she told me, "If that's all you can get, go for it." The look in her eyes said, *Please don't make me do this alone,* and I knew that my loyalty to her had to be greater than my desire to play and master my craft or further salvage what was left of my career. This very point in my life was when I knew she was the one for me because to this point, I had never chosen a woman over my career. Slightly reluctantly, I declined the offer, and I just began to pray heavily that God would open another avenue for me to continue to do what I love. Whether good or bad, you should know this lesson:

Lesson 31: Be careful what you ask God for because he might just grant your request, and it might not turn out to be the outcome you have desired.

I wanted to play so badly that I worked hard to get another chance, and I prayed on it constantly, and soon my prayer was answered. In truth, I really should have retired then and there and just transitioned to life after basketball, but I was superthirsty and wanted more success in my field—good old pride just wouldn't let me stop. At the time, I had about six people looking for jobs for me. I wouldn't commit to anything with anyone because of the last experience I had with an agent who lied and told me he had a job for me, but once I signed, the truth came out, and I was stuck dealing with someone I didn't trust.

An agent just happened to be on YouTube a day after Roz and I posted videos from the Bahamas games, and he e-mailed me asking if I needed a job. I ain't going to lie; I thought it was a joke, but Roz convinced me, as she has always done since meeting me, to network,

"If he can't do it, maybe he can put you in contact with someone who can." Hesitantly, I agreed and e-mailed him back. But first thing first was I had to come back for my son's birth; that was nonnegotiable. And I wasn't signing an agreement with him; I would only sign for him to get the agent's fee. That way, he had to work and show me if he could get the job done for me.

He came through, and I was offered a job in Slovakia. Ironically, it was the same team I had reached out to the previous season, but we couldn't negotiate a decent price (in my estimation), so nothing went down. Before I signed, I spoke with the coach and management to ensure that all my terms and conditions would be met. He personally wanted to talk with me, and that was a big thing for Roz and me because he wanted to know the quality of the person he was getting and not just a person with stats. After the conversation, we agreed on the terms, and I was about to take off on a new adventure with a new focus and direction.

Upon arrival—I kid you not—I was picked up by the wrong team and taken into Austria (neighboring country of Slovakia). After being there for a few hours, while in conversation, I realized that I was in the wrong place. Luckily, I met a friend that day named Markus, and he took me home and let me use Skype and just relax. He was such a good dude. After communicating everything with both sides, we figured out that I had been picked up by the wrong guy and instead got a guy who spoke no English, so how was I to know what was happening? It was crazy. But I humbled myself because I knew I wasn't in the position to be a jerk, nor should I be either, especially when I was being treated well. It was just a mistake that happened.

Finally at 10:30 p.m., the right people picked me up; and seven hours later, we were finally in Prievidza, Slovakia. I couldn't have scripted this whole scenario; it was so crazy and mentally draining you have no idea. After meeting up with the team, they seemed cool, but I could tell they were highly skeptical of me and what I could do, so I didn't have the greatest rapport with them in the beginning. After a few preseason games, I won them over, but they would really get confirmation on the first day of the regular season against the team's archrival from the next town. This game set the tone for me for the season as a leader and clutch player for this team.

The game finally arrived, and the start of another grueling season was upon us as we entered the gym of the enemy. Usually derby matches are when teams from nearby towns play against each other, and there are usually fights, lots of police, but they are great games to play in and to witness. This game would prove no different as it would go down to the wire and be a nail-biter. It was a tight affair that saw us down by two points with one minute to go in the game. We ran a play and let the clock run down close to the end…five…four…three…and somehow the ball found itself in my hands. And with one second on the shot clock, I heaved up a deep three-pointer, and like clockwork, it went in. We ended up winning by three points, and the season had begun with a bang for us. Through the first month, we had solidified, and we would be a top four team. We had won a good percentage of games, but looking to the calendar, eight games had come and gone. November had arrived, and soon it was time to head home. November 6 came, and I was on the plane home Sunday, bright and early, and man, I'm not even going to lie to you—I was sick to no end.

I had the runs like you wouldn't believe, and if you know me, then you know I'm not one to get sick, but I was a mess that night. After no rest all night, I was up early with Roz at the hospital, getting ready for the delivery. If you've flown from Europe to the States, you understand that if you don't get a good night's rest, you get jet-lagged big-time. I was in the waiting room, knocked out, as the nurse beckoned me to come in and join the festivities. As my son came out, I watched as they pulled him out of her belly, and I literally saw her insides and almost puked. But I had to see the delivery for myself, and what a proud moment it was to see him arrive. It was a new life that. a few months prior, I didn't want to be associated with; but thank God on that day, November 7, 2011, Jacobi Deshi Phillips was born. The craziest thing is, as soon as he was born, I felt fine, like I was back to myself and no longer sick. It was so crazy; I couldn't explain if I tried to. I guess I was so nervous on the inside, and that was my body's way of coping.

As much as I loved holding him, feeding him, and changing his diapers, in the back of my mind, I knew I had to go back to work and finish what I had started in the professional realm. In a blink of an eye, it seemed I was back at the airport, ready to board the plane and head back to Slovakia. After a ten-hour flight, I got off the plane and into a car heading back to my city. As soon as I got home, I got food and clothes and was off to the bus because we had a game that night. You can't imagine how exhausted I was. I didn't know if I was coming or going, but I knew I had to perform and snap out of it immediately for the game. It was a reality-check game for me because up until now, I had pretty much come through every time I needed to close out big games at home or even on the road. But that night, I would be faced with a tough challenge to close out the game, and I failed. Our coach got kicked out of the game in the first quarter, and we trailed by as many as fifteen points going into the fourth quarter, but we clawed our way back with six seconds left with the ball and down by one point. I live for these moments and the opportunity to control destiny.

I fumbled the ball in the closing seconds and barely got a shot off against them, and we lost. Man, I was blown, and I was pooped, a bad combination; and as I lay on the bus, I heard the blame game start. There was new doubt about me, but I realized early when things are good, you're the man; and when they go bad, you're hated. For the next few weeks, I would have to regain the trust of my teammates and fans as we cruised into the Christmas break with one game against another championship contender right before the holidays. As all of our games were against this particular team, it was a close contest, and we won by four points. I hit a few clutch shots as we escaped with a narrow win. You see, in all my years, the Christmas games are the hardest ones because you're so close to going home, yet you have to work and remain focused as well. Luckily, we did; and with a bonus of a couple hundred euros in pocket, it was time to head home. And my baby Ja'hnniah was arriving three days later—awesome.

Off the court, Jacobi was getting huge; and Skyping with him, Roz, and Mei-Lin was so much more exciting. At the same time,

I was sending pictures and e-mails to Ja'hnniah so she could feel a part of the process as well. Truthfully, it was hard to reach out to her because, at times, I know she was feeling left out and slightly abandoned in the whole process, but that gave me more focus to bring her into the fold as much as I could and make her feel welcomed and loved even more.

Before I would head home, I was awakened to some horrific news. Roz's close friend had been murdered by her estranged husband. These types of things upset me. Someone is so selfish to the point where they would take a human soul for no apparent reason other than the belief that "if I can't have you, no one else can have you." Even in the midst of excitement about Jacobi, this broke Roz's heart; thus, it killed me too. The woman was a good woman, mother, and loyal wife to a selfish estranged coward who ended her days in such a selfish manner. This crushed Roz, as well as her other friends, to bits and pieces. In every group of friends, there are pieces needed to maintain balance in the group and allow everyone to coexist with the right dynamics, and now they'd have to dig deep and find a way to bridge the gap left by her loss. This would be tough, knowing that, as soon as I touched down, I would have to head to the funeral soon after. Unfortunately, this was life as we understood it to be, but trust that it was ugly.

A long nine and a half hours later, I landed, and there was my little man and my other baby Mei-Lin waiting for me. There's no better feeling than knowing and feeling that love only family can give to you. The funny thing is you could tell Ja'hnniah felt the same way as she exited her flight and saw the love and excitement upon her arrival. I would be home for two weeks; that's unheard of in professional sports. The maximum is usually a week, including flying time, but I was certainly going to make the most of the time.

Before the fun, we had to head to Pennsylvania for Tarina's funeral. Basically, I landed, and the next morning, we were off to the funeral. It was a very tough and horrible timing for an event. (It's not as if death could be better planned for, but with kids involved, this occurring before the holidays makes it much more tragic.) In the short space of time I knew her, I can honestly say she was a beautiful soul inside and out and very down-to-earth, cooler than the other side of the pillow. However, for reasons beyond our control, she was taken. But God knows best, and even though we don't agree or understand, we have to trust why he does certain things and why those things sometimes leave us feeling lost with many questions. Yet as the song says, we will understand it better by and by. At some point, words are hollow, and the hurt and pain make it hard to trust God and believe in his will being done. It's nothing worse than seeing people you love mourn over a senseless death.

I can't even fake it. I thought because of the funeral, the break would be nothing but an emotional roller coaster for Roz and would ultimately be a quiet, somewhat somber holiday. But thank God her resourcefulness and resilience were at an all-time high, and she straight thugged through her emotions to ensure the kids had a blast. My mother and Ja'hnniah came through to visit as well. In November, I encouraged Roz to invite her mother over for the holidays to make a new tradition for our family to spend time together, fellowship, and just relax. On Christmas Eve, we took the kids to Dave & Buster's for some fun and entertainment, as well as expend the extra energy they needed to get out. We had done our shopping beforehand to ensure more family time and fun for Ja'hnniah and Mei-Lin. On Christmas morning, and like always, everyone meets in our house and open presents. The excitement and joy you see in your kids' eyes is priceless, and it is my favorite part of the holidays.

Later, Roz's parents came over for dinner, and it was just what the doctor ordered. We all had an incredible time, just relaxing, seeing our parents meet and bond—it was a great feeling. With little Jacobi in our midst, it made for a great time and a reason for celebration in the midst of all that had happened. Unfortunately, more drama came when my daughter's worst fears came true when she realized she wouldn't get to hang with her mother; it broke her heart.

The worst thing for a man is to see his woman, or his daughter, cry for no apparent reason; it's supertough. My heart was broken, but I had to be strong, and the sad thing was, hers was broken even more. She had been with her grandparents and was supposed to see her mom, but unfortunately, something came up, and it didn't happen.

At this point, I was just like man. This break was crazy. It just seemed like no matter what good was occurring, the bad was always creeping in and overshadowing the love and positivity in our lives. As tough on the exterior as she might seem, Ja'hnniah is a very sensitive child. She's always been like that for as long as I could remember. And to hear her utter thoughts of being left out and feeling unwanted, it just tore me in half.

After finally consoling her, I went to my bathroom and began to cry and pray to God, just asking him why this poor child always had to suffer and how I could make this pain go away. It was a long thirty minutes, but I needed it. Maybe I needed to mourn Tarina as well, but as a real man, I'll say this: tears are therapeutic for the soul. Real men cry and have no problem admitting their emotional frailties, especially when it comes to family.

Fortunately, we were getting Tarina's boys for the New Year's holidays, and that would lighten the mood and allow Ja'hnniah to have fun and not think so heavily about her pain and disappointment. New Year's Eve was awesome, and the kids danced and played the whole time, opened their gifts, and really had a blast. Tarina's oldest son, Tyhrie, was very angry; and even amid the fun, I could see the anger streaming through his eyes. But as the days went by, his eyes lightened, and he began to glow with fun and excitement as he always does. It is one thing for adults to experience extreme pain, but when you see it in a child's eyes, it's heartbreaking, and the pain you feel for them is much deeper than what you feel for yourself.

My final three days of the break were spent just trying to soak up the love and ensure that Ja'hnniah and Tarina's boys felt love and realized how special they were. Soon it was my time to fly out. After hugs and kisses, it was time for me to mount up and finish the job I had started in Slovakia. During the break, Roz and I had gone ring shopping to see what was out there; and to our surprise, we saw a hell of a deal, so I got the ring for her. But I was very clear and adamant that I wasn't going to give it to her until I felt ready and asked her politely not to rush me, and that's the exact way I said it, with a straight face. I know myself, and I'm not good when someone pressures me or gives me an ultimatum. It usually doesn't end well at all, so that was real talk.

The ring was supposed to be ready and set to her liking the day before I left, but I faked Roz out and told her I didn't get it and we would have to wait until summer for me to give it to her. In reality, I planned to surprise her with it at our family dinner that evening. As the day wore on, I spoke with close friends, telling them my plan and looking for suggestions to make it funny or maybe romantic. Truthfully, I knew that I never wanted it to be elaborate, nor did I want to attract a lot of attention during the special moment when I would ask Roz to marry me.

Man, I can honestly say I had the runs. I couldn't stay off the toilet. It was like I was reliving Jacobi being born all over again. We went to Uncle Julio's for dinner, a usual spot for our family to go and hang out; but tonight was a moment in time that would mark a special commitment that, before I had met Roz and grew to know her and love her, I had never seen myself making. Don't get me wrong, my relationship with Ms. Peaches was excellent, but it was during the height of the drama with Ja'hnniah's mother, so it truly had no chance, and I don't think mentally I was ready for it then. But this space of time God had set aside for me to ask Roz to love me for who and what I was and to accept the baggage I had—help me unpack it and sort through it so I could be a better me.

For all the romantics out there, don't go our route; for the comedy lovers, I didn't go that way either. I did it in typical Sulli fashion, and it was quiet and simple. As I pulled out the ring, Mei-Lin began to scream uncontrollably, and the tears began to flow down Roz's face as I asked her to marry me. She was choked up for a second, so she didn't answer. I was like, "Uh, yes or no, babe?" She smiled and said yes, and my soul mate and best friend had consented to be with me until our last breaths departed us.

Instantly we got on our phones and told everyone the news. I just confirmed with my people it was done; but Roz, in her typical fashion, called, e-mailed, and texted pictures of the ring to her friends and family. I was just happy to see the joy on her face because, like me, she had gone through a lot of things emotionally, even with me. She had to endure the pain of me not wanting to have Jacobi, from us going from a booty-call, hookup type of relationship to an "I can't live without you" bond. I just sat back and basked in her glow. She was so happy, as was I. Just a few years prior, I had run good women away because I was afraid to involve them in my drama and wasn't ready to wed, but finally, I had come to that point in life, and it was a beautiful occasion.

As good as those moments were, unfortunately, the time had come for me to return to my job. But I can honestly say it was on a good note, knowing that a huge part of my life was steady, and now all I had to do was go out and use my God-given abilities to ensure success in the athletic realm. The second half of the season started like the first. We got off to a great start and pushed off to a 5–0 record to start the round. Things were looking good on paper, but our coach decided we needed a new spark to help us get over the hump to finish the season strongly. We got this clown in—and man, from the moment I saw him, I was totally against him being there, and my initial feelings would soon become the sentiments of the entire team. He was a cancer and was spreading through our group, and we had our longest losing streak while he was there. He was a player who thought he had it all, but clearly, there was a reason why he was just getting a job in the middle of January and early February.

After that project failed, we went back to our normal ways; but going into the final five games, they brought in another player. Again, I wasn't feeling this either. In my years of playing, my experience has been that bringing in new guys always jacks up the chemistry of the team and messes up the team's rhythm. The coach and I sat for like an hour and talked. It was his first head-coaching job. I was older than he was, but he took my counsel in most matters concerning basketball. In truth, his earnest due diligence and, of course, allowing me to go home to see my son being born sold me. He took on a new guy who basically was the energy guy to help us get across the finish line in the final run to end the year. However, when he first got there, I was beyond disgusted; but even with my competitive nature, I held firm to my New Year's spiritual resolution, which was not to curse. During the first half of the year, I was so rude and vulgar at times I know I was unbearable, and I wanted to be better with my language and also better with my teammates. And me being more positive and not cursing definitely helped us so much. Literally, the second half of the year, I didn't curse. I may have slipped up a maximum of five times (probably not even that many times), but it was the first step to getting more of a spiritual grip on my life.

On court, the season was coming to an end, and Roz and Jacobi came out to see me. It was amazing to see how much he had grown and how clever he had become. To see your child from day one and watch him grow in close proximity was something I've never done before, and believe you me, I would enjoy every second of it. He still wasn't sleeping through the night, but just to have them around just before the playoffs was so refreshing, and it eased the tensions for me by having a breakaway from basketball. We traveled to Austria, where Roz, Jacobi, and I straight ran the streets all day just exploring, having dinner, and then driving back home. It was a long day but was a much-needed getaway from my city to just enjoy more common civilization.

Prievidza was a small town. Its main attraction was a huge grocery store and McDonald's, and that's the gospel truth right there—no excitement whatsoever. No Starbucks, Burger King, KFC, nothing. We were so far in the woods it wasn't funny. So you can imagine my surprise in Austria to see TGI Fridays, Starbucks, Pizza Hut, and all the pleasantries I had experienced along my other travels. To get some good old American cuisine with my fiancé and my son was just phenomenal. Honestly, the little joys in life—like spending time with loved ones, enjoying your favorite foods—are so big and important, and they make the world a much better place. This trip was living proof. It was only ten days but was a much-needed breath of fresh air, and let's face it, being with my lady made me much happier and pleasant as well.

During their visit, we played three games. We won two and lost the final game against a team we would later see in the playoffs and consequently relinquished the top spot going into the playoffs. That was huge because instead of a much easier road to the finals, we would now have to face possibly the most difficult team matchup in the league. You see, in the playoffs, it doesn't matter what place you're in. What matters is if you win more games than other team to move on to the next round, and boy, would we ever be tested.

They had Euro League experience and a much bigger budget, but in game one, we controlled the game. Unfortunately for me, I came down with an extremely high temperature two days before the game, and I was sick beyond words. I had a 102 temperature and was throwing up at every second. It was highly unlikely that I would play, so it seemed. However, like always, I would find a way to muster the energy to ensure we had a chance to win. Luckily, on that night, we won. Game two wasn't so good for us, and we lost by seven points. We really played so badly on a whole, but we still were right in it as came to the waning minutes of the game. But we were unsuccessful.

Game three could have been our biggest letdown when we lost the home-court advantage, and that put our backs against the wall. The other team celebrated and looked at our fans as if to say, *No way we are losing this series now.* Once again, I was so worn out, but slowly I was regaining my energy. But it was rough, and we lost. In the do-or-die game four on their court, the gym was packed, and they even had the celebration paraphernalia lined up. But this nail-biter game would go down to the very last whistle before a winner would be decided.

The initial push out of the gate was strong from them. They wanted to pound us and win easily, but we were quite resilient and wouldn't waver, especially knowing this was our last chance! With four minutes to go, the leading scorer and oldest player—me—fouled out. Looking back, it was so providential that this happened because, later on, other guys would step up and make plays when I might not have been able to. In the last three minutes, we saw the dunk of the year, a chest-to-chest clash at the rim, where my teammate annihilated his opponent and propelled us to a one-point win on the road and set up a critical game five at home where we would live to fight another day.

Game five was a tale-of-two-halves game where they beat us down in the first half, and we ran them out of the gym in the second half en route to a seven-point win. It was a straight fight, but we held on, and this would be the springboard for our moving forward and seeking future success. The semifinals were up next, and we would face a team we lost to the majority of the times we played during the year.

Game one would be my statement game as we straight destroyed them and moved on for a twenty-point win. In this game, I would finally be healthy again; and with the rest, it was evident that I was back to my old ways. The first game always allows you to send a message, which we especially needed in this instance as we didn't play them well during league play. The game would show we surely wouldn't be playing in the same manner, nor would we allow them to dictate the game to us. Game two was close, and we really should have won it as well, but some bad execution in the fourth quarter helped us lose by six points. But we were superconfident still. We allowed them to do some things they liked to do, but in the end, this game was about one or two possessions where we lost focus and were punished as a result.

Over the next two games, we would close out the series by routing them by twenty points again and by about twelve points to move on to the finals. After the game, we saluted the fans as we did in previous rounds, and reporters came running. I've never been one to be in cahoots with the media, so I was extremely brief but thorough when I said we expected to win the finals and that we would show maximum effort to make a championship a reality.

Just think, a few months prior, I was deemed washed up, unemployable, and professionally, things were in disarray. But that's the beauty of God and his mercy. Even when I didn't deserve his favor, it was shown to me. The proof was me leading a team with players whose average age was twenty-three years old to play in the finals. It was something the team and club hadn't achieved in almost twenty years! The whole ride home, the guys were going crazy and just bouncing around. But I was lightweight in a zone and wouldn't let my excitement or intensity be swayed because I still had a point to prove, and my goals weren't met yet!

The game has its ups and downs, but you can
never lose your focus of your individual goals,
and you can't beat because of your lack of effort.

-Michael Jordan

At this point in time, this saying summed up my mission and reason for not being overly happy. I knew that we were about to compete for the highest medal of honor of the season, and that was for the championship. Any sportsman of worth will agree and sing in chorus with me that you're defined by championships and wins— that's how you cement your legacy. Here in Prievidza, I was trying to cement a legacy to where, even in fifteen years' time, I could walk in a gym owned by the team with my kids and see my name hanging in the rafters and witness history from years past, still being respected and celebrated.

Game one was against the regular-season champions from Komárno, Slovakia, as they rode in on a high, having won eighteen games in a row, almost a league record, but records and streaks are always meant to be broken. The first game was a good, old-fashioned slugfest, where we couldn't buy a basket with a golden ticket. We were just off and lost by eight points, and people began to murmur that Komárno was going to sweep us and sweep us easily.

In game two, we made it known very clearly with a strong per-formance from me that we were a force to be reckoned with and there's no such thing as a divine-right winner. We were cooking on all cylinders as we cruised to a convincing seventeen-point victory and set the stage for a do-or-die game for us there. For us, this was a final, knowing that if we had to go there for game five and close them out, we would lose—in essence, this was our game five. Our goal was to keep the game close and allow their inexperience and the pressure break them when it counted most. The plan was perfect as the closing moments of the game slowly strolled around, and we were up by one point with ten seconds remaining, and they had the ball on an inbounds ball. We switched every screen, or movement, that could get them free; and to our surprise, they threw the ball in directly to us, and we ran out the clock. The team of destiny some five days ago now looked like a team on the ropes going into our home for the fourth and potentially final game of their season. It's funny how things and situations can change in a matter of a few moments. Nothing had been won yet, but clearly, we had put ourselves in a very good and solid position to complete the series and be called champions if we could just muster up another win.

Game four was on a summery Wednesday evening and was to be an eventful game that had everyone on edge. The tone was set early, and neither team would back down or waver. Someone would have to take the championship from the other team. The first half was a seesaw battle. As halftime came, we were up 36–34; but in truth, we still hadn't hit a lot of shots, so I was feeling comfortable about the result. The third quarter followed the same script. Up by two points, down by four points, up by two points—this game was shaping up to have an absolute crazy ending. In the fourth quarter in the waning moments, I began to seize the opportunity to step up and solidify my leadership and help push us over the line. With two minutes to go and up by two points, I used a screen and roll and shot a tough floater off the glass only to see them come back down the court and score.

Then another screen and roll with a shimmy to create just enough space for a fadeaway jumper off the glass with two opponents on either side of me, off the glass for a basket. Another tough bucket, but by this time, I can say that things really started slowing down. When someone gets like this, we say they're in a zone. During the last two minutes, I was unconsciously in a zone, and the defenders were at my mercy as we finally made it to the end as champions of the league. From a team with little hope of entering the tournament to celebrating a title was a remarkable feeling and accomplishment. The finals were over, and we were the champions! That's an awesome feeling, and to top it off, I was named MVP, so the personal and the professional met as a result of hard work and dedication.

During all of this excitement, I was given a recall to play with the Great Britain (GB) Olympic team for the 2012 games. You can't even imagine how psyched I was. Truthfully, I knew this was what I deserved, and I knew it would open crazy doors for my latter years of playing and financially put me back in a position of much-needed financial security with a new baby and my girls getting bigger. A championship, an MVP, and GB Olympic hopeful—things were definitely on the up-and-up, but I always remained patiently grounded throughout the whole process. As the season's final payments were given and good-byes were shared, I headed back home where "Operation Get Right for the Olympics" was on. In truth, my family would basically never see me this summer; but in my mind, I knew what it could do for me and the family long-term. But God had other plans, and things that I would soon find out were more important than my wants.

Precamp was in Houston, and even though there was resistance for me to have and get Ja'hnniah, we bought tickets so that even she could see me before the long haul began. Essentially, camp was the middle of June through the Olympics if you made the squad, and I had all intentions to do so, and the squad's dynamics were set up that way as well. Just as things were in play and set up, I found out I wasn't eligible because of a technicality in the rules and wouldn't be able to compete. I can honestly say that was one of the most disappointing days in my life to date. I was beyond furious, I'm not even going to front. I aim to keep it 150 percent. I was pissed with God as I walked into church, like, *What did I do wrong to miss this, God?*

As disgruntled as I was, I heard the message that I needed to hear, and I wouldn't quite understand until later what relevance it might have for my life at the present. The minister's message was that God places us in situations at certain times, and there are no accidents. You're there because it's part of his will and design for your life. I heard the words, but they wouldn't hit home for a few weeks yet. That week, Ja'hnniah actually came on the day I was due to go to camp, but it was good to finally see her and spend time with her.

When the news broke that I wouldn't be playing, my better half began planning an array of events. The first event was to head to North Carolina to meet with Jacobi's and Mei-Lin's godparents for a week of fun in the sun and just relaxing. Along the ride, I received news that totally broke and shocked me to bits; and if the source was anyone else, I wouldn't have believed it. I was told my daughter was acting a right fool, being very bossy and bullying others. I really had to catch myself and make sure I heard correctly, and even after, I was in shock. Trust me, that wasn't going to fly and would be dealt with immediately, but Roz said to wait until after the trip to keep it in-house.

Unfortunately, more of that behavior occurred in North Carolina, and you should know I straight shut that down. We sat her down and began to ask a series of questions, and I learned a lot more about where the behavior was learned. Nevertheless, she was punished, and I realized that just a spanking would not suffice. We took the last few outings away from her to show that bad behavior wouldn't be tolerated or glorified in our household in no way, shape, or form. The rest of the summer, she was on lockdown, and trust me, I'm worse than a prison warden when you try and get over on me. She definitely got the picture, but unlike a lot of parents nowadays, I micromanaged her to a fault. It took a solid month before I eased up, but at the end of the day, it had to be done to ensure it wouldn't be a reoccurring bad behavior.

As the summer drew on, there was a trip to Florida for a week, and it was an absolutely fabulous time. It was also the first time for Ja'hnniah to see the Big Apple, New York. The summer finished on a high, and as Ja'hnniah left to go home, I remembered the words of the pastor. It dawned on me why my situation didn't work out as I wanted, and relief and understanding began to unfold. You see, if I hadn't been there, I would still be in the dark about my daughter's behavior, and her anger would be uncontrollably high now.

On the personal-job front, I was back at square one; but like always, I didn't fret. Deep in my spirit, I knew something would come up.

CHAPTER 13

ONE LAST GO-AROUND

Do not go where the path may lead, go instead
where there is no path and leave a trail.

—Ralph Waldo Emerson

I can't even lie; the summer brought a whole new meaning and appreciation to the phrase "It takes a village to raise a child." Our network of support had ultimately shown me the anger of abandonment and hurt my daughter was feeling and how she was acting out to show her disapproval for the whole situation. I can also honestly say I'm glad I figured that out early enough to try and curb the behavior before it got out of control and then there's no turning back! From a parental point of view, I got it. If I weren't around, my oldest would be so far gone with her ways, and the quality time and fun wouldn't have been the same because Roz couldn't do the same things with the three children that we did as a family when I was there. From a sport and job front, it was really stagnant; and in August, if it's stagnant, that's not a good look at all. It's crazy how I was just chilling, and unlike the year before, I was even more confident that things would work out for me.

A few teams were interested, but the money I was hearing and negotiating for when my name was in the Olympic conversation was vastly different, and in truth, my pride was slightly tugging at me not to take anything. But this time around, I had a better half who implored me to take another shot for the big payout, humble myself again to show my worth, and use the financial setback as fuel again to succeed. So it was settled. Around the beginning of October, I would play in Germany under my same coach as the year before in Slovakia. After signing, I found out that four guys from the previous team would also be there, so it was almost a reunion. But the goal was, first and foremost, another championship. It would be tough as I soon would realize that anything worth having in this life is surely worth fighting for, and after my summer, I was more than willing to fight to show my worth.

I literally signed a week before the season started, so I had one full week of practice before we officially started up. But it was all good. I knew the plays from the previous year, so it would be a quick memory learning curve and back to work. We got out of the gates quite well, opening 3–0 only to lose two in a row. It was crazy, like we were following the same script as the season before. Doubt began to creep in our squad, but we kept working hard to ensure that losses to lowly ranked teams wouldn't keep us from looking at the big picture and progressing as a squad. We hit a nice winning streak, and just around the time my family was coming in November, we had cemented a top spot. Truthfully, this would be first season in my career when there literally was no easy game or a game where it was a given that we do what we know to do and expect a victory. In this league on any night, anyone can beat anyone, and that was great motivation for us. Off the court, I did hang out with my teammates and tried to be more sociable than I was in Slovakia, but I was focused on proving my worth again.

Coming up to the Christmas break, we had a tough road game with one of the teams at the lower end of the tables; and to be fair, we really got smacked around in the first half and were losing by twelve points. But our coach ripped into us and let us know it would be hell on us when we got back if we didn't play our style of play and impose our will. I didn't play the whole third quarter except the last three minutes and helped us go on a run to secure a four-point lead. The fourth quarter was the same. I just created chances and helped our team crush them and secure a fourteen-point win and start my Christmas break off the right way: in first place and winning along the way. This time of the year was always the best for me, hanging out with friends, going to church, and just embracing the break.

Like clockwork, my mom missed her flight, and I would have to go out later to get her. But we would spend the holidays together; that was the most important thing. I finally got Meme (my kid's nickname for their grandma), and we rode home just catching up and got her up to speed with our plans for the holiday. We were just enjoying a quiet moment before the storm of kids hit the next day. I took Roz to get her Christmas gift. She wanted a Louis Vuitton bag, and for me, I had no problem spending that type of money on her because there's no monetary value to put on the love I have for her, so it was cool. To any man out there, trust it's a hard process to get to this stage where it's not that deep to spend $1,000 once in a blue moon to ensure your lady is happy. At the end of the day, the purse may get old, but the appreciation she will have every time she looks at it and remembers the sacrifices you've made to make her happy will never get old. Trust me, it's a worthwhile purchase no matter what it is. Better you spoil your lady than someone else!

Having said that, I also learned a valuable lesson of getting to know my kids much more than on a personal level and really know them for who they are and their actions. Mei-Lin wears her heart on her sleeve and is sometimes slightly overdramatic while masking her pain and insecurities with comedy. Jacobi is the spitting image of me. There's no gray area, and just like me, there's no mistaking what you're going to get with him. He's also very stubborn; that's my boy. Then there's Ja'hnniah, extremely sensitive, somewhat sneaky, has a huge, huge heart but will hold on to things and can be spiteful. She'll mask it by smiling, but deep down, she has so much pain that when it's triggered, it manifests itself either by tears or anger. Some people may say, "Uh, okay, why did he put his kids on blast like that?" I didn't put them on blast; I simply showed that they're human. Maybe while reading, you can see similar characteristics in your kids or yourself. The point is that knowing your kids and yourself is always better than finding out things the hard way. During the Christmas Day festivities, it was amazing to see Jacobi and Mei-Lin light up and enjoy their gifts, but I wanted to see Ja'hnniah's expressions too and to know how her day was.

I tried to reach out to her, but I didn't hear from her until the end of the day. It was cool because she was supposed to come over the next day to be with us. Unfortunately, that didn't happen; and once again, my baby was heartbroken. For me, it was the last straw. I just went up to our room and began to cry as if I had been the one to be let down or hurt, or as if I were a kid. Again, I'll be the first to say I'm not perfect, not even close, but when it comes to my kids, I do my best to do right by them. And it's tough, even as a Christian, when others don't share the same sentiments as you. Roz didn't catch me, but man, I stayed in there for a solid fifteen minutes and prayed and cried until my heart was less full and stressed. Sometimes the pain can be so unforgiving and harsh, but without it, you can never fully appreciate happiness. For me, finding out I couldn't see my Ja'hnniah was harsh, but I remained calm with the solace that she would be at my wedding and, in the summer, we would make up for the time we would miss being together during the holidays.

Our tradition continued with our families meeting up for Christmas Day with the addition of Roz's uncle and her grandmother as well. It was an awesome time with all the family, playing games with her cousins and seeing the kids just relax and enjoy each other; it was an absolutely amazing time. I'll be honest, I was definitely not in the best of moods; but it wasn't fair to spoil everyone else's mood, so I just lay low and tried to have a great time as well. I did find joy that warmed my soul even with Ja'hnniah not being there, and that was in seeing Roz and her family bond more and the happiness it brought her. At the end of the day, her bonding and creating a closer bond was so gratifying, especially understanding the strain or the lack of closeness they had before we met. It was so good to see her smile and really and truly be happy among her family. The time and energy of the season would stay on a high as the next day, the family of Roz's close friend who was murdered the previous year would come down, and a new tradition was formed to ensure that we'd bring in New Year's with them.

Tyhrie, Deon, Dylan, and Caleb would come down to hang out, relax, and just have a blast; and hopefully, this would serve as a reminder of the good times amid the drama they had to deal with. In this juncture of life, losing a mother to a senseless murder is traumatic, so we started this tradition to reach out and get them. And to be honest, they love coming down and hanging out, and we love having them.

Before I left, I did get the privilege of attending church; and like it was as a kid, if you're alive and don't have a previous engagement, then you will go to church, stay awake, and listen. So that Sabbath morning, we all got up bright and early and headed out to church. As always, it was therapeutic for me to hear a good word, especially since I was due to fly back to Germany that night. After hearing a great word, on the ride home, I was hit for another loop as my mom would totally shatter my image of the perfect relationship she and my father had, or so I thought.

She told me that I had a brother and a sister and that my father had them before he met her but had never told her until one day she pried and saw money orders and small bits of information about them. She told me that when we went to Cleveland to meet his family, he'd go and visit them for long periods at a time. Man, you can't imagine how furious this made me. I just sat there as she began to tell me more and tried to explain, but I was too mad to even listen. It all just sounded like excuses, and I firmly had to catch myself before I totally disrespected my mom and hurt her feelings. Anyone who knows me knows when I see deceit, I question anything and everything associated with the situation. So immediately I was like, "Is there anything else you want to tell me, Mom?" I could see the tears in her eyes as she realized how bad of an idea it was keeping that information from my sister and me, but unfortunately, the deed was done, and the repercussions included a furious son.

This definitely wasn't what I wanted to hear as I was about to leave my family and return back overseas, but that's life. It's never scripted unless it's TV. As we rode home, for the rest of the ride, I said nothing at all to my mom. It was unusual because with age, we had become very good friends. I still respected her; she was still my mother, but this was too much for me. As I came home, I went straight to the room, and Roz could see I was beyond pissed. As she opened the door, I blasted out, "Babe, you know my mom never told me I got siblings. What's up with that?" She could see the pain and anger because, to me, family is everything. Even if the relationship isn't the greatest, you can't dismiss that people are your blood, or at least that's how I feel.

The beautiful thing about finding the woman who is made for you, there are certain things only she can say to you that make sense, and you'll accept even when you don't want to hear them. Amazingly, I just dropped the anger and moved forward after asking my mom to get my siblings' information because I felt I was due that at least. After she obliged and apologized, I let it go. That was a huge step for me to not harp on it and tear into it until somebody would be in tears, and I'm not one to cry easily. But that's what happens when you connect with a good woman and start to make changes for the betterment of your life. You realize that there's so much more to gain from a happy life then a bitter, resentful, and vindictive life.

A few hours later, the hugs and kisses were shared, a cup of Starbucks in hand, and the grind of going back to work was on the brain because, in ten hours, I would land and have an evening practice. Once again, it would be a quick turnaround. The hardest part of the year for me was being there, leaving the confines of comfort to go on that foreign venture, but that's what I did for a living. However, this time, when I left, I could feel that this wasn't going to happen much anymore because things had changed for me personally and professionally. It was time to look for a new venture in life. Finally, after a long flight filled with mixed emotions, hurtful feelings about Ja'hnniah and my siblings still burned deep even though I thought I was just going to get over them. This prompted me to add a new challenge in my life, and that's thirty minutes of uninterrupted prayer and listening to God the first thing every morning so I could be connected to God more.

I can honestly say the first few weeks, and sometimes even now, it's rough training yourself to clear the mind and just focus on God and commune with him. I'm trying to let you know that when I tell you I struggled, that's a kind way to put it. I couldn't get the minutes in without my mind wandering. I was like a kindergartner in a candy shop trying to be patient. It's mind-boggling how hard it is to concentrate and clear the mind to commune with God for even just a short time. If you're honest and you think of all the garbage or silly things we do throughout the day, our mind records it all and comes right to the forefront when you want to concentrate. That's what I went through, and even now, I have to mentally block out everything. But with time and practice, I began to see how personally and professionally I became more at peace with everything surrounding me.

The beginning of the second half of the season was a bit topsy-turvy. The first few games we won barely, but definitely not convincingly. The turning point of the season was our first thirty-point loss on the road. Man, it was so bad we went into a shell and lost three games in a row, and people started to be ask if we were good enough, did we need another player, and if someone was going home. Truthfully, we ended the season strong enough in second place with a few tough wins and losses, but it was safe to say that going into the playoffs, I wasn't as nearly so sure of our success with this group of guys.

Unfortunately, my predictions would turn out to be right as we went out of the playoffs in the first round. I was so mad I was fouled on the game-winning shot that would have propelled us to the next round, but unfortunately, it wasn't meant to be. For the first time in a long time, I'd tasted defeat, but for the first time since I don't know when, I wasn't really pissed or even remotely pissed. It was really weird for me because normally, I'm the worst and can't be around anyone or do anything because the game would have consumed me. But oddly enough, I wasn't feeling this way. Deep in my heart, I knew it was over for me with basketball—sad but true. That night in Jena, Germany, I knew I would never play professionally again. In truth, it was almost like a relief, like a burden had been lifted from my shoulders. But now I had to think, *What was next for me?*

Roz had been talking with me about different ideas and plans, but truthfully, in eleven years, I never seriously thought about what

I could do or what I was good at aside from playing ball and chasing women. Now it was even more evident that a new era was beginning, and I had to start looking into new avenues of reinventing myself. For the two weeks that I was stuck in Germany, I had to take a closer look at myself and figure out how I could use my gifts and be successful. Let me tell you, the hardest thing in the world is preparing for the unknown, especially coming from playing ball. Your skill sets are very limited unless you're a poster boy for a team (meaning you do a lot of promotion and advertisement activities to learn more of the business side of entertainment). What would I do now? How was God going to use me to be better for my family, friends, and most of all, be a better witness for him? All these questions were rolling through my head, and I had so much time on my hands. But soon it all would be revealed to me in such a powerful way.

CHAPTER 14

DON'T TALK ABOUT IT, BE ABOUT IT!

*For what is a man profited if he shall gain
the whole world, and lose his soul? Or what
should a man exchange for his soul?*

—Matthew 16:26 (KJV)

L ooking over my life down through the years, I can honestly say that I've been blessed and highly favored. In this final chapter, I want to show and use a couple of analogies to help push you toward success and avoid some of the pit stops I encountered along the way. I'm going to use the magnetic resonance imagining process, or more commonly called the MRI, to break down my life and decisions through the years. Depending on what is being scanned, usually an MRI has four steps or parts. Here are the steps to success and happiness I have learned.

Step 1: Preparation

Before any exam, you're always prepped. Things have to be taken out of your pockets, belts and chains removed, and they explain the rules of what's needed for a successful scan. For me, my life's preparation was my spiritual foundation, the best gift any parent can give in my humble opinion. The rules we follow day to day are quite important man-made rules. However, my parents drilled and instilled the importance of knowing and respecting God's laws for my life and my betterment. Stealing from my teacher, lying, getting expelled/suspended—those weren't good either, but they helped form me and prepare me for life and understand the consequences of life. When you do bad, there are punishments that you'll have to suffer. The final step in preparation is very imperative, and that is the losing of things in order to have the scan. Sometimes we hold on to so many things instead of trusting God and leaving them at his feet and letting him fight our battles for us. When we do these things and follow instructions, it helps us make a smooth transition to the next phase.

Step 2: Placement (Positioning)

With the MRI scan, no matter where the facility is, there are protocols to the positioning of whatever is being viewed. With most machines, you must lie still on a table that slides into a narrow tube. Despite the loud sounds and annoying beeps, you must remain motionless. They may even give you earphones with music to help you relax, but it can be tough to relax. For me, placement (positioning) early in life was sports, and my tube was to be the best at whichever sport I wanted to be associated with. Along with positioning, you have to put yourself in the best place for you to accomplish your visionary paths.

I was blessed in Bermuda to have great friends who helped me achieve my goals, but more importantly, I wasn't afraid to declare from a young age that I would get paid to play basketball and soccer professionally. In Sentinel Hill (Southampton, Bermuda), I spent many days learning the basics of soccer alone until I began to master the art of the game. Often being the last picked and being teased fueled me to be better.

When everyone else didn't believe in me, I found avenues to get better and propel and place myself and skills in alignment to be the best I could be by being placed with the Fenton Drive basketball squad, even playing soccer with the Devonshire Colts. There are too many names to mention, but know that you're not forgotten. Even those who hated on me, thanks for helping me place and position myself and move on to the next phase on my path to success.

Step 3: Testing Time

MRI exams usually run from fifteen minutes to ninety minutes, depending on the extensive pictures needed to see the damage or area of concern. Real talk, this step or phase is when you find out how badly you really want your dreams to come true; but with that, you can't forget the discipline needed to keep your dreams alive. With soccer, I signed an A-League professional contract and had the potential to sign higher contracts elsewhere, but I lost my desire and got complacent in just accomplishing the dream. Without discipline, I just crept down to lower leagues and never fulfilled my full potential.

With basketball, I was invited to and went to a few NBA camps and runs and had a great chance to make it; but after getting money playing ball, I lost the drive and work ethic needed to stay in that arena and make a team. I also didn't humble myself when opportunities arose. Consequently, I never played in the highest European competition, nor did I make the NBA. Playing in an illustrious European competition, the Elite Eight, I was so bored I went to the bar and had drinks with an owner who was there to watch me play and—win, lose, or draw—offer me a huge contract after the game. But I got tipsy with him and had a great time, and he knew that I wasn't ready for the money he wanted to invest in me.

I was a woman magnet and just loved the thrill of the chase more than I did my career up until the last few years. Many women I did wrong, hurt, and just used them, but in this testing period, I went back to each of them and apologized. And it was truly humbling to hear how you made someone feel when you thought it was just fun. Getting spat on, doors closed in your face, and hugs accepting my apology—it was truly a daunting experience and was the turning point in my career when I actually manned up and faced the demons that haunted me. It also helped me seek professional help about my personal demons, resentment toward my parents, and anger toward God for my dad dying. I was allowing myself to heal and be available to be used by God.

The hardest test was being a dad. My dad wasn't emotional; in fact, I don't even remember him ever saying *I love you* or ever kissing me. That's pretty sad, but in truth, he could only act like his dad had, and so on through past generations. Until I met Roz, I never knew or understood how important hugs, kisses, and just listening can be for a child's development. Again, I had to learn, and it was a test of patience and how badly I wanted to be a good father for my kids' betterment. All the things I longed for from my dad, I've now learned to give to my kids daily, and the generations of the drought of love by men in my family is over. I've broken the mold, thank God.

What I'm saying is that during the exam or test phase, you'll see and experience many things in life; but you must be true to what you believe in, follow your dreams, be honest with yourself, and allow the best you to come front and center. Success can be closer than you think.

Step 4: Results/Conciliation

This phase is where you find out your fate (surgery or rehab) and the steps to ensure that your health is improved. The fruits of your labor usually bear the results of your work in this life, and these steps have led me to openly and freely share my struggles and pains that, even as a Christian, I've experienced and many other experiences as well. I'm praying that the difficulties, challenges, and negative things I've experienced help you to avoid the same traps and snares and allow you to focus on the positive to help you strive to be better.

> *Personally.* After years of chasing one woman after the other, God gave me a wonderful woman just for me, even when I didn't deserve it! From having to drink to be able to function normally

and deal with problems and situations, whatever they may have been, to now enjoying date night or just being outside in the front yard with my kids, enjoying them growing up and just evolving into a better person and place in life. I am happily married, with three kids, and a picket fence in my front yard—it's a beautiful thing.

Professionally. God granted me the ability to say that, as a Bermudian, I'm one of the few athletes to play professionally in two different sports, three years of soccer and twelve years of professional basketball, winning numerous awards and team accolades along the way and leaving a solid legacy in the professional ranks of the sports world.

Spiritually. I've grown and come to return to what I was taught by my parents. I have been baptized again, and I am actively involved in finishing the work of Jesus for his soon second coming. Most of all, I want to be a true example to not only my family but to all I come into contact with or whose paths I may cross. I'm not in any way suggesting I have arrived or that I'm perfect, but I have been changed. And I pray that what you've read will help you find and make changes in your life to be the best you possible. I'm not saying I'm perfect, but I'm trying daily to be better.

Crazy how life can seem all good in one moment and then so chaotic in the next. What lies around the corner for me? Where would I be working, was I really suited to be full-time dad? So many questions to be answered, stay tuned the reality of the new world is on the horizon.

ABOUT THE AUTHOR

Sullivan Phillips is married to the lovely Rosalynn Law-Phillips, and they have three amazing kids. Ja'hnniah (15), Mei-Lin (14), and Jacobi (6) complete their joyous union. Sullivan played professional basketball and soccer for fifteen years before becoming a basketball coach and motivational speaker after retiring. Sullivan also runs a Mentorship program for young men, is starting a nonprofit, and most of all he prides himself on being Christian.

Printed in June 2019
by Rotomail Italia S.p.A., Vignate (MI) - Italy